A Treacherous Accusation

An Arabella Stewart Historical Mystery-Book 7

D.S. Lang

Ebook ISBN   979-8-9867318-4-1

Paperback ISBN   979-8-9867318-5-8

Cover Designer: Karen Phillips

Copy Editor: Alyssa B. Colton

This book is a work of fiction. All events, incidents, entities, characters, names, and locations are products of the author's imagination or are used fictitiously. Any resemblance to real events, places, or people (living or dead) is purely coincidental.

Chapter One

December 1921

"I'm glad we came," Arabella Stewart said as Jax Hastings tucked her hand into the crook of his arm before leading the way down Main Street to the town park. Expectation lifted her spirits. The difficulties of the past few years grew dimmer as the future shone as brightly as the Christmas star.

"I am, too." He closed his fingers over hers as they ambled along with the crowd gathering to see the ceremonial tree lighting.

Before America's entry into the Great War in April 1917, the tree lighting—the unofficial start of the town's holiday festivities—had taken place every year. Then, with so many of Moreley's young men heading to France with the American Expeditionary Force, the town fathers had thought it callous to carry on with the typical festivities the following December. By the time the Armistice went into effect in November 1918,

1

influenza ran rampant in the area, so no public cele-
brations took place.

In 1919, some effort was made to draw visitors, but
no one had come and many storefronts had been
empty. Last Christmas had seen a slight uptick in traffic.
This year, sizeable crowds were once again expected.
Bella smiled as she glanced around. The lighting mostly drew townsfolk, which she loved. Not only was every
shop festooned with decorations, both the constable's
office and town hall doors boasted wreaths with bright
red ribbons. Lights burned in the stores, which were
almost all staying open on this Monday night. Soon,
the towering blue spruce on the edge of the park would
again be lit with electric lights, as it had been for several
years before the war, influenza, and economic down-
turn. Excitement bubbled inside Bella. The ceremony
was only one event she would attend with Jax. The next
two weeks would be filled with fun and festivities, just
as the last few had been. Back in September, Jax had
offered to fill her calendar with engagements for the
rest of the year—with a special engagement as 1921
ended. Bella had agreed with delight and anticipation.

Both Ballantyne, her resort, and Moreley, her home-
town, were getting back to normal after several tough
years. Bella's life and her world were definitely on the
upswing. Jax's life was, too. Three years after his major
war wounds, he finally had surgery to fix his shoulder
and arm. Now, a month later, the pair was enjoying
each other's company again. For the first time in five
years, Bella looked forward to the holiday. Although
several places at the dinner table—places once set for
her brother, parents, and grandparents—would remain
empty this year and always, Jax would be there. As her

spirit soared, she squeezed his arm. This Christmas would be magical.

He patted her gloved fingers. "You all right?"

"Very much so." All right was a tepid phrase to describe her feelings. Excited. Ecstatic. Enthusiastic. Those words rang truer. She would tell Jax later, when they weren't in a crowd. Not that she didn't savor the smiles and greetings from her neighbors. The jolly atmosphere brought back happy memories and evoked cheerful anticipation. After loss and sorrow, Bella looked to the future with confidence.

As the December dusk descended, Bella and Jax chatted with others in the crowd. A brisk wind picked up, and Bella pulled her wool scarf up with her free hand.

"Are you cold?" Jax asked, concerned darkening his green eyes.

"Not now that the cold air isn't hitting my neck."

His gaze ran over her. "I haven't told you how pretty you look in your new ensemble." Jax kept his voice low, so only she heard him. "The hat is charming."

Warmth spread through her. "Thank you."

The colorful lights blinking on drew their attention. Oohs and aahs followed. As enchanted with the beautiful glow as she had been when the town first used electric lights as decorations, Bella leaned against Jax and let the radiance seep into her heart and soul. The high school choir and a combination of local church ensembles performed popular carols, while the crowd sang along. When Bella gripped Jax's arm tighter, he laid one hand over hers while his clear baritone rang out. Bella lifted her voice to join his.

For the next half-hour, music filled the air. Finally, the mayor invited everyone to gather at the high school for the holiday potluck. The dishes provided by Ballantyne had already been taken, so all Bella and Jax needed to do was go. But she was in no hurry to leave the park. Sharing these moments with Jax was something to savor. Bella was only vaguely aware of the crowd dispersing until a woman's voice, her French accent obvious, cut through the night.

"Jackson, why is this lady being so familiar with you?"

Bella swiveled to face the intruder, who was focused solely on Jax. In the dim light, seeing clearly was difficult. While the woman looked familiar, Bella couldn't place her. She looked up at Jax, whose square jaw had gone rigid. Simultaneously, his arm stiffened. Long moments passed before he spoke.

"What are you doing here, Celeste?"

His question sent Bella's attention back to the newcomer, and she stared in stunned dismay. Celeste. Celeste Bouchard. Three years had passed since Bella had seen the French nurse. That one occasion was a distasteful memory, distasteful enough to make her stomach roil. What was the woman doing in Moreley?

The Frenchwoman laid her small gloved hand on Jax's chest, which had several passersby stopping to look. Bella tightened her hold on his arm and, heart pounding, waited.

"What am I doing here? Surely, you can guess," Celeste replied.

"No, I can't." With his free hand, he removed hers from his person and took a step back.

4

Bella let go of his arm and shoved her hands into her coat pockets. Instead of reacting to her, Jax kept staring at the Frenchwoman.

"I have been looking for you ever since the war ended. You knew I escorted patients to the hospital in Nantes. Even when I could no longer work, I was nearby. If you had written or come, you could have found me." Celeste's voice was soft with entreaty.

"Why would I look for you?" Jax's brow furrowed, as if in confusion.

Bella's mind filled with the long-ago day in France. The day of her brother's burial. The day Jax had walked away from her with Celeste Bouchard. Powerful and painful memories threatened to swamp her. As they did, Bella was swept back to when she had first and last seen Celeste. Bella fought back the anguish that had nearly overcome her three years ago and threatened to do the same now.

Jax had explained the situation months ago and sincerely apologized. Since then, the barriers between them had slowly disintegrated until they got back to where they had been during December 1916. Or had they? If the Frenchwoman had been a mere acquaintance, why had she sought Jax out? Bella did not have to wait long to discover the answer to her silent question.

"Jackson, surely you would not forsake your wife."

While Celeste's assertion echoed in Bella's ears, whispers and gasps from onlookers joined it. Bella couldn't make out the comments of her neighbors, some of whom had lingered after the event, but she was very aware of the stares.

"What?" Jax's voice was sharp with rebuke. "That's ridiculous, and you know it. Why would you say such a thing?"

"Oh, Jackson, do not deny the truth. Before you left France, I wanted to see you, but I was in confinement. Then, I was ill for some time after the birth of our boy, so I could not get to America right away. I wrote to you. All letters were returned. Finally, I got to my uncle's home in Cleveland some months ago. When I saw an article about a case you solved as a Prohibition agent, I contacted the Bureau. It took time, but someone there was kind enough to provide your whereabouts." She clasped her hands together and held them to her chest, as if in supplication.

The Frenchwoman's words sent Bella's pulse racing because Celeste had evidently been with child. Jax's child? Surely not. Bella turned to him, but his focus was on the other woman.

"I can't be the boy's father." Jax's jaw tightened. "It's impossible."

Celeste laid a hand on his forearm. "Do not say such things. Taking care of a child is not cheap or easy. Xavier needs and deserves your support."

"Support?" Jax echoed the word, as if in disbelief. "You want money from me?"

"I would rather have you as part of our lives." Her voice was soft with longing and petition.

Bella stood frozen in place. While she heard the exchange, absorbing the woman's words proved almost impossible. Nothing Celeste said meshed with what Bella knew, or thought she knew, about the other woman. The folks remaining in the park had formed a semi-circle around the trio. Some continued to whisper, while others stood and stared. Bella wanted to curl up in a ball and roll away, but she needed to hear Jax's answer. She needed to know this woman was lying.

"That won't happen. You've come to the wrong place and the wrong man," he shot back. His chin came up and his shoulders lifted. Everything about his demeanor indicated hard resolve.

"I have come to my husband, the father of my child," Celeste asserted. Her firmer tone lost its note of entreaty. "Do not forsake us any longer, Jackson. You did not know about him when you left France, but you knew I was your wife and yet, you sailed away without a thought for my future. I thought better of you."

Jax's jaw dropped as he stared at her. "We aren't married. We never, ever were. I don't know what you're thinking by coming here and making such a ridiculous claim."

A low, throaty laugh escaped her. "Jackson, we are husband and wife. We have been for over three years."

Bella gasped at the import of the Frenchwoman's continued assertion. The sound again brought Jax's attention to her. "Bella…

Before he could continue, Celeste turned toward Bella. "Miss Stewart?"

Unable to form any words, Bella simply nodded. The Frenchwoman—with porcelain skin, deep brown eyes, and nearly black hair—was stunning. Slight of figure, the top of Celeste's head barely came to the middle of Jax's chest. Bella felt like a sturdy oak, an oak with its leaves being ripped off with every sentence spoken, while the former French nurse more resembled a graceful willow. Clad in a magenta velvet cloak with a matching hat, she looked far more fashionable than she had when Bella last saw her in a French nursing uniform. But her coiffure was the same—an elaborate twist with a few strands artfully escaping to touch her face. With one hand, Bella fingered her more modern bob. Jax seemed to like the style on her, but he had once mentioned missing her long hair. With determination, she fought off the errant thoughts and spoke, "I'm Bella Stewart."

"I knew your brother, Matthew. He carried a photograph of you. I saw it when he was one of my patients. And I saw you in passing after he died. He was a wonderful man, just like Jackson." She slipped her hand into the curve of Jax's arm. "I am Mrs. Celeste Hastings."

The name had Bella swallowing hard over the lump suddenly forming in her throat. Speaking, even breathing, seemed beyond her capability. She simply gaped at the woman.

Jax shook off Celeste's hold and pulled away from her. "You're not Mrs. Hastings."

"Oh, Jackson," the woman said in a silky but scolding tone, "I feared you would not be pleased to see me. Not when you never sent for me as you promised. But I thought you would wish to help our child, so I came to tell you."

His nostrils flared with a harsh intake of breath. "We. Do. Not. Have. A. Child." Jax enunciated each word separately. Color rose in his lean cheeks while a muscle in his square jaw worked.

Celeste laid her hand on his chest in a gesture of pure possession. "We do, my darling husband. We most definitely do." With her free hand, she reached into her pocketbook, extracted a photograph, and held it in front of Jax. "Look. This is Xavier. Your son. Our son."

Jax glanced at the picture but shook his head. "He isn't mine, and you know it."

"Jackson, let us talk privately." Celeste put the picture away and lifted her chin.

"We have nothing to discuss. I'm not your husband or the father of your child. We barely knew each other."

His attention flickered to Bella, who had to look away. As she did, their small audience once again made her feel exposed. Conflicting urges—the need to hear the truth and the fear of it—tore at her.

"But you are, and I can prove it." A grin curved Celeste's button-mouth.

"There's no way to prove we're married because we aren't now and never were."

"But I have our license, Jackson. It is dated nine months before Xavier was born."

The lift of her chin and set of her jaw telegraphed obstinacy or certainty. Bella wasn't sure which. Her emotional crash—from joyful to anguished—seemed to take her logical mind with it.

"Why are you accusing me? It makes no sense. If you have a child, he isn't mine." Jax ground out the words.

Color flared in her cheeks, and Celeste briefly glanced away. For several moments, she appeared to mull over his responses. When she focused on him again, determination was back in her expression. "Xavier is your son, and I am your wife. We need you. A good man supports his family. You will regret it if you do not."

"I don't have a family, and I'm for sure not supporting you." As he spoke, his voice rose in volume. "My advice is to leave town right away, or you're the one who will have regrets."

More murmurs went through the people looking on, but one person—a man of middle years and raw-boned build—spoke up. "You're a disgrace, young man. A complete disgrace. I never believed you should've become our constable. Now, I know I was right. Threatening a young woman, a guest in our town? Despicable. Even worse, I heard every word. The lady is your wife. The mother of your child. She deserves respect, even reverence." His craggy face flushed with anger. "See if you can go back to the Prohibition Bureau, because I plan to do everything in my power to keep you from being our constable again." He turned away from Jax and introduced himself to Celeste as Lyle Fikeland. Both his countenance and tone softened when he did.

She responded in kind. "How lovely to meet you, sir."

Fikeland shook his head. "I'm sorry Hastings was rude to you. I'm on the Moreley council and, if I can make your stay more pleasant, call on me at the hardware store. It's in the middle of town."

"Merci," she replied. "I hope Jackson will do what is right and help me and our child. I thought he was a good man, or I would not have married him."

Fikeland's pale gray gaze shot to Jax. "You're trying to spurn your wife and youngster while courting another woman. Disgusting." His attention went to Bella. "I hope you recognize what a cad he is now, Miss Stewart."

Celeste's brow furrowed as she looked from Bella to Jax. "You are wooing her?"

"He has been for weeks. Looks like it's getting serious." Another voice came from among the onlookers.

"Maybe not now," an additional person added.

Bella did not identify the sources. Shivers, from emotional upset instead of cold weather, rippled through her. Her voice seemed to be frozen in her throat, while her feet felt like they were deep in ice. Speaking and moving were beyond her.

A small gasp left Celeste when the onlookers spoke, but her expression didn't match. Her slight smile indicated no surprise or unrest. She wasn't startled. Not at all. "Jackson, how could you? We have been apart for a long time, but that is no excuse. I have looked endlessly for you, and I thought you must have tried to find me. Perhaps not."

"You were aware of where I lived, so you could've contacted me long before now," Jax said. His tone indicated his patience was completely shot.

"As I said, I sent letters, but they came back unopened," Celeste said in a wobbly voice. "Perhaps, you got them and returned them yourself. Xavier and I are struggling. My aunt and uncle can only do so much for us. I help in their bakery, but it is doing less business." She wrung her hands.

Jax put one hand to his head. For several moments, he said nothing. Finally, an inaudible sigh left him. "If you're really in financial trouble, I can give you a couple hundred dollars. But you need to go away and leave me alone."

Celeste gaped at him. "You cannot buy me off, and so little money would hardly keep us for a few months. Surely, you have more concern for your boy, if not for me."

"I'm not listening to any more lies." Jax ground the words out. "You'd be smart to leave town, Celeste, because you won't get any money from me." He turned to Bella. "Let's go."

Before she replied, he grasped her elbow and moved her past the remaining townsfolk. Bella's cheeks burned with embarrassment. How she hated to be a spectacle, but she was. The murmurs behind them revealed as much.

When they were out of earshot, Jax spoke again. "I'm sorry she showed up and created a scene. I'll get her out of town as soon as I can, although I've got no idea why she came here with her sorry tale. It's all lies."

Bella's pulse pounded in her ears. Celeste's appearance put her off-kilter, and the woman's accusation added to her dilemma. Some time and space might help. As would getting away from prying eyes, and there were more than a few folks staring at her and Jax. She walked toward his Chevrolet Chummy, parked a bit down Main Street, and he followed.

"I don't know why she came here, and I'll get rid of her as soon as I can."

She stopped to face him. "You offered her money. If you have no ties to her, why would you do that?" Bella didn't keep the hurt and confusion from her voice. While she wanted to believe Jax, old memories and his proffer of funds kept her in check.

"Her struggles made me feel sorry for her, but I shouldn't have said I'd give her money. She sure didn't appreciate the gesture, and I won't be offering again."

His words barely permeated her consciousness. "I'd like to go home."

"Go home?" he echoed. "We were going to the school for the potluck supper."

"Everyone will talk about Celeste showing up and about us. And you and her. I don't want to face people and be stared at and gossiped about." Nor did Bella want to be the target of sympathy—genuine or feigned. When Jax didn't immediately reply, she hurried on. "Please. Take me to Ballantyne." The resort, which she co-owned, was her home and her haven. ,

Jax didn't move. "You can't possibly believe I married that woman and had a child with her. You know me better."

Whatever Bella might have said was halted by her best friend's arrival.

"I'm sorry we're late." Ida Byington, with her fiancé Griff Biggins at her side, stopped in front of the other couple. "I hoped to get away from school earlier, but some students were still on campus."

Biggins had been the Ballantyne golf professional for nearly a year, and Ida—a teacher at a nearby boarding school—had met him when she visited. They hit it off immediately and began courting in short order. Bella struggled to smile at the couple. Their joyous expressions should be returned by Jax and her, but he looked as grim as she felt. "I'm sure it was hectic, but I'm glad you're spending the holidays at the resort."

"We'll be able to get to all the other festivities with the two of you," Ida said. "The dance, the play, caroling, and such. Of course, we'll be busy at Ballantyne, too, and I'm looking forward to everything. Griff is, as well." She looked up at the tall, dark-haired man beside her with love in her hazel eyes.

Griff's grin, directed at his betrothed, faded when he turned to Bella and Jax. "Everything go well with the lighting?"

13

"Of course," Bella gestured toward the tree with its colorful lights, but her pleasure over the festivity had waned.

Lyle Fikeland stopped by the Chummy before the conversation could continue. "Hastings, you're a disgrace to this town and to your parents' memories." His gaze went to the other couple. "I don't know how any of you can bear to associate with him." Fikeland stared at Bella. "Especially you. The man is married with a child. Maybe you didn't realize until tonight, but you do now. Show some sense and get away from him." Lyle stomped off without a backward glance.

"What is he talking about?" Ida asked.

Mortified by the ongoing scrutiny, Bella focused on her friend. "I'll explain later. Right now, I want to go home."

Ida studied Bella for a long moment. "Of course. Griff and I will take you." She released her fiancé's arm and took Bella by the hand.

"We need to talk." Jax's tone was tense. "You know what Celeste said isn't true. You know she was involved with…" His voice abruptly stopped as he shot a glance at Ida. Jax shifted from one foot to the other. "She was involved with another American, not me. He's probably the father of her boy. I'm certainly not."

Ida spun toward Jax. Seconds ticked away as she stared at him. "What? Some woman accused you of being her child's father. You say you aren't, but why come to you? Why not go to the other man? That would make more sense."

While Bella appreciated her friend's loyalty, she only wanted to get away. And without Jax revealing details about Celeste's lover. Or lovers. Had there been more than one? Was Jax in that number?

Jax bowed his head. "It would if he was still alive…"

Bella interrupted him. "Do not say one more word." She stole a glance at Ida, who seemed more confused than ever. "Will you and Griff drive me back?"

"Of course," Ida said.

"Bella, I understand why you're upset," Jax spoke rapidly. "But Celeste is lying."

"Celeste," Ida echoed the name. "What is her surname?"

"She says it's Hastings," said another passerby.

"Bouchard. It's Bouchard." Jax looked at the other man, who shrugged and moved on.

"I've heard that name," Ida murmured.

"We met some French girls, and she was one of them, I think." Bella said. Not true, but Ida didn't need to know more about the intruder. Because she didn't want to be subjected to more gossip or have Jax reveal any more about Celeste and her American soldier, Bella tugged on Ida's arm. "I'm getting cold. Let's get in the car."

Jax reached and took Bella's hand when she walked past him. "Please talk to me. Please listen to me."

She shook her head. "Not tonight."

"Tomorrow morning," he said.

"I can't. Ida and I are visiting a friend in Sandusky. I'll call you when we get home." Bella knew they had to discuss the situation when she was calmer…and when her best friend wasn't around to overhear hurtful news.

A harsh breath left Jax, but he nodded. "All right. Later tomorrow, we'll get this straightened out between us."

"We will." Despite her uneasiness, Bella tried to inject optimism into her voice. She forced a smile, or the semblance of one, and walked away with Ida.

Chapter Two

J ax fought the urge to insist Bella allow him to drive her home. Clearly, she wasn't ready to listen. Why, why, why had he offered to give Celeste money? The answer came quickly. Because he felt sorry for her, just as he had in France. He'd made a poor decision then, and he'd just made another one. Hopefully, the outcome would not be as long-lasting.

"I feel like I missed some details," Griff said. "Not that you have to tell me. But if you want to talk, I can spare a few minutes. That'd give Bella and Ida some private time, too."

With one hand, Jax removed his cap while he finger-combed his blonde hair with the other. "Celeste Bouchard was a French nurse, whose brother was mortally wounded and found by an American platoon. When she discovered where he was, she came to care for him. Some of us met her in the field hospital." The revelations barely scratched the surface, but Jax was not prepared to reveal every detail at the moment. "Things got complicated when she became involved with one of my fellow officers."

"And he's apt to be her husband and the boy's father," Griff said.

Jax's gaze strayed to Ida and Bella before returning to Griff. "Not her husband but, if there's a child, he's probably the father."

"Why would she come to you?"

Although answering the question might give Griff insight, Jax wasn't lying to protect a dead man. Not anymore. "He was killed in France at the start of the Meuse-Argonne offensive."

"Before they could marry," Griff suggested.

Jax exhaled sharply. "He wasn't planning to wed her. At least, not that I know." He couldn't help looking back at the two women climbing into Griff's roadster. Mostly at one of them—Bella.

"Ida's fiancé died around that time."

Alarm filtered through Jax as he turned to the other man. Griff was a smart guy, and he had likely put past knowledge together with current circumstances. Or he was mulling over the possibilities. "He did."

A female voice broke into their conversation. "Griff, are you coming? Bella and I are getting cold."

"I need to take the girls home," Griff said. "I'm sure you haven't revealed everything, and I don't expect you to. But I don't want Ida hurt."

"Neither do I." He hesitated a moment before offering a tad more insight. "That's why I've kept the secret about Celeste and her American lover for years. I finally told Bella last spring, but she'll say nothing to wound Ida, and neither will I."

"Good." Griff nodded before walking to his vehicle.

For several moments, Jax watched as the roadster drove away. With mixed emotions, he got into his own vehicle. He and Bella had planned to eat at the school potluck. Going alone was out, but the hour was still early, so he drove to nearby Boxwood instead of heading home. Supper at the village diner seemed liked the best idea, since no one there would have witnessed the contretemps between Celeste and him.

Jax figured correctly. Only two people were in the small diner. One was a fellow veteran, Burton Cratton.

"Join us," Burton called out when Jax walked in the door.

"Thanks." Jax shed his coat and sat down.

"Did you know Victor Gaspard in France?" Burton asked.

"We met in passing." Jax looked at the Frenchman. "Good to see you again."

For a moment, Gaspard's dark gaze—shadowed by mauve smudges—went to Jax. Recognition, along with some indefinable emotion, crossed his face. After mumbling a response, Victor focused on his food. Burton continued the conversation, so Jax followed suit but, out of the corner of his eye, he saw the Frenchman eat as if he was in a rush to get some place. Had Gaspard been at the lighting and heard the scene with Celeste? Jax inwardly chastised himself. They were both French but didn't necessarily know each other. He needed to shake off the incident for now. Jax glanced around the nearly empty restaurant. "Awfully quiet tonight."

A half shrug lifted one of Burton's broad shoulders. "Many people are in Moreley for the tree lighting. My folks went, and they're staying for the big potluck. I had to work late, or I'd be there, too. I'm surprised you aren't."

Their conversation was interrupted by the diner proprietor taking their orders. When he left, Jax commented. "I was, but I didn't feel like the potluck." Although Jax had not seen Burton in months, he figured his friend knew about his courtship with Bella. News traveled fast between the two towns, but Jax did not mention her. He didn't want to talk about what had happened. Not yet. Again, he looked at the Frenchman. "You didn't want to go, either, Victor?"

His head came up, and Gaspard briefly met Jax's gaze. "I am busy with my shop." He put his napkin on the table and stood. "Thank you for joining me, Burton. And you." The last was added as his gaze flickered over Jax. "I must go." He pulled a cap over his dark hair and shrugged into an old army jacket before leaving the diner.

"What's up with him?" Jax asked as he watched the other man go outside.

"No idea," Cratton replied. "He often stops here to eat on his way home. There's always at least one of us veterans having a meal. I worked with the French army for a while, so he and I got to know one another, which is one reason he moved here. All his family died during the war or soon afterward. We corresponded when I got back and before he came over."

Jax absorbed the information. "You know him much better than I do. We met in France. I can't say we were well acquainted, but Matt and I stayed at his aunt's guesthouse in Paris when we had weekend leaves once. Victor recommended the lodging to us, and I talked to him later to say thanks because his aunt was very gracious." Bittersweet memories surfaced. He and Matt had spent those days with Bella, the last time all three had been together. The heavy weight of past loss and current discord burdened him. Jax continued eating, but the food became tasteless because all his senses were focused on long-ago times. Matt Stewart, his best friend and Bella's big brother, had died in the trenches. Although Jax always felt the loss keenly, he was especially up-ended now. Matt would know what to say to Bella, and he'd back Jax up in doing so.

"I've heard Victor's business is struggling. He talked a little when I first sat down with him, but he's reserved most of the time." Burton laid down his fork and brushed a lock of auburn hair off his forehead.

"He was wearing an American army jacket," Jax said.

"It belonged to Bill Addison. He and Victor got close during the war, which is part of why Victor settled here."

"Even though Bill died."

"Bill had told his mother about Victor, and she was set on him coming. To take Bill's place, in a way. Of course, I knew Victor, too, and welcomed him."

"I see." Since Jax had only met the Frenchman in passing, he let the subject drop.

For a few minutes, the two former soldiers caught up. When the food came, they both dug in. While they ate, Jax relaxed. The hot food and friendly conversation eased his mind. Tomorrow morning, he would talk with Bella and work out the problem of Celeste Bouchard.

The owner let Jax and Burton stay and chat long past closing time, and it was after ten o'clock when Jax reached his home. Weariness filled him as he mounted the porch steps.

He opened the screen door to find a paper tucked between it and the wooden one. His heart beat faster. Had Bella come back to town looking for him? If she had left a note, wouldn't that be a good sign? After heading to the parlor and turning on a lamp, Jax opened the missive to see only two sentences: Meet me behind the café at eleven-thirty. If you do not come, I will take our marriage license to Miss Stewart. C.

As anger and anxiety collided inside him, hope disintegrated. Bella wasn't the one wanting to see him. Jax longed to tear up the paper and ignore the order. But how could he? What if Celeste showed the fake certificate to Bella? What if Bella accepted the document as real? He could not risk it.

An hour later, he left his house and headed to the meeting place. The potluck would have ended long ago. Now, all was quiet, and Jax saw no one until he entered the alley. A petite, feminine figure moved toward him.

"Jackson, I am glad you came."

"I had very little choice." Jax stopped a few feet away from her.

In the dim light, her features weren't clear but, when she replied, annoyance undergirded her words. "You could have agreed to give me money earlier."

"I thought you wanted to be a family."

"Would you like that?"

Jax ground his teeth. Now that they were alone, she was not so quick to have him as a husband and the father of her child. Not surprising. "You and I were never involved, so you don't really want to create a family together. You want money, and I offered you some because I feel sorry for you. Or I did until you produced a spectacle in front of the town."

"But you are most worried about Miss Stewart. If you had not been so mean, we could have settled matters already, and neither of us would need to be here now."

"If you weren't lying, neither of us would be here at all." Exasperation filled him. "Let me see the supposed license."

She reached into her pocketbook, extracted a paper, and extended it to him. When Celeste didn't let go, Jax tried to wrest it away.

"I will hold it," she said. "The light is good enough for you to read each word."

While resentment rose inside him, Jax bent his head. Scanning the paper, he felt increasingly sick. Both of their names were on the document. His French was good enough to make out the date but not much more. While the license looked genuine, it wasn't. "It's a fake." It had to be, since the two of them hadn't married. But why go to so much trouble? Was she so desperate? He glared down at her. "I don't know how you managed this, but it isn't real."

Her chin lifted a fraction. "It is very real, and others will accept it. You would be wise to arrange payment, Jackson. A lump sum now, and I will go away. You will not hear from me again."

"What if I'd rather be a husband and father?" When she didn't immediately reply, Jax continued. "Not so interested in that, are you?"

"Of course, I am," Celeste said. "I will have to send for Xavier and the rest of my things, but I could move into your house, our home, right away. Perhaps, Monsieur Fikeland would reconsider hiring you back as the constable, if the two of us are together." A grin curved her lips.

The strength of her assertion, and her triumphant attitude, made Jax wonder if she would make good on the threat of going to Bella. He studied the firm set of her delicate jaw and the bright glitter in her dark eyes. Celeste's certitude alarmed him. The woman seemed intent on perpetrating her lie, her treacherous accusation, which could ruin the rest of his life. Would Bella listen to him or was her mind made up? He planned to plead his case but, if he lost his job, Jax might not get other work in Moreley. He could return to the Prohibition Bureau, but asking Bella to go with him was unthinkable. Ballantyne was in Bella's blood, heart, and soul. Jax loved the place almost as she did, and he could never—would never—take her away from it. Panic provoked his next words. "Do yourself a favor and get out of town. Take the first train tomorrow, or you'll be very sorry you stayed because I'll make whatever's left of your life pure misery." The statements were more a threat than a promise, but pressure might move her. And Jax needed to move her.

Celeste's gaze briefly shifted away before returning to Jax. "You would not wish to harm the mother of your child." She wiped at nonexistent tears with the back of her hand. "Please, please. Do not forsake us."

Her artificial histrionics further infuriated him. "I'm not arguing anymore. Get out of town or regret it." When Jax spun on his heel to walk away, he saw Sam Push in the back door of his café. Dismay lined the proprietor's face.

"Miss, can I help you?" Push asked.

Celeste rushed toward the man. "My husband is angry. Very angry."

Jax stared at her in shock and dismay. She had not asked for help, but she had reinforced her lie. Not only was he not her spouse, he wouldn't harm her. Or any woman. Before he could object to her claim, Sam addressed Jax. "Lyle Fikeland and others who were at the lighting ceremony have been telling everyone about your confrontation with this young lady, and I couldn't believe my ears. Now, I have to wonder if the war changed you. I wouldn't have believed it until tonight." The man turned back to Celeste. "Do you want to come inside, miss?"

"No, monsieur, but I thank you. Jackson and I need to discuss our future." Her voice was soft with regret and hope.

The woman sounded sincere enough that she could make a living on the stage. Jax gritted his teeth. "We have no future because we've had no past."

A harrumph left the café owner. "If you need help, call out, miss. I won't be leaving for a few more minutes." Then, Push closed the door, leaving the pair alone.

As soon as the proprietor disappeared inside, someone whistled, which made Jax turn to look down the narrow alley. A man, cloaked in shadow, stood some fifty yards away. Jax narrowed his gaze, but he only made out a silhouette.

Celeste also spun at the sound, and a shiver rippled through her. "I must go. Plan to give the money to me in the morning. Five thousand dollars. If you do not, perhaps Miss Stewart will convince you—after she sees our wedding certificate."

The threat made Jax swivel back to face her, but curiosity about the stranger stayed with him. "Bella won't believe you have a real license. She speaks fluent French and can read the details." He wasn't sure her knowledge would make a difference, or that seeing the supposed document wouldn't crush her. His focus was on getting Celeste and her male companion out of town. "When I prove it's counterfeit, I'll make sure you, and whoever is with you, go to jail."

"No one is with me. Why would you say such a thing?" Her reply came quickly, almost spasmodically. The whistle came again, and Celeste briefly glanced in that direction. "I must go. Get the money ready. I will be at your house at ten o'clock tomorrow." Celeste, without taking time to tuck the paper away, darted toward the male figure.

Her sudden departure caught Jax flat-footed. As soon as he regained his equilibrium, he ran after her, but his arm—still sore from surgery—impeded his speed. Besides, she was fast and reached the man twenty yards ahead of him. As he followed, Jax stared at the stranger but got only a fleeting impression—the man was wearing a greatcoat and the top of Celeste's head did not reach his shoulder.

As Jax trailed them, the pair slipped into the cross street. By the time he got there, they were out of sight. He spun around and around but saw no sign of either figure. Unsure which way they had turned, he headed toward the hotel. The pair must be staying there. Jax rushed to the back door and ran right into the desk clerk. "Did a man and woman just come in here?"

"No. I haven't seen a soul for an hour or more." Korbert Lannigan, the desk clerk, stared at Jax for a long moment. "Why are you out looking for people? I thought you was still getting over surgery and not back to work."

The mad dash after Celeste proved Jax wasn't completely well, and he worked to catch his breath. "I am, but I was talking with someone in the alley and she ran off."

Lannigan's eyes widened. "Your wife? Lyle and some others was telling me about her. I was working, so I didn't see the goings-on at the park."

Jax drove his fingers through his hair. "I'm not married. Never have been."

"Uh-huh."

Clearly, the man didn't believe him. Did anyone after the scene at the tree lighting? Except for his service in France, Jax had spent all his life in Moreley. Didn't folks know him better? But Lannigan had come to Moreley after Jax left for the Prohibition Bureau, so the two were almost strangers. "The man was wearing a greatcoat. Have you seen anyone in one?"

The desk clerk's attention darted away. "Nope."

The one-word answer and dismissive gesture signaled an end to the exchange. Lannigan must know nothing. Or not want to reveal what he knew. "Thanks. I'll see if I can find them some other place."

"Good luck," Lannigan said, but his tone held no sincerity.

Jax left the hotel with a heavy heart. Wanting to locate the Frenchwoman and her associate, or accomplice, he walked around town. Most homes and businesses were dark. Finally, Jax headed back to the park. The Christmas tree still glowed with electric lights, and Jax went toward it. As he did, a vehicle drove by, but the driver didn't slow down. Since Jax was in clear sight, being ignored felt like rejection and disapproval. Usually, fellow townsfolk waved or honked in greeting. His mood kept plummeting. Maybe the automobile belonged to early visitors, not a resident. Jax hoped so. He didn't want to think he had become an outcast due to Celeste's ugly lies.

For an indeterminate time, he sat on a bench and considered all that had happened since early evening.

Briefly, he pondered getting his vehicle and heading to Ballantyne to talk with Bella. But the hour was late. Too late for a visit. Over and over, he weighed what to do next. Celeste was tenacious, but he was convinced she wasn't alone in her quest. She had hurried off, as if frightened not to heed the stranger's call. Why? Victor had rushed away from the Boxwood diner, too. Were the incidents related?

With only glances of the man in the alley, Jax couldn't describe him. Only two details were clear. Celeste was more than a head shorter than the stranger, just as she was with Jax. And the man had been wearing a greatcoat, one the same shape as French soldiers had worn. Not much to go on, but Victor fit the profile on both counts.

Frustrated and exhausted, Jax finally headed to his house after two o'clock. Another automobile passed as he left the park. This driver sped on, too. Gloom settled over Jax like a shroud. He had never felt so alone and bereft in his entire life.

Once home, he went to bed. But sleep was a long time coming.

Hours later, banging on the front door yanked Jax from a deep sleep. He hadn't dozed off until well after five. A glance at the clock revealed only four hours had passed since then. With a low groan, he rolled out of bed, pulled on his clothes, and descended the stairs in his bare feet. The incessant knocking continued.

"I'm coming," he called out. Jax yanked the door open to find Nolen Rogers, his former deputy and the interim constable, outside. Beside him was Mayor Cawlings. Both men looked grim, but only Nolen appeared edgy. "Can I help you?"

Nolen shifted from one foot to the other. "I need to talk with you, Jax."

The statement revealed little. Jax focused on Cawlings. "You need to talk with me, too?"

With one hand, the mayor brushed his dark hair back from his face. "I don't want folks accusing young Rogers of favoritism. This case must be conducted with the utmost professionalism."

Jax rubbed his eyes. Grogginess plagued him. What was going on? He hadn't discussed Celeste's blackmail attempts with any authorities. Had someone else? Was Nolen investigating her? That would be helpful.

Jax stepped back and waved the pair inside. "We can discuss things in the parlor."

Nolen quickly responded. "That's a good idea." He stepped forward as he spoke.

Cawlings was slower to react. "I suppose it'll be acceptable."

The reply seemed odd, but Jax led the way with a glimmer of optimism. Maybe an investigation would convince Celeste and her friend to leave town. He didn't care about having them charged with extortion. Having them gone, and the accusation retracted, would be enough.

After the three men sat down, Nolen pulled out a notepad and pencil. "I know a little about Miss Bouchard from during the war." He cleared his throat and glanced away from Jax. "Of course, I've heard about your encounters with her, since she came to town. But gossip isn't evidence."

"Have you seen the fake marriage certificate? Is that why you're here?" Nolen's behavior struck Jax as out of character. Did confronting the Frenchwoman bother him? Why? Maybe because she'd had a love affair with Alan Brewster, Ida's dead fiancé, which Nolen already knew. The men had served together in France but, more than that, Nolen had disapproved of Brewster's involvement with Celeste. As had Jax.

"We've both seen it," Cawlings put in. "The license looks very real."

The revelations provoked anxiety. "Did she come to the office with it?" Jax kept his attention on his former deputy. Why would she do a such a thing? Did her treachery expand to making the town turn on him? He had done nothing to merit that kind of revenge. Not to her or to anyone else.

Nolen licked his lips and swallowed several times before replying. "No, we found it when we searched her hotel room looking for clues to her death."

"Death." Jax echoed the word with shock. "Celeste is dead?"

"That's why we're here," Cawlings put in. "Her body was found shortly after dawn. She'd been bludgeoned and thrown into the creek at the far end of the park. Doc examined her. He figures she was hit hard with a rock and dragged into the water. As far as he can tell, there was no water in her lungs, so she probably died from the blow to the right side of her head."

Jax's insides roiled with horror. For long moments, he sat frozen in place. Slowly, the mayor's observations coalesced, and an ugly realization hit Jax. He was a suspect in Celeste's murder. At least to Cawlings and maybe to other townsfolk. Lyle Fikeland came to mind as one person who would think the worst of Jax. What about Sam Push's reaction last night? And the others who had witnessed the scene at the park. Not reassuring. Neither was Lannigan's response to Jax's queries. Small bits of evidence could be as powerful as one major clue. No wonder Nolen looked apprehensive.

The mayor spoke again. "A mitten was found in the park. A green knitted one. Didn't a lot of you boys receive them while you were in France? And in different colors?"

Again, Jax struggled to absorb the information. Then, he pulled up memories of boxes from home. "Mostly khaki ones through national organizations, but we got different shades from smaller groups and individuals.

Everyone did, as far as I know." Jax clasped his icy hands together. "I assume the one you found would fit a man?"

Nolen nodded. "Yep, it would." His freckles stood in stark contrast to his ashen face.

"You got mittens yourself, didn't you?" Cawlings made the query.

"I did," Jax admitted. "Some of the boys would re-member that, since mine were bright green. I got them at the field hospital when I was wounded the first time, but I don't have them anymore."

"Interesting." Cawlings paused before asking another question. "When did you last see Miss Bouchard?"

A sigh left Jax because he figured Cawlings already knew about the meeting behind the café. He must have been busy gathering information in the time since the body was found. "We spoke for a short time late last night."

"What did you two discuss?" Cawlings asked.

The mayor's tone and expression indicated he knew the answer. "She wanted money from me. Five thou-sand dollars. She said she'd be here this morning. If I didn't give it to her, she'd show the license to Bella."

"And you threatened her." Cawlings made it a state-ment, not a question.

Once again, Jax reminded himself that prevaricating was a poor strategy. "I said she and her friend would be sorry if they didn't leave town."

Cawlings did not react to Jax's answer. Instead, he veered into fresh territory. "When did you get home?"

"Shortly after two," Jax replied.

"You got home after two o'clock. Why not come right back after meeting her?" Cawlings asked.

The mayor was doing what should have been Nolen's job, which annoyed Jax. The mayor could be presumptuous, and he seemed to be now. "A man whistled at Celeste, and she took off. I ran after them, but my arm is still healing, and the pain impeded me. They got away. I went to the hotel, but the desk clerk hadn't seen them. From there, I looked around more."

Nolen, notepad still in hand, retrieved a pencil from his pocket and started writing. "We've been at the hotel, and Korbert Lannigan mentioned you being there just around midnight. He said you rushed off when Celeste wasn't there."

"I didn't rush off. He wasn't any help, so I went out to look more," Jax said.

"You walked the town for over two hours?" Mayor Cawlings sounded skeptical. "It got pretty cold last night. Not exactly a fine time to stroll around."

Jax glanced at Nolen, whose stricken expression provided no solace. "I went to the park and sat there for a while." His stomach knotted. One vehicle went by as he had entered the area, and another passed when he was leaving. Both were witnesses to his presence near the murder scene. Although Jax didn't know if Cawlings and Nolen knew that, he saw no point in hiding the facts, which would come out eventually. "A couple of people driving by the park saw me, I'm sure."

An uneasy silence preceded Nolen's next comment. "Did you recognize the vehicles?"

"I can identify the makes and models. One was a Willys Overland. The other was a Paige Englewood. A couple of locals have the same ones."

His former deputy jotted the information down. "What about the man with Celeste? Can you describe him?"

Jax replied with the two details about the figure—the man's coat and his height. "She denied someone was with her, but she left with him. I'm sure of that."

"That's a vague description for a supposed accomplice," Cawlings said in a disbelieving tone.

Her accomplice and maybe her killer. Jax drove his fingers through his hair. "It's all I can say for sure."

"And you planned to confront both of them? Was that wise? If they were crooks, as you allege, he could've been armed while you weren't. Or were you?" Cawlings maintained a calm demeanor, which further grated on Jax's nerves.

"My service revolver has been in the nightstand drawer since I got home in October." Although it meant nothing in terms of the case, Jax offered the detail because he wanted to be forthright. After investigating several homicides, he knew hiding information created suspicion—and he didn't want more doubt falling on him.

"But you say you were being extorted. Why not call Nolen and get him to talk to this Frenchwoman?" Cawlings asked.

Indeed. Why not? "I should have." Jax bowed his head. Why had he met Celeste late at night? Why hadn't he contacted Nolen? Why had he acted rashly? One answer arose: he wanted Celeste to leave town as soon as possible, so he could repair the breach with Bella.

"You've been a lawman for a few years now," the mayor observed. "Would you accept your excuses from a suspect?"

The man had Jax there. "I'd look into someone telling a similar story in a comparable situation."

"Which is what Nolen is doing." Cawlings turned to the acting constable. "Go ahead."

Actually, the mayor was doing most of the interrogation. His former sergeant and deputy only briefly met Jax's gaze. To put Nolen at ease, Jax said, "I'm ready and willing to answer questions." He wasn't. Not really, but he would cooperate.

Nolen gave a slight nod. "Sam Push said you and Celeste argued in the alley behind his café. That was around eleven-thirty?"

Jax confirmed the information and everything else the café owner had revealed. He admitted his anger during both meetings with Celeste. Doing otherwise would be foolish, since there were witnesses to the confrontations. An entire group had seen them after the tree lighting. But she had not asked for a large sum of money until they were alone. His insides knotted. "She was lying about our involvement. I barely knew the girl in France." The latter statement was for Cawlings, since Nolen already knew as much.

Nolen tapped his pencil against the notepad. "Did she show you the license?"

"She did. My French is poor, so I could only decipher the names and dates," Jax replied. "But it's fake because we didn't get married."

"The two of you were at the same field hospital on the date named." Cawlings made the statement with certainty.

How had he learned about that? When Jax saw the color rise in Nolen's face, he knew. Not that Jax blamed the younger man for making the admission. The entire truth had to come out, and sooner was better than later. "I was. Most of the boys who were in France with me could confirm it, since it was the day after Matt Stewart died. I don't think any of us will forget the date we lost him."

Something akin to relief crossed Nolen's boyish face, but sorrow shadowed his eyes. Clearly, he was glad Jax wasn't angry about the younger man revealing a pertinent detail. But Nolen obviously still remembered Matt's mortal wounding.

"If you don't disagree, we won't need to question any of them. It's a minor point." Nolen spoke with more certainty.

A harrumph left the mayor. "Perhaps not so minor. It establishes a relationship between the two of you."

Jax ground his teeth until he feared they might crack. "I admit being with Celeste at the field hospital that day. You don't need to question anyone else. However, running into her there doesn't constitute a connection, and it was a happenstance." An unfortunate one in more than one way. "I was in another field hospital when I heard about Matt. I went right away, but I was too late." He swallowed hard over the lump of grief that always threatened to choke him when he remembered the loss and pain and regret. "I didn't plan to meet Celeste. In fact, I was surprised to see her there. That's the truth."

"Time will tell." The mayor turned to Nolen. "And I believe confirmation from the other men is necessary."

The mayor was right. If Jax was running the investigation, he would confirm every detail. "Fine."

After a brief nod, Cawlings glanced back at Nolen. "Go ahead. We need to wrap this up."

"Yes, sir." Once again, Nolen looked uncomfortable. "About how long did you and Celeste talk last night?"

"Twenty minutes, maybe." But the exchange had seemed endless. "Sam Push heard us and came out. After he went back inside, the stranger whistled twice, and Celeste said she had to go. Celeste was obviously uneasy." Since his former deputy was taking notes, Jax repeated the details. Nolen wasn't to blame for his current plight, so Jax maintained a calm tone despite the anxiety clawing at his insides.

"Sam didn't mention seeing anyone else," the mayor said. "As for you not catching up with them, how did you plan to go back to work on January first? Only a few days ago, you said you'd be ready. What if you had to chase down an actual crook?"

The mayor's continuing disbelief wasn't encouraging. Before responding, Jax took a long breath. He needed to remain composed, at least outwardly. "I didn't realize my arm would be a problem until I darted after her. Mostly, it's doing well."

"I see." The mayor's tone indicated he didn't. "What about Sam not seeing this other person? How do you explain that?"

"He'd gone back into the café by then."

"That's unfortunate," Cawlings said.

Again, Jax took a moment to rein in his dismay. "That man could be the killer. There aren't a lot of visitors in town yet, so you could question all of them. And the hotel staff. Someone else had to see him at some point." The words tumbled out of Jax, and he was reminded of several suspects in past cases who had reacted similarly. Such voluble retorts smacked of desperation. Despite being innocent, Jax definitely felt cornered and defensive.

"We already talked to some folks and searched Celeste's room. That's how we found the marriage license." Nolen's troubled expression spoke volumes. All bad.

"Every hotel guest was interviewed already. There aren't many yet, and none has been seen with the victim. Or seen her with another man. While two had seen her in passing, the others hadn't gotten even a glimpse." Cawlings' tone was serene, but his expression remained dour. "I've helped, since finding the murderer is important. This Christmas will be the first one in several years when the town will welcome visitors again. We don't need an unsolved killing."

Cawlings was the ultimate middle of the road, take no controversial stand glad-hander. While he wouldn't make outright accusations against Jax, the mayor wouldn't hurry to defend him, either. Not when he was more interested in announcing the case was closed than he was in solving the murder. "The man might not be staying at the hotel."

The mayor's dark gaze narrowed. "Where would he stay? The Eddingtons will open their boardinghouse to overflow guests next week. That leaves Ballantyne. I spoke with Mac myself, since Arabella was heading out of town this morning. They only have two visitors. Young men who checked into separate cottages. Their families are arriving soon."

The urge to find out how much Cawlings had told Mac took the forefront in Jax's mind. He resisted asking. If Bella had left early, she wouldn't have gotten any information, but word was evidently out in town. Jax didn't want to consider how she would feel when the news got to her. "If Celeste's accomplice is also her killer, he might've left already."

"You think he came into town for less than a day?" the mayor asked.

Cawlings' tone indicated the idea was preposterous, which made Jax feel even warier. "It's possible."

"But not probable," Cawlings added. "On Monday, Miss Bouchard came in on the noon train. How do you think this stranger got here?"

"Is she the only one who got off at that time?" Jax asked.

"No," Nolen replied. "We stopped at the train station. Mr. Geneve wasn't in, but I spoke with the chief porter, who didn't know how many people got off. He was too busy to count. We'll have to go back and see if we can learn more."

"Good." Jax hoped the stationmaster knew something useful. Although Nolen was the acting constable, he and Newton had served as deputies together for going on a year. Both were skilled lawmen.

Another harrumph left the mayor. "Newton has some years as a deputy behind him, which is a good thing now."

"In Boxwood. Nolen knows this town much better," Jax pointed out. He looked back at Nolen. "Do you have other questions?"

"I should probably look around a little." Nolen spoke with hesitancy.

"Of course." Jax followed Nolen as he searched. Cawlings followed.

Afterward, the mayor cited a meeting before leaving Jax and Nolen on the front porch.

Once Mayor Cawlings was out of sight, Nolen laid a hand on Jax's arm. "I'm sorry about the mayor coming along. I don't think he trusts me."

"It's fine. Like he said, he wants to avoid the appearance of favoritism." Jax forced a smile. "I'll be proven innocent when more details emerge."

"I know you will." Nolen shoved his hands into his coat pockets. "I reminded the mayor about your surgery on the way over, but he insisted you could have wielded a rock with your left hand."

"I could have," Jax reluctantly agreed. "Since you said the blow was to the right of her head, the mayor is right."

Nolen grimaced. "I know."

"Thanks for trying, though."

"I'll keep trying," Nolen replied. "Knowing the man waiting for Celeste was wearing a greatcoat might help. Could you tell the color?"

"No, but it reminded me of the coats worn by French soldiers." Jax scratched his head. "I can't be sure, though." Should he mention Gaspard? But what evidence was there against the Frenchman? Next to none, so Jax waited. Maybe he could learn more on his own before telling Nolen.

Nolen again made notes. "That could be helpful. We'll definitely check into it."

"You're planning to talk with the two drivers who saw me last night." Jax made it a statement.

Dismay blanketed Nolen's freckled face. "I have to."

"I know you do. You need to pursue this case like I'm a stranger."

A long moment passed before the younger man replied. "I know, but you aren't, and I wish this wasn't necessary."

"It'll all come out fine because I didn't kill Celeste." Jax spoke with more confidence than he felt.

"I never thought you had."

The support lifted Jax's sinking spirits. "Thanks. If you have more questions, I can come to the office."

"I'll call if that's necessary." Nolen studied Jax's face. "I wish you had told me about Celeste trying to get money from you."

"I wish I had, too." Jax shoved his hands into his jacket pockets. "The whole situation stunned me, and I wanted her to leave town right away."

"That's understandable. Seeing Celeste and hearing her accusations had to shock you, especially since Bella witnessed last evening's squabble. I'm sure her being there made it all worse."

"Much worse," Jax admitted. "She was pretty upset, and I don't blame her." How did she feel now? Did he want to know?

"She won't stay upset with you."

"I hope not. I really do." But hope could evaporate like mist in sunlight. Quickly and without a trace left behind.

Chapter Three

That morning, Bella was back in town to board the train for Sandusky, since she and Ida had decided not to drive due to snow. While Ida picked up a few items at the mercantile, Bella went to the post office. On her way back to Main Street, she ran into Nolen Rogers.

"Good day, Bella." Nolen doffed his cap.

His glum expression didn't match the greeting, but Bella forced a smile. "Hello, Nolen. How are you?" She fully expected an effusive response about his temporary stint as constable and about his sweetheart, Jillian, so his reaction surprised her. The pair had not been courting for long, but they were smitten with each other, and Bella expected a betrothal soon.

"Not good. Not good at all."

"I hope no one's giving you a hard time." Bella knew some of the townsfolk thought he was too young for the position. While in his early twenties, Nolen had left all traces of boyhood behind in the trenches of France. "You're more than capable of handling your duties."

He shook his head. "It's not that." Nolen doffed his cap and ran his fingers through his close-clipped red hair.

"What's wrong?" Had he and Jillian had a tiff? Since she was the clerk in the constable's office, any personal issues would make working together a challenge. Or maybe he had heard about Celeste being in town. Did he know more about her relationship with Jax? Was there more to know? Bella had been ready to apologize for her hasty reaction. Now, fresh uneasiness assailed her.

Nolen glanced up and down the street before replying. "Celeste Bouchard is dead. Someone murdered her."

"Dead? Murdered?" Bella echoed the words in shock. "Who would've done such a thing?"

"I don't know," he murmured. "Her body was found around dawn. We're still gathering evidence and doing interviews. Nothing conclusive so far."

"Do you have many leads?"

A stricken expression crossed his face. "We have several. A couple of witnesses who passed the park very early this morning, and a mitten was found close to the body. A couple other potential clues, too."

"That should help. Anything else?" As Bella studied Nolen, she noticed the dark smudges beneath his eyes.

He glanced away and back. "I'm afraid so." A heartbeat passed before Nolen continued. "There was a marriage license in her suitcase. I don't read French, but I could make out the date and the names."

Suddenly, Bella's pulse pounded in her ears. She didn't need to ask what names. "Jax and Miss Bouchard."

"He says it's phony," Nolen hurried to say.

The information barely registered. Early this morning, Bella had planned to apologize to Jax and assert her trust in him. Nolen's revelation threw up a major hurdle to doing both. "What was the date?"

Nolen's brow furrowed. "September 30, 1918."

The answer drove the air from her lungs. Drawing another breath seemed impossible as recollections crowded her head. That was the day after her brother died, while taking Jax's place on the line. Taken Jax's place and died. Had Jax wed the French nurse right after his best friend, Bella's only sibling, perished? The idea deepened her anguish. Alan Brewster had succumbed to his wounds earlier. Had Celeste been with child then? Had she appealed to Jax for protection? Or could Jax, not Alan, be the father? Misgivings sprouted like weeds.

"Bella?" Nolen's voice broke into her misery.

With grim determination, she responded. "I was just thinking back to that time."

He nodded. "I've gone over it repeatedly, since I got the call this morning. The evidence looks bad, but I believe Jax. He didn't marry Celeste, and he didn't kill her."

Nolen's sincerity sent guilt skittering along Bella's nerves. She should offer the same sort of support, but uncertainty hampered her. Bella had seen Jax and Celeste together on the date logged on the license. The look on his face—an expression of regret and remorse—was still clear to her, although three years had passed since then. Bella shook off thoughts of the past and focused on the present. "I'm sure that's true. Have you spoken with Jax?"

"I did a little while ago." He looked up and down the street before continuing with Jax's revelations. "Newton and I have a lot to do, and we'll investigate thoroughly."

Jax had evidently been forthright with Nolen, but the details were disturbing. "What other evidence is there? Anything substantial? Did the drivers see someone else near the park?"

He shifted from one foot to the other. "Nothing substantial. At least not to me, but Jax feels sure both saw him. That's circumstantial evidence." Nolen's troubled expression didn't lighten. "I'm going to call Richard Jenkins and see if he can help. Mayor Cawlings already warned me not to shape the investigation to help Jax, so I have to be careful."

The disclosure added to her dismay. "Does the mayor think Jax killed her?" While Bella didn't believe—didn't want to believe—he would conceal a legal union, she knew for certain Jax wouldn't commit murder. "Richard would be a big help. He has a lot of experience as a lawman, and he knows Moreley after taking Jax's place for a time." The older man knew and respected Jax, as well.

The door to the hardware store opened, and the owner stepped out. Lyle Fikeland's glare went from Nolen to Bella and back. "I hope you're not revealing confidential information about the murder case to Miss Stewart."

A blush blotted out the freckles on Nolen's face. "No, sir. Of course not."

"You better not be. The mayor said he'd make sure you don't let your longstanding ties to Hastings affect your actions, but I think you ought to be replaced." The older man scowled. "You were his platoon sergeant at the end of the war, and his deputy ever since. Except for when he went off to the Prohibition Bureau. I hardly think you're unbiased enough to investigate."

"Nolen will do an excellent job," Bella put in.

A harrumph left the older man. "You're not a disinterested party. What we need is an outsider to handle this case. Every merchant in town is counting on this Christmas to get us back to normal. We've come a long way in the past two years, and a strong holiday season will help us turn the corner. We can't afford to have potential visitors fearing they'll be attacked, particularly not by our former constable. A few are here already, but the bulk of folks are coming next week. This problem needs to be solved by then."

"I'm sure it will be," Nolen said. "We're doing a thorough investigation. We may have an answer soon."

"Good. Until then, keep the case information to yourself." Fikeland went back into his store without a backward glance.

Nolen ran one hand over his face. "Evidently, Mayor Cawlings told Mr. Fikeland everything."

"Fikeland shouldn't be criticizing you, since he ought not to be in the mayor's confidence. He's such a hypocrite. Always has been."

The slight twitch of Nolen's lips said he agreed.

"What about big leads?"

Nolen's amusement dissipated. "None that I like."

The statement sent Bella's spirits plummeting. A peek into the hardware store's window revealed Fikeland staring out at them. Bella quashed her questions. She'd have to get details later. "I know you'll find the killer soon."

He briefly followed her gaze. "I better get going."

"Good idea."

Nolen put his forefinger to his cap in a salute before moving on. For several moments, Bella watched him go. A lot was on his young shoulders. Getting help from Richard was advisable, and she was open to assisting, too. But how? Before an idea formed, Ida joined her.

"I saw Nolen talking with you. Is everything all right?" Ida asked.

It wasn't, but they needed to catch the train. "I'll tell you on the way."

The pair hurried to the station and boarded. After the train pulled out, Ida turned to Bella. "Something must be wrong. Both you and Nolen looked upset when you were talking."

Following a deep breath, Bella explained. "Celeste Bouchard was murdered last night."

A gasp left Ida. "Murdered. How awful. I assume they haven't caught her killer."

"Not yet."

"Do they have any leads?" Ida asked.

"A few." Bella summed up what Nolen had told her and waited for her friend's response.

"Jax met her late last night before walking around town? Why would he do that?"

"I don't know. He wanted to talk things over with me last night, but I felt confused and embarrassed. Before you and Griff arrived, Lyle Fikeland created a scene. Then, a couple of others added to it. That's why I wanted to get away." The previous night, Bella had gone to her suite without discussing the situation. This morning, she had only hit the high points. Low points, really. Now, she was torn between pouring her heart out and keeping her own counsel. The former was fraught with hazards. Months ago, Jax had shared the information about Ida's deceased fiancé and Celeste Bouchard. Not wanting to hurt her friend, Bella had kept the secret. But how could she explain more without revealing the truth?

"I understand. You had every right to be upset. I know Jax wouldn't murder anyone, and I doubt if he's married, because he wouldn't be courting you if he was." Ida chewed on her lower lip. "I heard him say she was involved with another American officer, one who died."

Bella studied her friend's expression, but found reading it difficult. "That's right."

Ida's brow furrowed. "Did you know before last evening?"

Again, Bella hesitated. Ida looked suspicious, which made Bella think back to their time in France and their shared confidences and worries. Abruptly, a memory surfaced. About two weeks before her fiancé died, Ida had mentioned her doubts about Alan not getting a day away from the line to see her. Other officers had gotten time off, so Ida was suspicious. Why hadn't Bella remembered sooner? Probably because so much had happened during the following weeks and months—Alan and Matt dying, seeing Jax with Celeste, the Armistice. "Jax told me last spring."

"When he explained about Matt's death, right?"

"Right," Bella murmured. While she had revealed why Jax had kept her at arm's length after her brother was killed, Bella had not included the details related to Ida and her former intended. Should she now?

"I know you, and there's something you're not telling me."

For a moment, Bella stared out at the passing scenery and mulled over how to proceed. Lying was out, but would the unadulterated truth wound Ida? When she felt her friend touch her arm, Bella shifted in her seat.

The other woman offered a tremulous smile. "You can tell me everything. I've probably already guessed part of the story, maybe most of it. During the last weeks before he died, Alan rarely came to see me. Alan used the excuse of not being able to get leave, but other officers got a day here and there. Although I never pointed that out to him, you might remember me being upset with Alan."

With reluctance, Bella nodded. "I hadn't thought about your concern over his behavior for a long while, but I recall it now."

"I was aware of plausible reasons for him staying away. Is he the officer who was involved with Celeste Bouchard?" Her voice trembled, but Ida offered a faint smile.

Bella laid one hand over her friend's. "He was."

Moisture filled Ida's eyes, and she blinked rapidly. "I can't say I'm surprised, and it shouldn't hurt after all this time. Especially not since I know now what genuine love is.

"Of course, it hurts." Bella recalled her friend's sorrow when Alan Brewster had died.

"I grieved for Alan, even when I wondered if he'd found someone else. I pushed my doubts down. I don't enjoy having been betrayed, but Alan and I got engaged in haste. You know how it was when America declared war. Emotions ran high. When we became betrothed, I was happy. Maybe not ecstatic, and I didn't want to show any misgivings later for fear it would get back to Alan. If our engagement made him feel better, kept him safer, I was fine with it. I figured we could see how we rubbed along after the war when we weren't swept away with emotions."

"You never told me, and I wouldn't have said anything."

"I know you wouldn't, but I felt foolish for agreeing to a betrothal when I wasn't sure."

Bella patted her friend's hand and released it. "Not foolish. If Jax had proposed, I would've accepted. But neither of us was ready for marriage."

"If you are now, and I'm sure that's the case for both of you, let him know you didn't believe Celeste Bouchard."

"I should've done that already." Despite her misgivings, Bella needed to let him explain.

"You can call him this evening. Besides, Nolen and Newton must be working on other leads. The trouble is, who else in Moreley knew Celeste?" Ida frowned. "If people find out she had an affair with Alan, maybe I'll come under scrutiny."

When the color left her friend's face, Bella shook her head. "That's ridiculous. You were at Ballantyne all that night."

"You went right to bed," Ida pointed out.

"But you and Griff must've sat up and talked."

A flush replaced the pallor in Ida's cheeks. "We did."

Bella could not help but chuckle. "In the lobby?"

"Yes."

"I'm going to surmise at least one employee saw the two of you."

Some of the tension drained from Ida's shoulders. "Three were in and out of the kitchen. The last one went to bed around midnight. After that, Griff went to the apartment over the pro shop, and I headed to the suite across from you. But she was killed in the wee hours, wasn't she?"

"She was, and Nolen told me how." Bella glanced around, but no one was close enough to hear. "She was hit in the head, probably with a rock, and dragged to the creek bank. That took some strength."

Ida's hand flew to her mouth as her eyes went wide. "How awful."

"It is," Bella agreed, "but they're looking for a man, so rest easy on that score."

"Resting easy will be an onerous task until the murderer is caught."

"I couldn't agree more."

"If you want to talk with Jax, reassure him, and help with the case, we could get off at the next stop and go back."

A big part of Bella wanted to do that, but she forced herself to stick with their plans. Bella shook her head. "Our friend and her family are expecting us, and we've had the trip planned for quite a while. I'll call him tonight when we're home again."

"Are you sure?"

"Yes, not much will happen in the meantime, and I want to talk with the conductor when he comes through for tickets. He might've seen Celeste."

"He surely isn't the only conductor on this route," Ida said.

"I'm not sure, but it can't hurt to ask."

Ida gestured to the front of the car. "There he is."

Bella could barely contain herself and, after exchanging greetings with the man, she made her inquiry. "A friend of ours came to Moreley on the train from Sandusky on Monday. We knew her when we served in France during the war."

The man looked from Bella to Ida and back. "You were nurses?"

"No, we were Army Signal Corps operators," Bella replied.

He smiled and nodded. "I hear you girls were important in the war effort. Making connections between the top brass and the soldiers at the front, and so forth."

Both expressed their gratitude. They had made contributions. The female operators freed men to fight, and they processed calls much faster than their male predecessors had.

"Was your friend alone?" he asked.

"We aren't sure. She's French." Bella provided a description and ended with, "Pretty and petite."

"Of course, I was the conductor on her train. I believe she was alone, but a young man stopped and spoke with her for a while. Maybe he knew her in France, too."

"Possibly, since she was a nurse. Do you know if he got off in Moreley?" Bella tried to tamp down her hope. Could this man be the killer?

"He did."

"Perhaps we knew him, too," Ida suggested. "What did he look like?"

A frown furrowed the man's brow. "Brown hair, maybe six feet tall, solid build. Not much to go on, I'm afraid."

"No, but thank you. Perhaps we'll see him when we get home," Ida said.

He put his hand to his cap brim. "I better move on. Enjoy the rest of the trip."

When he was out of earshot, Bella turned to her friend. "That's an interesting bit of information."

"If you can match it up with someone visiting town, it might be."

Bella nodded. "I'll definitely work on that when we get back."

After Nolen left, Jax got into his Chummy and headed back to Boxwood. News of the murder hadn't reached the little village, so he ate at the diner again. Since he was there after the lunch hour, the place was empty. Before leaving town, he went by Victor Gaspard's shop. A closed sign was in the front window, so Jax drove on to the man's residence—the only boardinghouse in town. He climbed out of his vehicle, went to the front door, and knocked. A small sign next to the mailbox read: Cotton, which jogged his memory. The elderly landlady, Mrs. Cotton, answered in moments.

Surprise blanketed her face before a smile formed. "Jackson Hastings. Come in, come in."

Jax swept off his cap and stepped inside. "I'm looking for Victor, ma'am. He wasn't at his shop."

The older lady's cheerful expression faded. "He's been struggling for a while. Business is terrible. He studied art in France, but not many local folks buy paintings or frames. He's tried woodworking, to little avail."

Her comments only reinforced what Burton Cratton had said in the diner. "I'm sorry to hear that. Do you know where he is?"

"I don't. He's been taking off a lot lately. Silent about his activities." She tsked, tsked. "I try not to pry, but he's all alone here. No folks left in France, either. I can't imagine where he goes."

Fresh dismay gripped Jax. "By lately, what do you mean? The last few weeks or the last few days."

The landlady's brow furrowed. "He left for a few days about a month ago. No idea where he went. Then, he was away over the weekend. He came home very late last night, so I had to speak with him. I don't like my boarders out until all hours." Disapproval underscored her statement.

"I understand," Jax said. "After midnight is late for most folks." Perhaps providing a time would elicit more details.

A harrumph left her. "He didn't get in until after three-thirty in the morning. I can't have that, and I told him so. He promised not to do it again, and I hope he sticks to his word. But he left after breakfast. Said he wasn't sure when he'd be back."

The revelation had Jax's heart hammering. "He was out last night and left this morning?" Although she had just said as much, he wanted to ensure he understood her correctly.

"That's right." She bit her lower lip as she studied Jax. "Did the two of you know each other in France?"

He answered with care. "Only in passing. We veterans all have things in common." Their last encounter stood out in Jax's mind.

"I'm sure you do. Victor doesn't speak about the war, but he moved to Boxwood due to meeting two of our boys during the war. Burton Cratton was one." A sorrowful look fell over her face. "Bill Addison was the other."

The landlady's sorrow echoed inside Jax. "I knew Bill. Made it through the fighting but succumbed to influenza."

"That he did. Near to broke his poor mother's heart. Victor and Bill evidently became fast friends. Since Victor lost his whole family, the two of them planned to come home together, much to Mrs. Addison's delight. When she lost her boy, she still encouraged Victor to come." The woman shook her head. "Poor thing. She passed not long after Victor arrived. Heart trouble. But Burton insisted Victor was welcome here, so he stayed."

Mrs. Cotton's revelations were interesting. Although getting details might not be easy, Jax planned to try. "Thank you, ma'am. I appreciate your time."

As Jax turned away, the lady's voice stopped him. "Do you want Victor to telephone you when he gets back?"

"Unnecessary, ma'am. I'll catch up with him another time. Have a good day." Jax decided to stop at the Cratton home and talk to Burton again, if he was there. Maybe he knew about Victor's recent travels.

Jax pulled to a stop at the curb and hurried to the house. A brisk wind and steady snow combined to put a chill in his bones, but that was nothing compared to the icy dread in his heart. He needed to talk to Bella soon.

Burton threw open the front door as soon as Jax stepped onto the porch. "I'm surprised to see you again. Glad, of course." He gestured inside the house. "Come on in. Ma baked cookies today, and she's always got fresh coffee on the stove. I just got home from work."

"I don't want to intrude." Jax hesitated on the doorstep.

"You're not intruding. My folks went next door to visit, so I've got the house to myself."

Jax followed the other man into the parlor, where a cheerful blaze flickered in the hearth. "Thanks. I won't take much of your time."

"I'm happy for the company. Let me grab cookies and coffee. In the meantime, make yourself at home."

After the other man exited the room, Jax perched on one fireside chair. He extended his hands and let the warmth spread through him.

Burton was back in only moments. When both men had refreshments, he looked at Jax. "I haven't seen you this often since we were in France. Something about your expression makes me wonder if this is a purely social visit."

Obviously, he wasn't cloaking his apprehension well. Jax shrugged. "Not purely social. We have a bit of a problem in Moreley."

The other man's expression grew grim. "I heard about the murder today at work."

When Burton didn't continue, Jax spoke again. "Did you meet Celeste Bouchard in France?"

Burton shook his head. "I didn't, but I heard about her." His gaze narrowed on Jax. "She and Lieutenant Brewster were involved, from what I know."

Jax braced his elbows on his knees and folded his hands in front of him. "They were."

"But she came to Moreley looking for you. At least that's the word going around."

"She came to the tree lighting last night and claimed I was her husband and the father of her child. Some people overheard our exchange. When I returned home, she'd left a note on my door saying I better meet her, so I did." Jax swallowed hard. "She had a fake marriage license, which she was using to blackmail me into paying her off. I was angry. Very angry. The café owner overheard the argument. I said she needed to get out of town or she'd be sorry, but I didn't kill her." Jax stared at the mug in his hands as he spoke.

Burton put up both hands. "I didn't think you had. No one who knows you would, either."

"Thanks," Jax replied, although he wasn't sure that was true. "I have a motive and no alibi, since I was alone after I met her behind the café late last night. We'd had harsh words earlier and again then. Witnesses overheard us both times. Even worse, I didn't go straight home after the late-night meeting, and others saw me out walking." Cratton deserved to know the details, since Jax wanted to find out more about Gaspard. Maybe he was grasping at straws, but who else might be involved?

For several moments, silence fell over the room. "I'm not sure how I can help, but I'm happy to try. You were a fine officer and put your men, all of us boys, ahead of yourself. I'd like to repay that."

While he appreciated the compliment, Jax focused on his current dilemma. "I don't need or expect repayment. I did my job like most other soldiers. What I need now is some information."

"Sure, I hope I have some."

Jax did, too. "I'm wondering about Victor Gaspard."

Burton frowned. "You think he's the killer?"

Jax shrugged. "I don't know, but I saw a man about his height with Celeste last night. I didn't get a good look, but he was wearing a greatcoat similar to ones worn by French soldiers." He sat back in the chair. "I just came from his boardinghouse, where I spoke with his landlady. Gaspard was out of town for a few days about a month ago, and he came in very late last night. Early this morning, he told Mrs. Cotton he'd be gone again for a time. Added to that is his failing business, and his sudden departure last evening at the diner."

Burton drummed his fingers on the chair arms. "You're the lawman, but all that seems suspicious to me."

"I agree, which is why I'm here. I was hoping you might know if Victor and Celeste were acquainted, or if you have any other details about him."

"I'm sorry, Jax. I don't. As far as Victor, he was at art school in Paris when war broke out. He was from a small town, but I don't know the name." Burton released a long breath. "I got to know him in France, and he was always reserved. Still is. Now, except for eating at the diner sometimes, Victor keeps to himself mostly. Even when he eats with some of us veterans, he doesn't say a lot. He mentioned going to Cleveland last month. When I asked why, he cited needing a change in scenery. It seemed odd then, and it seems odder now."

The information increased Jax's wariness, but he needed additional details. Many additional details. "You don't know if he's been in touch with other French immigrants?"

"No. There aren't all that many in Ohio. If he found a few in Cleveland, it wouldn't surprise me if he was friendly with them. But, like I said, he's reserved." Burton took a bite of cookie before speaking again. "You're investigating on your own? Aren't Nolen and Newton doing that?"

Jax nodded. "They are, but with only the two of them, they're spread thin. For right now, I'm trying to figure out who the man with Celeste was. She has an aunt and uncle who run a bakery in Cleveland."

A long breath left Burton. "Interesting. Victor has been gone with no explanation. He mentioned his whereabouts last time, but not every time. He could be the one you saw. When he comes back, I'll let you know."

"If he comes back." Dismay filled Jax. Nothing held Gaspard in Boxwood.

"Did Mrs. Cotton think he wouldn't?"

"She didn't say that. I just wonder if he will." Jax ran a hand over his face. "I'm not feeling optimistic."

"If he gets back, I'll let you know right away."

Jax got to his feet. "I'd appreciate that."

After the men said their farewells, Jax climbed into his Chummy and headed out of the small village. Briefly, he considered going to Ballantyne, but Bella was away for the day.

As he drove through the familiar countryside, his thoughts were filled with Victor Gaspard and any links to Celeste. Had they known each other in France? How could Jax find out? The questions plagued him.

To gain peace and solitude, Jax took a long drive before ending up at the cemetery by the Moreley Methodist church. Although he hadn't been there since the funeral for Bella's father, Jax unerringly found his grave which was beside that of Bella's mother. Both of her parents had made him feel like part of their family. As he gazed down at the markers, bittersweet memories took hold. Like so many others, the elder Stewarts had succumbed to the Spanish flu—and only months after Matt lost his life in the trenches. Reluctantly, Jax looked at the next marble slab. The one with his best friend's name:

Lieutenant Matthew Stewart
American Expeditionary Force
Buried in France, remembered at home

Moisture flooded his gaze, and the etching grew blurry. So many dreams had died in the war. One was Jax and Matt being co-golf professionals at Ballantyne. As always, his heart ached for his friend, who had died far too young. And for Bella, who had lost her big brother and her parents. She had suffered too much, and it killed Jax to cause her more pain. The look on her face when she heard Celeste's accusations replaced her brother's tombstone in Jax's mind's eye. Her stricken expression still cut him to the core. So did her abrupt departure.

He wiped away his tears. Surely, Bella would listen and believe him. If she didn't…Jax didn't let the possibility form. She had to believe him. She had to trust him. If not, the future was as bleak as the immediate past.

As dusk fell, he made his way back to his vehicle and headed home.

Bella and Ida arrived back in Moreley much later than planned. Heavy snow made their train late getting into the Sandusky station and getting back to Moreley. Their friend urged them to stay overnight, but Bella yearned to get home and see Jax. Midnight had come and gone when the pair finally walked into the Ballantyne Inn. Both women were exhausted.

Mac and Griff, seated in chairs by the lobby fireplace, rose to greet them. "I'm glad you called to say you'd be late. Otherwise, we would've been sick with worry. This way, we were only worried," Griff said.

"Aye," Mac agreed. "Tis a concern to have ye lasses traveling in such foul weather." Anxiety etched his lined face and shadowed his gray eyes.

After Bella slipped off her coat, hat, scarf, and gloves, she put them on the hall tree and went to hug him. "Sorry."

"Ye be home now," Mac said as he hugged her in return.

"Anything new?" Bella asked.

"Sit down," Griff replied. "We've got a bit of news."

Bella took the chair he had vacated. Mac returned to his seat, while Ida and Griff shared the loveseat facing the hearth. "What is it?"

"Richard and Jenny Jenkins are coming to help with the case, mostly separate from the constable's office from what I gathered when Richard called," Griff replied. "They're planning to stop here on the way into town tomorrow."

"Good. I have a couple of ideas to share with Richard," Bella said.

Mac looked grim. "I dinna like the mayor focusing on Jackson."

"Neither do I," Bella agreed. "Any guests arrive? With more snow coming, I thought some might come early."

"We had two arrivals today. Both have family coming. One has been staying at the hotel. The night clerk drove him out."

"Who is it?" Fatigue clouded Bella's memory regarding guests.

"Smithson Collier," Griff replied. "He said his family used to come summers and for some holidays."

Anxiety prickled along Bella's nerve ends as she thought about Smithson. Bella remembered him and his family from their previous visits to Ballantyne. Since Smithson was the same age as Matt and Jax, the trio became friendly. Witnessing the exchange between Jax and Celeste had thrown Bella off-kilter and evidently affected her memory. "I don't recall a reservation for the Collier family."

"Nor did I," Mac put in. "Tis under Everts. Mrs. Everts is his sister. She, her husband, and her parents twill be here tomorrow. Since the cottage be empty, we let him stay there. Mrs. Rogers said it be clean and supplied."

"It's fine. I just wondered. He served with Matt and Jax in the National Guard, and I didn't know what happened to him after the war." Could Smithson have been the man talking to Celeste on the train? He matched the conductor's description, as far Bella remembered. And why had he come early? "There's not much to do right now. The town festivities won't get into full swing until the Saturday night dance. He can ice skate, of course, and there was the tree lighting." Had he been there?

"What does he look like?" Ida asked the question.

Bella listened carefully when Griff replied. "About my height. Trim. Sandy brown hair and greenish eyes. Why? Did you know him, too?"

Ida shook her head. "No, just curious."

Bella knew her friend asked the obvious question because Bella hadn't, mostly due to her mental meanderings. But her memory was right in regard to young Collier's appearance. Smithson could have been the man talking with Celeste on the train. "I'll watch for him. I'd like to offer a welcome back." And find out if he had known Celeste Bouchard in France.

The puzzled expression did not leave the golf pro's face. "You'll run into him around here."

"Of course, I will. I'm just tired." Bella was worse than tired. She was anxious and exhausted.

Griff glanced from one woman to the other. "I've got a feeling you two aren't telling me everything. I'm not an amateur sleuth, but I want the killer found quickly. Otherwise, suspicion will linger on Jax. He doesn't deserve that." He focused on Bella. "Neither do you."

For several moments, Bella considered the assertions and concluded Griff and Mac should know as much as they did. "Ida and I spoke with the conductor this morning. He's on that train six days a week." She finished with what the man had said.

Griff leaned forward and braced his elbows on his knees. "Collier is on your suspect list."

"He is," Bella agreed, "but we need a lot more information. The conductor didn't see Celeste with anyone else, but I want to find out if she spoke with someone at the station. And who else got off at the same time. We know so little right now. Smithson's appearance and arrival could be coincidental."

"But you don't believe in coincidence," Ida added.

Bella gave a shake of her head. "Not where crimes are involved."

With a sigh, Griff sat back in the loveseat. "It's good the Jenkinses will be here tomorrow. They'll be far more help than I am. But I'll be happy to pitch in here, so you don't have as much on your shoulders."

"So will I," Ida said.

Gratitude formed a lump in Bella's throat. "Thank you. Thank you, both."

"Of course," Ida replied.

"I twill pitch in meself," Mac said. "Ye've nay let me do a lot, since Griff arrived. I've enjoyed a lighter schedule, but I can take on more now. Ye need to focus on finding the killer."

Bella beamed at her partner. "I can always count on you, Mac, and that means more than I can say."

"Tis true both ways," he assured her before stifling a yawn.

A chuckle left Bella when Ida yawned, too. "It's late. Let's all get some rest."

Mac rose. "Me bed is calling."

"Mine is, too. I'll see all of you tomorrow." After a round of good-nights, Bella went to her third-floor suite, changed into her nightgown, and climbed into bed. Despite her exhaustion, her mind reviewed the past few days, especially the suspects, over and over. Eventually, she fell into a troubled slumber.

Chapter Four

That night found Jax in much the same state, except he was alone. After tossing and turning until just before dawn, he managed a few hours of sleep and went to the kitchen around nine o'clock. He was on his third cup of coffee when someone rapped on the front door. With weariness dragging at him, Jax headed to answer.

Nolen and Newton stood on the porch. In France, Jax and Nolen had faced some grim situations, but the younger man had never looked so completely crushed. Newton, who had joined the Moreley constable force in March, appeared to be equally crestfallen. "What brings the two of you here?" He tried to maintain a cheerful attitude, but anxiety was marrow-deep. The presence of both lawmen seemed odd.

"As of this morning, we spoke with some witnesses," Nolen replied. "The ones who saw you walking around town and in the park. We've been investigating almost nonstop. We didn't turn up anyone who saw the other man."

Although he had already revealed being seen on the night of Celeste's murder, Jax's heart hit his heels. A chasm of silence fell in the hallway as Jax struggled with sick dread. The expression on both lawmen's faces were troubled, and neither could quite meet his gaze. Realization raced through Jax, leaving him barely able to breathe. "You're here to arrest me."

"I'm sorry, Jax." Nolen looked as bereft as Jax felt. "So sorry." His voice was a bare murmur.

Newton's tone wasn't much louder when he added, "I am, too."

Because both looked distraught, Jax aimed to make it easier on them. They weren't at fault. They were doing their jobs. "It'll get straightened out because I didn't kill her."

"We don't think you did," Nolen said.

"Of course, we don't," Newton agreed.

Jax held up one hand. "Don't say that again. You two need to be completely fair."

The men nodded.

"If you'll let me put shoes on, I'll be ready to go." But was he ready to be put in jail? Nausea rose in his throat. He'd never be really ready for that.

On Wednesday morning, Bella, at the resort, rose earlier than Jax did at his home. She ate a quick breakfast before becoming enmeshed in helping their maid sort out problems with the linens. The grandfather clock in the lobby was striking ten o'clock when she finally made a call to the Hastings house, with no success. Could Jax be out or was he sleeping late? The telephone was in the kitchen, quite a distance from Jax's room at the front of the house and on the second floor. She tried to call again around eleven. Still no answer. Where could he be?

Shortly before the noon meal, she went to the kitchen where Mrs. Rogers, the cook-housekeeper, was busy. Although they didn't have many guests, employees would arrive soon. Before she had time to talk with the older woman, the bell on the lobby counter had Bella hurrying out to see who was there. Surprise hit her when she saw Patrick Orlington. Griff had mentioned two check-ins the previous day, but they had never gotten around to naming the second one. Since she knew the Orlington family was coming, she should have guessed the other man was Patrick.

"Good morning, Bella," he said in a cheerful tone. "I missed you when I dropped my things off at the cottage. I wasn't here long, since I visited my grandmother after that."

She managed a greeting. "It's been a long time."

"A few years. I heard you were in France as an operator. Too bad we never crossed paths."

Although she thought the opposite, Bella nodded. "There were millions of soldiers and others involved, so it's not surprising."

His dark eyebrows rose a fraction. "Yet, I saw a lot of guys I already knew. Like Hastings." Patrick folded his arms across his chest. "I stopped in Moreley on my way back from my grandmother's place. He's the talk of the town."

The last comment, and Patrick's smile turning into a smirk, sent dread hurtling through Bella. She hated responding to his comment, but doing so might evoke a clue. "Really?"

His gaze narrowed on her. "You must know he was arrested for killing his wife."

Shock and horror hit her full-force as she stared at Patrick. Bella shoved her trembling hands into her skirt pockets. For long moments, she fought to steady herself and absorb the terrible news.

"From your expression, you haven't heard."

"Jax isn't in jail," Bella said. He couldn't be.

"But he is. I heard he got arrested earlier today. According to the local gossip mill, he was still in a cell when I passed through town minutes ago. Arrested and charged with the murder of his wife."

Nausea rose in Bella's throat, and she swallowed hard to keep it at bay. "Jax was never married." After the inane comment was out, Bella inwardly chastised herself. Murder—not marriage—was the issue.

A half-shrug lifted one of Patrick's broad shoulders. "If he was, I'm sure he didn't tell you." Patrick shifted from one foot to the other. "After all, the two of you were sweet on one another from way back. In town, I heard you were stepping out just lately."

Warmth flowed into Bella's face, but she couldn't deny the observations. "Gossip isn't fact. Jax wouldn't court me, or anyone else, if he was wed to some other woman."

"Or maybe that's why he left her behind. He wanted to court you, so maybe he figured his name would be enough to protect her and the kid from ostracism."

The sick, sinking sensation inside Bella intensified. "Is that what folks at the café were saying?"

"Yep. Not sure everyone believed it, but some seemed to." He leaned against the counter. Clad in an expensive camel hair Chesterfield coat, Patrick looked like the rich scion he was. "It's plausible. The French were grateful for our help, so saying she had a dead American husband could've worked to cover up the affair with Brewster. And maybe another one with Hastings. Not sure why she didn't stay away, except I also heard she wanted money. Plenty of witnesses at the tree lighting and another one later that night."

"Where did you get so much information in such a short time?" Had Patrick heard everything from town talk? Or did he have personal knowledge because he was Celeste's accomplice? Almost immediately, she reined in her suspicions. Wild speculation wouldn't help Jax. Did Patrick even know Celeste? And, if he did, why would he join her in blackmailing Jax? Bella's mind churned with bits and pieces from past and present. Shortly before his death, her brother had sent a note to her about a dispute between Jax and Patrick. Matt had not offered details, but he asked Bella to urge Jax to ignore Orlington's taunts, which her brother felt sure would surface after the war, whenever and wherever the pair met. At the time, Jax hadn't suffered debilitating war wounds, so Matt had most likely pictured some run-in at a golf tournament—perhaps one at Ballantyne. While Jax was far from hot-headed, he would directly confront cheating, cowardice, and dishonesty.

Patrick had shown all three at various times, which was sure to put the pair on a collision course. Would Patrick carry his vendetta as far as partnering with Celeste to accuse Jax? And what was the reason for their last quarrel? Asking outright was not apt to glean valid answers. Bella wanted to know who had been gossiping, but it made little difference. Spreading tittle-tattle was common, and not always intended to cause harm. But it often did. Refuting Patrick's assertions would get her nowhere fast, so Bella throttled her impulse to vigorously defend Jax. "I haven't been in town for any length of time these last couple of days."

"You'll get an earful when you go." His gaze narrowed on her. "With you two stepping out, he had a powerful reason to kill the woman. She would've been in the way."

"Is that what people in the diner were saying, or are you spreading the idea?"

For a long moment, Patrick studied her face. "Are you questioning me in your role as amateur detective or as Hastings' sweetheart?"

Silence echoed in the lobby until Bella gathered herself and found her voice. "There's no such thing as an amateur detective. I've helped Jax in small ways. And, as you heard, he and I just started stepping out." Only part of her statement was true, but why tell all to Patrick?

He smiled. "You've helped Hastings with cases. I heard as much through my sister. She told us all about the big case at her school last spring."

Bella had forgotten about Patrick's sister being a student at Boxmore Hill, a nearby girls' boarding school. Of course, he would know about the missing employees—a teacher and the receptionist. And about Bella and Jax investigating. "I have, but primarily as a driver and notetaker." Not the complete truth, but close enough for Orlington.

"I see." His tone clearly indicated he might not see what she wanted him to. "I suppose it came as a shock to have the French nurse come to town."

"It was a surprise," Bella admitted before turning the conversation to his family's arrival. "When will your parents and sister be coming?"

"Day after tomorrow," he replied. "My father has trouble taking time off."

"But you don't?"

Patrick's nostrils flared with a sharp intake of breath. "I'm not working at all right now. Or getting paid. I came into work hungover too often. The old man didn't like that. He's still miffed. Probably worried I'll get arrested in a speakeasy raid and taint the family name."

With Prohibition in effect, plenty of illegal bars had cropped up. Bella could easily imagine Patrick, who had always been a playboy, frequenting them. But how was Patrick funding his activities if he had no income? Would that drive him to extort Jax? "How do you get along without a steady source of income?"

"I got a small inheritance from my maternal grandparents. It won't last forever, but I'm fine for quite a while. Right now, the old man thinks I need a lesson in standing on my own two feet. Like I didn't have to do that in France. Of course, he wasn't happy about me being shipped out, but he couldn't pull enough strings to keep me at home."

Bella remembered the elder Orlington as imperious, so she could easily imagine him trying to keep his only son out of the trenches. "You'll go back to working for your family's business, won't you?"

"I'd rather not, but money is a necessity."

Needing money moved him up a notch as a suspect, but why admit as much? Did he figure on outsmarting her and everyone else? From what she knew about him, Bella would not be surprised. "It's certainly nice to have more than is needed."

"Definitely."

Before Bella replied, Ida stepped into the lobby. Her hazel gaze fixed momentarily on their guest. "Hello, Patrick."

He put one forefinger to his brow in a quick salute. "Ida, how nice to see you after so long."

"Thank you."

Bella noticed her friend didn't say seeing him was nice. Before Patrick could reveal the terrible news about Jax's arrest, she directed a statement to her friend. "I was going to help Mrs. Rogers with the noon meal before Patrick arrived."

Ida shook her head. "I'll do that." She gave Patrick a nod before heading to the kitchen.

When she was gone, Patrick shrugged. "I don't think your friend likes me, but she never has. I ran into her at golf tournaments when she and Alan Brewster were courting. Never friendly, either of them. I knew her a little more from social events in Cleveland. I hear Ida's old man lost everything, so she's teaching. My little sister is one of her pupils."

Bella ignored most of his comments. "Ida enjoys teaching."

Once again, his lips quirked into a smirk. "I'm sure she does. According to my sister, Ida is popular with the students. My sister mentioned you teaching temporarily at Boxmore Hill last spring. But I suppose it was really to investigate the disappearances of those two women."

"No one knew anyone was missing when I went to substitute." Which was the truth, but why was Patrick returning to the topic? Was he trying to see if she was involved in the current case? Or figure out what she might already know?

"How handy for you to be there to scout around for clues with Hastings."

After a long breath, Bella responded. "The school is in the Moreley jurisdiction, so Jax and Nolen were on the case."

Patrick put forefinger and thumb to his chin. "Nolen Rogers. He's from here. I'd almost forgotten. Pretty awkward for him having to arrest his former lieutenant."

Since Patrick didn't sound or look to be gloating, Bella was forthright. "I'm sure it was." In order to maintain control, she fought back imaginings of the arrest and incarceration. Jax shouldn't be behind bars.

"It'll be worse if Hastings goes on trial and gets convicted."

Again, the man spoke in an even tone that revealed no gratification. Maybe he wasn't hoping Jax went to the electric chair. Maybe he wasn't involved. But what was the grudge between the two men? More than distant run-ins?

"After a big meal, I need a nap," Patrick said, "so I'm off to the cottage. Good to talk with you, Bella."

Since she couldn't echo the statement, Bella nodded. "Let us know if you need anything."

As soon as Patrick left, Ida poked her head out of the kitchen. "The meal is ready."

Bella tried to regroup before facing her friend. "All right."

"What's wrong?" Ida asked. "You look as white as a sheet."

Sharing the information about Jax proved to be difficult. The lump in Bella's throat and the knot in her stomach had her going weak in the knees, and she leaned back against the counter for support. "Patrick stopped in town on his way back. People in the café were talking about Jax because he was arrested this morning." Bella's voice was thick with suppressed emotion. "I need to call Richard and Jenny. They were already planning to come, but I hope they'll leave right away, if they haven't already. I'll tell everyone here after the call."

Ida slid an arm around Bella's shoulders. "Jax isn't guilty, so he won't be in jail for long."

Bella nodded, but fear gripped her. She picked up the telephone with shaking hands and waited to hear Richard's reassuring voice come across the line. When it did, she blurted out the terrible news. The older man immediately offered support and promised to be on the road within the next thirty minutes. After hanging up, Bella wrapped her arms around her waist and took a few reassuring breaths. The workers, all of whom knew and liked Jax, needed to hear what had happened.

As she entered the kitchen, every head turned toward her, and Mrs. Rogers gestured to an empty chair. "Sit down, my dear."

"In a moment." Bella fought to maintain her composure. Drawing a breath seemed impossible. She took several shallow ones and plunged ahead. "I just found out Jax was arrested for murder this morning."

Gasps and murmurs went through the group. The men were wide-eyed, and the ladies appeared to be on the verge of tears—the same as Bella. When the shock wore off, several people offered to help Jax however they could. Everyone asserted belief in his innocence. Unable to say more, Bella stood stock-still.

Ida rose from the table. "Let's go into the family quarters and wait for Richard and Jenny."

Bella agreed. Griff followed the women and started a fire. "I'll bring the Jenkinses back here when they arrive."

"It won't be for an hour," Bella finally said. "Maybe I should go into town now."

"No, let's wait." Ida settled on the loveseat and gestured for Bella to join her.

"You two get comfortable. I'll ask Mrs. Rogers to fix a plate for you, Bella," Griff said.

With her stomach in a mass of knots, Bella couldn't eat. "Thank you, but I'm not hungry."

Griff glanced at Ida, who gave a slight nod. "All right." Then, he left the room."

Ida patted Bella's hand. "I'm so sorry about Jax's arrest, but Richard will see that he doesn't stay in jail for long."

Bella wanted to believe her friend, but doubt and anxiety hampered her. She revealed her conversation with Patrick Orlington. "I wish Matt had let me know what happened between Jax and Patrick in France. They met in golf matches several times, and Jax won each one."

"Which annoyed Patrick."

"Absolutely. Patrick got accused of cheating twice, and they had loud confrontations."

"Jax is usually so circumspect, not that I blame him for not letting Patrick tell lies."

"But something had to happen in France," Bella said.

"If Patrick knew Celeste Bouchard, he'd go along with a plan to humiliate and extort Jax, especially if something else happened between them in France. But did he know her?" Ida asked.

"I'm not sure. Even if he did, would they stay in touch? That seems like a stretch."

"Maybe, but when she got to Cleveland, she might've contacted him. His family wouldn't be hard to locate, not when they own a big business with their name on it."

"You might be right. But there are other possibilities."

"You, Jenny, and Richard will sort through everything and find the killer in short order. Then, we can enjoy the Christmas dance on Saturday night, like we planned." Ida offered a reassuring smile.

Bella tried to smile. The dance was only three days away. Not much time to catch a murderer and clear Jax.

Time hung heavily until the older couple arrived.

After bringing them into the room, Griff glanced at Ida. "We were planning to get more greens to decorate the inn and cottage porches. We could do that now."

Ida went to stand by Griff. "A wonderful idea."

Once Ida and Griff were gone, Bella gestured to two chairs. "Please sit down."

Jenny, a blue-eyed blonde in her fifties, settled near the fire. Richard, with gray mustache and hair, took the seat across from her. "I can't stay because I want to see Jax as soon as possible. Being arrested had to be tough on him, and on Nolen and Newton." He cleared his throat. "Nolen gave me some information yesterday when he asked me to come. After I spoke with you, I called him, and he added a little more. The deciding factor in the arrest seems to be the drivers who saw Jax near the park around the probable time of the murder. And the mitten, since Jax admitted he had the same color. Jax mentioned a Frenchman living in Boxwood to Nolen after his arrest. Do you know anything about the man?"

Bella's brow furrowed. "I've heard a former French soldier settled there. I don't go over there often, so I haven't met him."

"Victor Gaspard is the man. And you didn't know him in France?"

"I met a few French soldiers, but the name isn't familiar," Bella replied. "Was Jax acquainted with him? Is that why he told Nolen about Gaspard."

With one hand, Richard brushed back his gray hair. "That's part of what I want to find out. I want Jax's view and any other details he might have."

"I ran into Nolen yesterday morning," Bella said, "and he told me about the evidence, scant as it is. Lyle Fikeland interrupted us. He thinks Jax is guilty, and he's probably telling everyone as much. I wonder if his hatefulness was another factor in Jax being jailed." Her insides knotted with dread. Would many people listen to the hardware store owner? Surely not, but he was on the town council. How the man kept getting elected, she didn't know.

Richard massaged his forehead. "I heard about Fikeland at the tree lighting."

"We're so sorry you and Jax had to deal with him and Miss Bouchard," Jenny put in. Sympathy clouded her gaze.

As Bella glanced from husband to wife, she wondered if they knew she had dashed off that night. Embarrassment flamed through her. Because she should have stood with Jax, Bella resolved to see him as soon as possible. "I want to visit Jax and help with the case."

After exchanging a long look with his wife, Richard turned back to Bella. "Good. We can use all the help we can get, and you're an excellent sleuth."

"I'll do whatever I can to help," Bella assured him. "Maybe I should go with you to see Jax right now."

"I'd like to talk with him in private, and he'd probably enjoy seeing you in private, too." Richard smiled. "Perhaps you could drive Jenny into town in a half-hour. You two can chat, and I'll have some time at the jail to see Jax and maybe get more details from Nolen. He has some interviews scheduled, starting in about an hour, which means I need to get on the road if I want to talk with him first."

"Of course, I'll bring Jenny with me." An additional worry weighed on Bella's mind. "I'll be able to visit Jax, won't I?"

"I'm sure you can," Richard replied, "but I'll smooth your way."

"Wonderful. Before you leave, there's at least one other possibility." Bella explained about Smithson Collier.

With one forefinger, Richard stroked his chin. "We definitely need to dig into him. You say Collier was seen with Miss Bouchard on the train."

Bella nodded. "From the description, I'm sure it was Smithson. The conductor noticed them when he passed through collecting tickets, so he only glimpsed them. They might've spoken longer than a few minutes."

"And this conductor is always on that train?" Richard asked.

"Every day except Sunday." Bella chewed on her lower lip. "Maybe I should speak with him again. I could be at the station tomorrow when the train comes in. There's a fifteen-minute stop here. Sometimes longer if many people are coming and going. The conductor didn't see Celeste with anyone else on the train, but he only passes through the cars."

"I have to wonder if her accomplice would be so obvious," Jenny put in. "Perhaps we should see how many folks got off that train in Moreley."

Since the older woman echoed Bella's thoughts, she nodded. "I agree. The porters and stationmaster, Edgar Geneve, might've seen her talk to someone else."

"Let's put all that under consideration. After I talk with Jax, we may add more important details." Richard got to his feet. "With some luck, he'll be out of jail soon, and we can bring him into the discussions. I spoke with the prosecutor, and he's deliberating about bail."

Hope made Bella's heart race. "Thank you. There's one more person who might be a suspect." She summarized Patrick Orlington's motive and her exchange with him. "I didn't see him at the tree lighting, and he supposedly left for his grandmother's house shortly after getting here yesterday. I have no idea what happened between him and Jax that caused my brother to put a warning in his last note." Not that Matt would have known he wouldn't be writing to her again. Or perhaps, he'd had a hunch.

"That seems strange to me," Jenny commented. "As does his lack of income."

"I agree," her husband said.

The pair's response made Bella feel validated. "We need to find out a lot more because I don't know if he met Celeste or not."

"We have work ahead. For now, be patient. If need be, the three of us can go over everything until Jax is out, but I want his viewpoint on the suspects." With that, Richard took his leave.

For the next half-hour, the two women engaged in casual conversation. Bella was grateful for Jenny's efforts to distract her. But Jax stayed on her mind.

Chapter Five

Hours after being escorted out of his house, Jax shifted restlessly on the hard cot. He had been in more uncomfortable places, but none had sunk his spirits so low. Even a vermin-infested trench in France had been preferable. At least there, he'd had a purpose. At least there, he'd been free. Here, he was a prisoner.

His arrest had been a waking nightmare and not just for him. Nolen and Newton looked stricken when they cuffed Jax and led him out of his house. As the trio had headed to the jail, gaping townsfolk only made the procedure more humiliating.

Jax's gaze traveled around the small, familiar enclosure. After his mother's death, he had sometimes sat in this very cell to do his homework. Never in the farthest reaches of his imagination had he ever figured he'd be locked inside it. What would his father think if he could see his only son now? And what about his mother? They'd both be horrified. He was horrified.

A harsh breath escaped him. Gossip was probably running rampant through town as people discussed his arrest. Not that Jax cared about chit chat. Only the opinion of his friends mattered. Especially Bella's viewpoint. What did she think? Did she believe Celeste Bouchard's allegations? Did she think he had committed murder to silence the woman? Surely not. But she hadn't come to him. Or even called. Their parting after the tree lighting had been unpleasant. Jax had been as shocked as Bella to see the French woman and hear her accusations. Did Xavier actually exist? Celeste's word and a photograph were hardly inviolable proof. Why hadn't Celeste brought the boy along? The question came to his mind for the first time.

Jax drove his fingers through his hair as frustration gnawed on every nerve. As the accused, he was in no position to investigate. But who, other than Nolen and Newton, would? Both lawmen were constrained by the mayor, so they could not go far afield. Nolen had mentioned Richard Jenkins. Would the older man come? Could he help? And what about Bella? She was an extraordinary amateur sleuth. Might she investigate for him? Although he didn't blame her for dashing off the other night, Jax wished she had contacted him. She was supposed to be back from her visit last evening. Why hadn't she telephoned?

The sick knot in his gut tightened. If only he could go back...but how far back would he need to go to fix things between them? Back to when her brother died? Jax had been planning to leave the field hospital against doctor's orders when Matt had visited. His friend had given up a short leave to take Jax's place on the line and died days later. Regret and remorse had been powerful barriers between Jax and Bella for far too long. When he had finally told her why he'd maintained a distance after the war, she had not blamed him. Since then, they had grown closer and closer. Until Monday night. Maybe his arrest would create the ultimate break, and put the end to any hope of him being her husband. Misery settled on Jax like a death shroud. This Christmas was supposed to be magical for him and for Bella. It was supposed to be everything December 1916 had not been because war had loomed on the horizon. He'd planned to court her then.

His train of thought was interrupted by Nolen's voice. "Richard Jenkins is here."

Jax's head snapped up. Immediately, he shifted to a sitting position. Richard, a retired senior constable, and his wife had only returned to their home in Karston, a nearby town, two weeks ago after his stint as temporary constable in Moreley.

"Thank you, Nolen. I'll be fine alone with him," Richard said.

Nolen nodded. "There's a stool over here," he said, pointing to the adjacent wall.

"Thanks," Richard replied before sitting down. The man's gaze burned with an intensity that Jax had never seen. When he spoke, banked fire was in his voice. "What in the heck were you thinking?" he asked in a cutting tone. "Threatening someone. Anyone. You're a lawman." The older man paused for a moment before saying, "One of your best qualities is your restraint. At least I thought it was."

Jax set his elbows on his knees and put his head in his hands. Refuting the accusation was futile, because he had acted rashly. He had argued with Celeste publicly. Even worse, he had threatened to run her out of town and make the rest of her life miserable. Not that he would have done either, but he'd been completely lost to restraint and propriety, something a lawman should never do. "I'm sorry, sir. There's no excuse for my lack of self-discipline. None."

For several long moments, the older man said nothing. "You're not going to defend yourself?"

Reluctantly, Jax met Richard's gaze. "I have no defense. I misbehaved. Badly and stupidly. I don't expect you to come back to town and bail me out of the situation." An idea hit him. "Maybe you're back as the temporary constable."

"No, not that." Some of the ice in Richard's gaze melted. "You think I'd ignore you being charged with murder? You ought to know me better."

"I deserve to deal with it on my own." Of course, Jax had no idea how to deal with the situation. Not from behind bars.

A long, low breath emanated from the older man. "You have a lot of good qualities as a lawman and as a person. But you've been alone for a long time, and you are independent. Too much so. In this case, you could've called me when Miss Bouchard confronted you. You could've told Nolen about her threats. You could've asked him to go with you to meet her. But you handled it all alone." Richard let that sink in before continuing. "You didn't do very well in your interview, according to the notes I saw just now. You admitted you were angry with Miss Bouchard. You admitted you met with her hours before her murder. You mentioned drivers seeing you and said you had green wool mittens."

Jax shook his head. "None of it is secret. Many people overheard us after the tree lighting. The two drivers were probably townsfolk. As for the mittens, some of the boys would know I had bright green ones." He struggled to organize his thoughts. "But she was lying about everything. I never had a love affair with Celeste, let alone married her. The license is fake, but I have no way of proving it."

"I just saw it, and it looks real. Not saying it is, but the document is well done."

A harsh exhalation left Jax. "I know it looks genuine. But it isn't."

"We can try to get information from the French church where you supposedly got married, but that will take a lot of time." Richard's jaw tightened. "What I'd like to know right now, is why you met her late at night. You'd already talked and disagreed. Argued, really."

"She left a note at my house saying she'd take the license to Bella if I didn't come, and I offered her two-hundred dollars the night of the lighting. I shouldn't have because it made me look guilty, I suppose."

"Why did you offer money? That's also in the notes Nolen has."

Jax ran one hand over his face. "On one hand, I was upset over her accusations. On the other, I felt sorry for her. That night in the alley, she asked for a lot more, which made me furious. Maybe I should've paid Celeste off. But I'm not the father, and I was never her lover or husband."

"Paying a bribe wouldn't have ended the problem. She would've continued to threaten you, and you'd have been paying for the rest of your life."

A long, low breath left Jax. "That's what I finally figured. But I didn't figure on Celeste dying. Or on getting blamed."

Richard leaned back against the wall and folded his arms across his broad chest. "I can understand your thinking, and I can understand why you didn't want to bring Nolen and Newton into it. They would've been in a tough situation, but that's part of the job. And they're in a pickle now because they hate having you in jail. At the very least, I wish you had called me instead of handling it on your own. I could've spoken with her."

"I wish I had, too," Jax admitted. "I just wanted the whole situation to go away. Bella was upset when she heard Celeste's accusations, and I don't blame her."

"Arabella called me about your arrest. Jenny and I were planning to come over, but we left right off afterward."

Mortification nearly choked him. Bella already knew he was in jail. What did she think now? Was she glad she had stalked away the other night?

"I dropped Jenny at Ballantyne on my way here. Now, I'd like to get your view on everything. Did Arabella know the woman in France?"

Jax shook his head. "Not really. Bella saw Celeste with me shortly after Matt died. Unfortunately, that's the date on the license I saw." He explained the chronology of those days at the end of September 1918. "A confluence of events from three years ago and Celeste's appearance here upset Bella."

"Because she might believe you didn't introduce Miss Bouchard back then due to marrying the girl that day?"

Was that in Bella's mind? "It seems possible. Celeste was involved with Alan Brewster, Ida Byington's fiancé. He died before Matt."

The senior constable put the heel of one hand to his forehead. "Exactly what happened when the three of you crossed paths that day?"

Old memories, ones Jax had struggled to banish, reared up. "I didn't want Celeste to mention Alan Brewster, so I didn't introduce her to Bella. I'd already promised Alan to keep the relationship a secret. If Bella knew, she might've let it slip to Ida, who didn't deserve to be hurt." His decision had seemed sensible. In retrospect, it had been another foolish move. He should have talked more with Bella instead of hurrying off. But a few months ago, they had discussed and addressed the problem. Back then, Bella understood. Now? Jax feared this was one issue too many to overcome.

A perplexed frown put more furrows on Richard's forehead. "You've given me the overall picture, but your precise words and actions would be useful. What did you say to Arabella?"

"I said I was sorry about Matt dying and led Celeste off. I know it was stupid, but I'd made a solemn pledge to keep the secret." Admitting multiple mistakes wasn't easy.

Several moments passed before Richard replied. "Which is part of what led to the previous hurdles between you and Arabella." No judgment was in his tone or expression.

"That and me feeling responsible for her brother's death," Jax admitted.

"You two resolved that issue, didn't you? I thought things were good when we left for home a couple of weeks ago."

"They were. She doesn't blame me. At least, she didn't. I'm not sure now."

Again, Richard didn't respond immediately. "Do you still blame yourself?"

The question deserved proper regard, so Jax waited a moment to reply. When he did, he was completely honest. "I'm sorry Matt was killed, but I know it wasn't my fault."

For several moments, Richard studied Jax. "What's troubling you at the moment?"

"Other than being charged with a murder I didn't commit?"

A grin pulled up one corner of Richard's mouth. "Yes, other than that."

"Maybe Bella thinks Celeste was carrying Alan's child and came to me for protection. Or she thinks I lied about Alan and Celeste, and I was involved with the woman myself."

"Really? Why would she believe that?" The older man looked and sounded skeptical.

"From the start, she was suspicious about me being involved with Celeste because I didn't introduce them in France. Then, I kept my distance from Bella for a long while. Until last April really."

"Because of your unnecessary guilty conscience over her brother's death, not because you were involved with Miss Bouchard."

Jax nodded. "When I finally explained everything, including the relationship between Celeste and Alan, Bella understood, and she agreed to keep the secret.

She still is. Or she was. I don't know now." Weary and worried, Jax found organizing his thoughts difficult. He might repeat himself, but he wanted to make things clear to Richard. "Bella and I were planning to go to the potluck after the tree lighting. Ida and Griff were, too. All that was off after Celeste's accusations, and Bella went home. Not that I blame her. My exchange with Celeste attracted a small crowd and some wiseacre comments." And worse.

"Nolen mentioned as much when he called me."

"I was as angry as I was embarrassed. Bella was probably embarrassed and upset. She has every right to be."

"Have the two of you spoken since then?"

"No. She and Ida planned to visit a friend in Sandusky yesterday. They probably got back late, but she could've called then or this morning, so I'm not sure Bella wants to talk with me now." One hand gestured around the dismal cell. "Especially here."

Richard ignored the last remark. "Do you think the boy is Alan Brewster's child?"

The question brought Jax's focus back to the case. "I don't know. I don't even know if there is really a son. It's possible, but why fake a marriage license with me as the groom?"

"You're alive to blackmail. He isn't."

"Why not go to his parents? They're wealthy."

"They might've wanted a relationship with their grandson. Did Miss Bouchard immediately ask you for money?"

"Not too obviously when there were witnesses at the park. When I met her behind the café, she did." Jax wished he hadn't initially offered money.

"Then, I doubt she wanted family ties. More likely, just funds." Richard put a finger to his chin. "Or your suspicion may be right, and there's no child at all."

Weary resignation made Jax slump forward. "I've wondered about that, and you're probably right about everything. But what can I do? Even if I get off on the murder charge, Bella may be finished with me."

A smile softened Richard's expression. "I just spoke with her, and she's quite concerned about you."

Despite his grim situation, hope stirred inside Jax. With effort, he fought to cloak it. Concern was a somewhat tepid word. "That's good to know."

"A group of us is concerned, and we'll see that the actual killer is found."

The statement made Jax wonder what Richard had planned. "If you aren't coming back as the temporary constable, what are you doing?"

Richard shook his head. "I'm here to poke around independently. Your mayor is overseeing the official investigation, but Nolen and I spoke yesterday and today."

With one hand, Jax rubbed the back of his neck. "Mayor Cawlings' primary interest is getting the case closed quickly, especially with the holidays coming. An unsolved murder might keep folks from visiting. At least, that's his fear."

"Cawlings is a slick character, but I can't imagine he'd be all right with sending an innocent man to the electric chair. Especially not you. Although he can't take sides, he's glad I'm here to look into matters. I called him before leaving home just to let him know what I plan to do. Nolen and Newton can't work with us on freeing you, since they can't take sides, either."

The observation wasn't surprising. "I understand. As far as the case, someone might've put Celeste up to coming here. I don't believe she conjured up the fake marriage license by herself. She was a naïve girl when I knew her, and she seemed edgy when we spoke. The other night in the alley, some man whistled to her, which upset Celeste. When he whistled the second time, she went to him and they hurried off. I ran after them. The surgeon told me to take it easy for a while longer, and he was right. Running made my arm ache. Anyhow, by the time I got to the cross-street, they'd disappeared. I went to the right first but didn't see anyone at all. I retraced my steps and went down another couple of blocks. No luck. I stopped at the hotel, too. Nothing."

"But you were overheard by Sam Push. Right? I haven't been able to speak with him yet, but Nolen summarized things for me. Do you know if Sam saw anyone else?"

"Nolen and Cawlings said he didn't, but he went back inside after asking if Celeste needed help. And I looked around some more. No clues where they went. At least there weren't any until Celeste was found in the park the next morning."

"Sam wasn't eager to cooperate. He told Nolen that he doesn't believe you had anything to do with the girl's death." Richard's expression was grim. "He had no choice but to say what he heard."

"I understand." At least one of his neighbors wanted to believe in his innocence.

"Nolen and I were interrupted, so I got few details. Can you describe the man waiting for Miss Bouchard?"

Jax didn't respond because Nolen reappeared. "Sorry to interrupt, but Mayor Cawlings is here. He'd like to speak with you, Richard." The younger man cleared his throat. "And he said I should limit how long Jax talks with visitors."

"I'll be out in a couple of minutes," Richard replied.

Nolen nodded and left the pair alone again.

"How's the arm doing?" Richard got to his feet as he spoke. "Any ill effects from the chase? You said it slowed you down."

"Not lingering ones. It's early, but the incision looks good. There's a chance I'll have almost normal use of it. If I follow doctor's orders and take it easy." Jax glanced around the cell. "Not much else for me to do here."

Richard grinned. "The first part is great news. Does Bella know you could have a full recovery?"

Jax shook his head. "I didn't want to get her hopes up. She'd liked for me to go back to being a golf pro and work at Ballantyne."

"Would you like that?"

With his left hand, Jax lightly massaged his bicep. Although his recuperation seemed to be going well, he hadn't let his hopes rise that high. "If I get close to normal use of my arm, and Bella still wants me there, I would love it."

"I'm guessing Arabella hasn't changed her mind."

Doubt niggled along his spine. "I hope you're right. Working as a law officer isn't awful, but I've enjoyed not needing to carry a gun the last few weeks."

"You'd be happy putting it away permanently." Richard made it a suggestion instead of a question or statement.

Jax exhaled sharply. "I would."

Richard nodded. "Right now, I better go, since the mayor is waiting. I'll look into who came into town over the past few days. Jenny and Arabella will help when I do interviews. Both will do whatever else they can to find the killer. We all will. I've gotten a few more details from you, which is useful."

Bittersweet memories rose in Jax's mind. "Bella is always a big help and not only because I had trouble writing. She has great intuition and insight, which you acknowledged long ago."

"She does, and Arabella will always be willing to help you. My Jenny still assists me. Like now."

"Please thank her for me." Jax appreciated the support, but his mind was on Bella. Her reaction to Celeste's lies had cut him to the core. He'd rather permanently lose use of his arm than hurt Bella. And, despite Richard's conjecture, she had been hurt. By him. Again.

"I will, but we're all set on getting you out of here and having the charges dropped before a trial becomes a concern."

"Do you think that's possible?" The older man's assertion provided a flicker of optimism. Being in jail was frustrating and chastening. Although he appreciated support from his friends, Jax wanted to help prove his innocence, not be stuck in a cell.

"The local prosecutor agrees your reputation is excellent and should be taken into consideration, so he'll do what he can to set bail."

"What about the witnesses and the mitten? I had a pair of green ones, but I have no idea what happened to them. Plenty of other doughboys had similar ones."

"I know. The knitting project was big news once the Expeditionary Force was in France. My Jenny and her mother donated a few dozen pairs in all different colors. I wondered how you boys would like the brighter ones."

The reminder took Jax back in time. "Anything to keep our hands warm when we were sitting in the trenches was welcome. Right now, I wish I hadn't had the same color as the killer."

"So do I, but there'll be more details uncovered."

Jax might have been relieved if Richard didn't look grim. "Do you really think there's much chance I'll be released?"

"I believe so. Means, motive, and opportunity are the problem."

"Motive? Why would I kill Celeste? Don't people know me better?" Although aware of the evidence against him, Jax felt wounded by the lack of trust. Was Sam Push in the majority or the minority?

Richard released a long, low breath. "Everyone in town knows you and Arabella have stepped out. They also know you two were sweet on each other years back. Add to that you keeping her at a distance when she first got home, and there's food for idle chatter."

The information made Jax sick at heart. "People are gossiping about Bella and me and Celeste?" The idea appalled him. Bella had cringed on Monday night when people saw the confrontation. Now, she must be even more upset.

For several moments, Richard fell silent. "I got a little information from Nolen and Newton. It's been circulating that you didn't lower your guard with Arabella because you were wed in France. It's a small but vocal group pushing the idea."

Dismay knotted his insides. The gossip might be fueled by those who had stopped and stared while Celeste leveled her accusations at the park. "Which is why Mayor Cawlings felt pressured to have me arrested."

Richard nodded. "The local prosecutor isn't under as much scrutiny, and he has sway with Cawlings and the town council. Try to be patient while it works itself out."

"What about Bella and Ballantyne? Any association with a murder suspect could hurt her and the resort. Business is finally better, and they have a lot of reservations for over the holidays. That could change if tourists hear she's associating with a killer." The admission tasted bitter in his mouth. "Maybe she shouldn't be involved in the case at all."

A chuckle escaped the older man. "You can try to convince her, but I doubt if you'll succeed. She's set on helping."

A tiny sliver of optimism pierced the darkness encompassing him. If Bella was set on assisting in the investigation, she hadn't given up on him...or their relationship. "Do you think that's wise? I don't want either Bella or the resort to suffer because of me."

"Visitors will hear about the murder, but people already knew about the earlier two deaths related to Ballantyne. One right at the resort. Loyal guests aren't deterred."

With effort, Jax focused his thoughts on the investigation. "I suppose, and I know you'll do everything you can."

"It'll be a team effort," Richard assured him. "We have suspects in mind. One, you discovered."

"Victor Gaspard." Jax revealed what he knew about the man.

Richard jotted down more notes. "I'll definitely keep him in mind. But someone might've come into town with the Frenchwoman. Arabella mentioned two others. One is Smithson Collier." He provided an outline of the information.

Jax frowned. "We served together, but I can't be sure he knew Celeste. Or that he'd be with her in an extortion plot. He was mild-mannered."

"Think about him more. The other man is Patrick Orlington."

Dread pooled in the pit of Jax's stomach. "I've known him since before the war." Known and disliked him. "During it, we served in the same area. We weren't friendly before France due to him being a sore loser and a cheater. An incident overseas made matters worse, and he may still have a grudge against me."

"From what Arabella said, I believe that's the case." Richard revealed what he knew.

After hearing about the conversation between Bella and Orlington, Jax felt his apprehension grow. "I don't like him staying at the resort. Especially alone. He could sneak away from the cottage and into the inn any time. Smithson could, too."

"I don't think the killer will go after Bella, since it'd be perilous. But I'll talk to Griff and Mac to ensure they have proper security."

"Good. I can't wait to get out and help."

Some emotion flickered in the other man's gaze. "I'm sure you do, but you'll have to content yourself with only coming to meetings. As a suspect, you can't be asking questions or poking around for evidence. It wouldn't look good."

Jax chewed on his lower lip. "You're right. I'll mostly stay out of sight. When I'm out of here."

"Fine." Richard cleared his throat. "It'd be a wise idea for you not to be alone, either. Just in case something else happens."

Uneasiness assailed Jax. "What makes you say that?"

"We know you didn't kill Miss Bouchard, and it's unlikely a total stranger did. More likely an acquaintance. It could be Gaspard, Collier, or Orlington. But maybe it's someone else. I'm thinking Miss Bouchard might've balked at doing more than blackmail. Then, her partner got angry and killed her."

"What else could they do to get money?"

Richard took a long, audible breath. "Kidnapping Arabella comes to mind. You would've paid to keep her safe."

"I would have." The agreement came quickly. For a long moment, he considered Richard's supposition. "You may be right about Bella being used. I would've done anything they said to ensure her well-being. I think Celeste would've recoiled at being involved in an abduction, but she recognized Bella immediately."

"Interesting," Richard said in a thoughtful tone. "Maybe my copper's imagination isn't running away with me."

Nolen's appearance interrupted the conversation. "The mayor is getting impatient."

"I'm coming," Richard said. He looked back at Jax. "It may take a few days to get you free. Try to be patient."

"You and Jenny are staying at my house, aren't you?"

"We only got here a short time ago, and she's out at Ballantyne. Arabella will bring her into town. Then, we were planning to see if we can get a room at the Eddington boardinghouse."

"You two are always welcome at my place, and it'd be good for me to have one of you there, so I'm never alone. If I get out."

"Probably wise, and I appreciate the offer."

A genuine smile came to Jax's lips. "Jenny spoils me with her cooking, so I'm the one who should thank you." After his surgery, Jax recuperated at home. The presence of Jenny and Richard, who had already been in his home when he was with the Prohibition Bureau, had been reassuring and helpful. "The key is under the back doormat."

"As usual. I can find it easily," Richard said with a chuckle. "We'll focus on freeing you and proving you're not guilty in steps."

"Yes, sir," Jax said. One step at a time was an excellent strategy. But a hard one. He yearned to proceed in leaps and bounds to the point when he was set free and proven innocent.

"I'll be back when I can," Richard said before turning and heading down the hall to the office.

Chapter Six

A t the same time, Bella was pulling her Ford into a parking place on Main Street. Jenny Jenkins sat in the passenger seat.

"Thank you for driving me to town," the older woman said. "I see our Winton in front of the constable's office, so Richard must still be there."

Bella's heart seemed to bounce like a ball inside her. "Maybe I can talk to Jax soon, too."

Jenny shifted and laid a hand on Bella's arm. "I'm glad you want to visit him. I understand seeing him with Miss Bouchard and hearing her accusations upset you."

After Richard left the inn, she had admitted her reaction to Jenny. "I've known Jax most of my life, and I shouldn't have jumped to the wrong conclusion so quickly. I guess we have more to iron out than I thought."

After giving Bella's arm a soft squeeze, Jenny sat back in her seat. "The two of you were childhood friends, and you had crushes on one another later. That doesn't mean you know everything you should to be husband and wife. That's a unique relationship, my dear, so courting is a fine idea."

The older woman's words resonated with Bella. "You're wise."

A chuckle escaped Jenny. "Some wisdom comes with age. Are you coming into the constable's office with me?"

"No, I need to stop at the mercantile. Mac wants shaving soap. I'll be over afterward." Although she could do her errand later, Bella felt the need to stoke up courage before facing Jax. He had looked so defeated before she left him at the park. How much worse did he feel now? With no family, he was very much alone.

"I know Jax will be happy to see you," Jenny said, before going on her way.

Bella was eager to see him, too, but also nervous. Surely, Jax wasn't guilty. He couldn't be. Over twenty years of memories proved his goodness. As a young boy, he had taken responsibility for stealing from a local shop because the buddy who committed the crime would have been sorely punished at home for the transgression. After Bella and a friend, as youngsters, had left cigarette butts behind the barn at Ballantyne, he had stepped forward to take the blame again, knowing she would have been disciplined by being barred from playing in her first big golf tournament. Other recollections filtered into her mind and joined with the confrontation in the park. Then and there, Jax could have asked Celeste if Alan Brewster was the father of her child. He could have revealed the pair had been lovers. Bella had hushed him. And he had listened instead of defending himself.

As she walked down Main Street, Bella felt ambivalent emotions. The town was decked out for the holidays with storefronts boasting displays of Christmas goods and every door having a wreath. Only two days ago, her spirits had soared as she considered sharing the holiday season with Jax. What would happen now? Nothing positive until the killer was found. A male voice broke into her dismal thoughts.

"Bella Stewart, how lovely to see you after so many years."

The greeting had Bella turning around to see a young man with sandy brown hair grinning at her. For several moments, she tried to place him. Finally, his name came to her. "Dewey Fikeland. It has been a long time." Dewey had lived in Moreley most of his life, from the time his parents died until he went off to France. But he had not come back since then.

He moved forward to grasp both of her hands in his. "You're as pretty as ever."

"Thank you," she replied. Dewey was the same in some ways. His Adam's apple still bobbed as he spoke, and his pale blue eyes blinked along. Once tall and gangly, Dewey had filled out, and his demeanor seemed different. As a boy, he had stuttered and stammered when asking her to dance at town events. And he'd thrust bouquets of wildflowers at her without saying a word. Now, his hands clasped hers in a firm grip, and his voice rang with confidence.

"It's the truth. Pretty as a picture."

"Are you in town for Christmas?" Bella asked, ignoring his compliment.

"I'm visiting Aunt Dorothy and Uncle Lyle. I haven't seen them since I left for the ambulance corps, which is far too long." When he grinned, his oddly spaced teeth were obvious.

"I'm sure they're happy to have you." Bella pulled her hands free of his grasp and stepped away.

He continued to beam at her. "I should get back more often, but I stayed in France after the war. So many villages were hard hit by the Germans, some virtually destroyed. Drivers were needed to ferry building supplies, food, and such. Not as dangerous as driving back-and-forth to the front. Very necessary, though. Rewarding, too. Folks were grateful."

As a boy, Dewey had often sought admiration. His current comments indicated the same sort of neediness, so Bella obliged him. Besides, drivers like him had made major contributions during and after the war. "You ambulance drivers endured difficulty and danger to save the lives of many soldiers." Even to her own ears, the statement sounded stiff and formal. But Dewey appeared to appreciate it.

His smile intensified. "It wasn't easy, but I'm glad I volunteered and got there ahead of our local boys. The French were thankful, since they needed help so badly. The Brits, as well. It's too bad more men didn't go before America got into the war."

Despite his pleasant countenance and tone, Dewey sounded critical of their fellow Ohioans, which scraped Bella's heart. "Our neighbors in the National Guard went as soon as they were called up." Loyalty and love dictated her next words. "My brother was one of them."

103

A frown knit his brow. "I haven't seen you since Matt died. I'm so very sorry. He was a fine person, and I know the two of you were close. Dewey patted her shoulder before closing his fingers around it. "My deepest sympathies for losing him and your parents."

His gesture, meant to be reassuring, felt more like a dead weight. Did he still harbor a boyish crush for her? Bella hoped not. His attention had been overbearing. Although two years behind her in school, Dewey had often tagged after Bella. Because she didn't want to hurt his feelings, she answered carefully. "I'm not alone. Mac MacLendon is my partner at the resort." He was also her honorary grandfather.

"Good to hear." He let his hand fall away. "When I was at the mercantile, I heard you and Hastings were stepping out. It's awful he's been living a lie, and embarrassing for you. Folks are sympathetic, since they know you were misled."

The statement disturbed Bella. Being the subject of gossip was bad, but having people believe Jax lied was worse. Most of what Dewey knew undoubtedly came from his uncle, who had made an unpleasant situation much uglier. "The facts will come out, and most people will withhold judgment until then. As they should."

For several moments, Dewey stared at her. Finally, he smiled again. "Of course. Only a handful think he's guilty. Sadly, my uncle is one of them. I don't share his opinion, and I want to aid you any way I can."

Bella couldn't hold her tongue. "Your uncle never liked Jax. Or Matt, my father, my grandfather, or Mac." The assertion came out with more force than she intended.

Dewey blinked rapidly. "No, I guess he didn't. You must realize I never felt that way. I admired your grandfather and Mac. Your dad and brother, too."

Omitting Jax's name didn't surprise Bella, but she didn't comment on it. When they were kids, Bella had gotten disgusted with Dewey hounding her—wanting to carry her books, giving her flowers and candy, monopolizing her time at town events, and following her whenever she came to town. Finally, she had complained to Matt and Jax, who took it upon himself to intercede. Dewey had accused Jax of grabbing him by the neck and threatening to box his ears, something which was highly improbable and denied by Jax. Nonetheless, Dewey had been upset for an extended time. His uncle had gone to Constable Hannibal Hastings, Jax's father, wanting action taken. The senior Hastings had lectured his son about being more circumspect, which was Jax's normal behavior anyhow, and took no additional action. The entire episode left a foul taste in Bella's mouth and lowered her opinion of the Fikeland family, which hadn't been positive beforehand. "Sorry. His feelings aren't your fault."

"I disliked none of them." His voice lowered a fraction when he spoke again. "And I always more than liked you. Still do."

While the words were benign, his tone and expression gave them more intimacy than appropriate. Bella wanted to keep young Fikeland at arm's length. "It was nice to see you," she replied, "but I need to get back to the resort." She planned to see Jax first but didn't share the detail.

A long moment of silence opened before he nodded. "I understand. My aunt mentioned the annual play. I'd love to escort you. Perhaps next Friday evening? It's being presented Thursday through Sunday, so another night would be fine. And I'll be at the dance this Saturday. I'd be happy to pick you up."

Mention of the events reminded Bella that she had planned to go with Jax. Surely, he would be out of jail by then. But would he accompany her to a public occasion? Probably not now. Not unless the killer was found. "I'm sorry, but I'm going with friends." True, since she and Jax had intended to attend with Ida and Griff. She forced a smile. "Enjoy your stay."

After bidding Dewey goodbye, Bella rushed off to do her errand before going to the constable's office. But her emotions were in a turmoil. Customers in the mercantile were discussing the case when she entered. Although they fell silent while she shopped, Bella heard them take up where they left off as soon as she went out the door. Pressure weighed her down. Celeste's killer needed to be caught right away.

Richard had only been gone for twenty minutes when Nolen appeared again. "You have a visitor, Jax. I'd let you meet with her in your office, but that might lead Mayor Cawlings to choose another interim constable. Again today, he said I better not give you any special treatment unless I want to be replaced."

Jax wondered who Nolen meant by her. Maybe Jenny. But wouldn't she have come with Richard? Possibly Bella. His heart raced at the latter chance. In his reply,

Jax focused on Nolen, not his next visitor. "Do nothing to compromise your position. And it's not my office now." He did not let himself think about the odds of it ever being his again. "Just show whoever it is back here."

"It's Bella," Nolen replied. Briefly, he hesitated. "I'll get her."

Long inhale. Long exhale. Jax repeated the process three times before Bella approached his cell. As she advanced, his heart sped up. Keeping his composure proved to be a sore trial, but he said, "Good afternoon," in what sounded like a fairly normal voice. He rose to his feet, started toward the bars, and halted. Touching her was out of the question. Not that she would come close enough for him to reach out. Although she had been away yesterday, Bella might have heard the town tittle-tattle by now. From her reaction the other night, she was probably still upset. With him. His hands tightened into twin fists. He would give anything to avoid having her hurt. But she was here to see him, so all could not be lost. The dim light masked her dark eyes, but the slight smile on her lips was clear. Some of his tension drained away.

"Good afternoon," she murmured, taking the stool that Richard had used.

He cleared his throat of lingering emotion. "Thank you for coming and thank you for helping with my case. Richard said you were, and I appreciate it." The statements sounded formal and forced, but Jax felt ill at ease. He had so much to say. Too much to blurt out at once. How should he begin?

"You would do the same for me," she replied without hesitation.

As reasons went, this one offered little in the way of personal concern. "Yes, I would," he replied. "Not that you'll ever find yourself in a similar predicament."

An uneasy silence ensued before Bella spoke again. "You might as well sit down."

Since the only place to sit was the hard bunk, he perched there. When Bella didn't speak again, Jax said, "What brings you here?"

Her lips twitched. "What do you think brought me?" Humor laced her tone. "I'm here to discuss your case, since I'll be working with Richard and Jenny to clear you."

Bella still had said nothing personal, but knowing others believed in him was balm to his soul. "Richard was here a little while ago"

"I know. He dropped Jenny off at Ballantyne, and we all spoke briefly. She stayed and, since I hadn't seen her for a while, we chatted." Bella bit her lower lip. "Newton, Jillian, and Nolen all know you're innocent, too." Her voice lowered when she continued. "It's especially hard for Nolen. He wanted to take a leave so he can help us find the actual killer. He just told me."

Jax was quick to react. "I don't want him to do that. He needs to think about his own future. Cawlings and the council might give Nolen a chance to take over as head constable permanently."

Her eyes widened. "When you left the Prohibition Bureau, you planned to go back to your old job. At least, after you've healed from the surgery. Have you changed your mind?"

Deciphering her underlying emotions proved challenging. Bella planned to help investigate, but how did she feel about Celeste's accusations? He wasn't ready to ask that question. Not after her rushing off the other night. Part of him wanted to blurt out excuses and another apology. Another part felt hesitant, so he eased his way along. "I'd like the job back, but I'm hardly in a place to pursue doing that—healed or not." He gestured around the cell. "If the town doesn't want me as constable after this, Nolen should be hired. He needs to watch out for his own best interest, not worry about me." Although Jax didn't mention the possibility he'd be tried and convicted, the possibility lingered in his thoughts.

"He's loyal to you." She chewed on her lower lip. "I heard the news about your arrest from Patrick Orlington this morning. Since our staff was in the kitchen for the noon meal, I told them. They all believe in you, and a couple spread the news. A few fellow veterans called already. They'll do anything to help."

Her revelations were a double-edged sword. On one hand, gratitude threatened to overwhelm him. On the other, hearing Orlington's name on Bella's lips disturbed him. "Richard mentioned Orlington."

"Patrick checked in when I was away and went to visit with his grandmother."

Jax slumped back against the hard wall. "Orlington isn't the type to dance attendance on an elderly lady, but he got to Ballantyne after Celeste was killed. Right?"

"True, but he could've been around Monday evening and lied about it. Did he know Celeste? In one of his notes, Matt mentioned Patrick being in the field hospital when Alan died. Matt had gone to see Alan and ran into Patrick. I hadn't thought about it until Patrick walked into the inn today. But my brother didn't offer specifics."

Her revelation gave Jax pause. "I didn't know about them running into each other. Matt never told me." But why would he? And when would he have done so? The Meuse-Argonne offensive had been on, and Allied soldiers were active all along the Western Front. Chances of chatting had been few and far-between.

"I don't think Patrick was badly wounded, but something happened that alerted Matt." Her expression grew solemn. "In his note, Matt also mentioned you having a run-in with Patrick. He didn't say exactly what, but he made it sound serious." Her dark gaze swept over him as if looking for confirmation.

What else had Matt shared? Probably enough that Jax needed to be forthright. He drove his fingers through his hair. "Orlington and I had a major confrontation, but I don't see what he could have to do with Celeste's murder. After the war, Patrick headed home to work in his family business, which is outside Cleveland. Although her aunt and uncle live there, it's improbable that the two of them met and conspired to blackmail me. Orlington doesn't need money."

Bella revealed Patrick's current financial situation and summed up with, "He doesn't want to work for his father, so additional funds might be attractive."

Surprise and dismay collided inside Jax. "Indeed, they might. And the rest of the family isn't here yet?"

"No. Only Patrick is." She hesitated before asking, "Is whatever happened in France reason enough for him to hold a grudge? Matt made it sound dire, and I know Patrick was a poor sport in golf tournaments. But that couldn't cause your trouble in France."

"It didn't. It was a problem that turned into an ugly situation." A frown furrowed Jax's brow while a period of silence ensued. "You know he was drafted, but he got put in our Guard unit."

"I remember, but what happened between the two of you? Matt didn't explain. He just asked me to make sure you didn't react if Patrick brought it up. I'm sure Matt was thinking about the two of you facing off in a tournament. I know Patrick got snide on a couple of occasions."

Her revelations brought back more memories. Matt had always backed up Jax, and vice versa. He wasn't sure the confrontation with Orlington was important to the case, but it was possible, especially considering Bella's exchange with the man. "Orlington served near me. He was a terrible officer. More concerned with glory than strategy or his men. We locked horns during the start of the Meuse-Argonne offensive. He wanted to advance before we got the order. We would've lost half of our platoons. Maybe more. But Orlington led from the back, so his life wasn't on the line like the rest of us."

"I'm not surprised," Bella murmured. "What happened when you argued with him?"

Jax's jaw tightened. "Nothing. Orlington wouldn't listen, so I went to our commander. He took my complaint seriously. The major reprimanded and reported Orlington for ignoring orders, which he'd done before. That ended any chance of him being promoted from second to first lieutenant."

"But you were promoted," Bella observed.

After a nod of his head, Jax replied. "So was Matt."

"On top of your history with Patrick, that seems like a reason for him to resent you and want to get even somehow. He was always an arrogant cad."

"A cad, a snob, and a cheater, too." Jax mentally went over his relationship with the former officer. "Even so, it's hard for me to believe he'd go to so much trouble after all this time."

"Maybe you're right, but I don't think we should completely discount him. He had to know Celeste, since he was at the field hospital where she volunteered." A grimace formed on Bella's face. "Patrick fancied himself quite a catch, as I recall."

The statement brought Jax to the edge of the cot. "Did he flirt with you?" Jax was well aware of the man's propensity to trifle with all the young ladies. "He always thought he was irresistible."

A half-shrug moved her shoulder. "I found him quite resistible. Still do."

"Good." The admission was out before Jax considered it. When Bella grinned, he shook his head. "For now, we've got to focus on the murder and the suspects. Did anyone mention Victor Gaspard to you?"

"I heard about him, and I agree he's a suspect. I knew about a French soldier settling in Boxwood, but I haven't met him and didn't know him during the war. Did you?"

"Just a little. Matt and I stayed at his aunt's guest-house that weekend when we came to Paris to see you."

"I remember the weekend. I still have the photograph of the three of us. It's on my vanity table."

A smile lit her expression.

"You sent me a copy, and I put it in my tunic pocket. After getting home, it was in my desk drawer until I joined the Bureau. I keep it in a drawer then and now. Mine is pretty tattered." Abruptly aware of how far they had gone from the case, Jax refocused his comments. "Anyhow, Gaspard may be a candidate for investigation." He followed with what he had learned in Boxwood. "He may not have been acquainted with Celeste. Maybe I'm grasping at straws by looking at him as a suspect."

"He is definitely someone to investigate. I'm sure Richard will start there. Also, when Ida and I were on the train, I spoke with the conductor. He's often on that run to-and-from Sandusky, so I asked if he had seen a Frenchwoman, and he had. It must've been Smithson Collier."

"It's hard to believe he'd get involved in blackmail or commit a murder. I already told Richard that, but we didn't get to finish because the mayor showed up. But Collier staying at the hotel for a couple of days is odd."

She pulled a notepad and pencil out of her pocketbook. "I'll talk with the Jenkinses later. The three of us will be the mainstays of the unofficial investigation. We don't want to duplicate our efforts, and I can share whatever you didn't get to say."

Renewed worry swept through him. "Be careful poking around, Bella. I'm grateful you're willing to help, everything considered. I don't want you taking chances, though. One woman has already died." Should he mention Richard's idea about a kidnapping plan, or did she already know? Uncertain, he hesitated to bring it up, "I don't want you being too involved."

Her gaze came up, and she shook one forefinger at him as if lecturing an errant pupil. "You cannot keep me from working on this investigation. You aren't running it. Richard is." Her terse tone matched the gesture. "It would pay for you to keep that in mind. Just as it would pay for you to avoid issuing any warnings or directives to me."

Her huffy tone didn't come as a surprise. He deserved the reprimand and the reminder. At present, he was in no position to make demands or give advice to anyone. Jax hung his head. "I said I was grateful for your support, and I am. More grateful than I can say."

"But you want to issue one of your typical warnings," she shot back. "I will not heed them, so you might as well save your breath. All of us plan to proceed whether or not you agree. You've said you're appreciative. Leave it at that."

"Yes, ma'am," he murmured, but the effect was spoiled because keeping the laughter out of his tone was impossible. Jax looked back at her. "Using your teacher voice is a good way to take charge of a situation."

Bella shook her head. "Jackson Hastings, you are utterly incorrigible," she said, but amusement underscored her words, and the corners of her mouth tipped into a smile.

Briefly, he grinned back at her, but his good humor faltered. Before they discussed the case, they had to clear the air. "Bella, about the other night…"

She cut him off. "I'm sorry I rushed off, but I was stunned and all those people were gaping at us and talking about the situation. That was upsetting, too."

"I understand." Jax ran a hand over his face. He might as well find out if she had heard more nasty gossip. "Richard said there's talk around town about me not courting you as soon as you got home because I was already married."

For a moment, she looked taken aback. "I heard a bit of it yesterday before Ida and I boarded the train, and today Patrick mentioned what he heard in the café, but it's nonsense. I paid no attention because I know you didn't marry Celeste, and I don't believe you were involved with her. Except for keeping her affair with Alan secret."

Relief slackened every muscle in his body. "I'm so sorry she showed up and ruined the evening. We both looked forward to it."

"You'll be out of here soon. We can still get to a few holiday events."

Her hopeful tone tore at him. "Richard thinks I need to stay home, if I'm released. I'm not sure about you being seen with me. It could reflect poorly on the resort and hurt business." He had said the same to Richard, but he wanted to gauge Bella's reaction.

"That's ridiculous," she shot back. "I don't care what other people think. I know you're innocent. I hurried off the other evening, but I was shocked. Besides…" Her voice trailed off.

"Besides what?"

Bella ducked her head. "Celeste is so pretty and petite."

The response held him momentarily mute. "You're prettier than she is. Much prettier." Her glossy brunette hair, cut in a bob, framed her lovely features to perfection. Although he couldn't make out her eye color in the dim light, Jax knew they were deep brown.

When she lifted her chin, doubt shone in her gaze. "But not petite."

"You're perfect just like you are." He imbued each word with certitude, because she was. Didn't she know that?

"Thank you."

"No need for thanks. It's the truth." Over the years, Jax had always thought of Bella as confident and courageous. Her intrepid spirit had led her into scrapes as a child and to France as an operator. It made her an outstanding detective. "And you aren't just lovely on the outside. You're sweet and kind, strong and brave. And resilient. You came home to find Ballantyne on the verge of closure, and you fought to save it."

"With help," she murmured.

"True, but along the way, you assisted me in several homicide cases, even when I tried to stop you." He injected a light note into his voice.

"You didn't want my help."

He shook his head. "I wanted your help, but I didn't think I deserved it. We're past all that now."

Jax cleared his throat. "As for courting, it's only on hold. Of course, if I'm stuck here, I won't be taking you out anyhow."

A bright smile lit her face. "We'll make sure you're out of here soon, and we'll see that the killer takes your place. Now, what else do I need to jot down?"

Jax took a moment to regroup and refocus. "When I met Celeste behind the café, she left with a man. After he whistled twice to get her attention."

Surprise rounded Bella's eyes. "I hadn't heard that."

"I told Nolen and the mayor. I'm not sure if Richard knows, since we got cut off, and there was a lot to cover."

"I'll tell him. Any other important details?"

116

"He was waiting down the street, so I couldn't see his face." Jax provided the details and included the meager description.

"A man about your height with a greatcoat similar to a French soldier's." Bella replied to Jax.

"It's not much to go on, but both Smithson Collier and Patrick Orlington are about my height. Victor Gaspard is, as well. Gaspard would've had one of those coats."

Bella looked up from her notepad. "We'll need more details about all of them. Smithson doesn't have a vehicle with him, but he was in town the night of the tree lighting. We don't know about Gaspard, and Patrick might have been. We can't be sure."

"Do you know what Orlington is driving?"

"No, but someone at the resort will have noticed, so I'll ask when I get back. What about Gaspard?"

"He's got Bill Addison's old Packard. They got friendly in France and, as I told you already, Burton Cratton was close to Gaspard, too. But

Gaspard doesn't share a lot."

"Still water runs deep, as the saying goes." Bella jotted more notes. "That's three possibilities to pursue." She rolled the pencil between her hands. "I'm not sure about my other one."

"You've got an additional suspect?" She had mentioned two ideas, but what was the source of the next one? "Have you been asking around town already?" Anxiety filled him.

"No, not really, but I ran into Dewey Fikeland before I came to see you."

Dismay hit Jax hard. "What's he doing back in town?" Dewey had been a thorn in his side as a kid, and his uncle was one of Jax's main detractors.

"Visiting his aunt and uncle. This is the first he's returned since going to France in 1916. That alone is interesting."

"When he left town, Dewey was vocal about never returning."

"I remember." Bella licked her lips. "You may not recall, but he was pestering me often for a while. I tried to be nice but disinterested. Dewey kept on and on. Finally, I told you and Matt."

"I remember." What Jax also remembered was his protective instincts. When he'd told Matt that Dewey ought to be warned off, his friend had suggested Jax perform the task himself. And he had. "Young Fikeland didn't appreciate me interfering."

"You weren't interfering. I was glad you talked to him, but I thought Matt would. Or the two of you together."

A long exhalation left Jax. "I was pretty upset after you talked to us. Your brother suggested I give Dewey what-for, and I was glad to do it."

Surprise rounded her eyes, and for several moments, she gazed steadily at him. "Thank you. He didn't bother me nearly as much after that."

"As it should be." An idea occurred to Jax. "Did he hound you today? Or say something about me? He must know I'm in jail. I'm sure his uncle is gloating over the situation." Maybe Dewey was, as well. As he thought back to the long-ago confrontation with the younger man, Jax recalled a threat. *You'll be sorry you stuck your nose in. Wait and see.* The malice in Dewey's tone and demeanor had stunned Jax, but he hadn't thought about that day in years. Surely, Dewey hadn't harbored rancor the entire time.

"Dewey insisted he didn't agree with Lyle about you harming Celeste, but he also mentioned how sad it is that you lied to me. Of course, I defended you."

Bella's observations brought Jax back to the present. Although her support warmed his heart, Jax issued another warning. "I appreciate it. Just be careful about being too outspoken on my behalf." He smiled to soften the directive. "We don't know who killed Celeste or why."

"I was careful with what I said, but I couldn't let his comment pass. The Fikelands are pompous prigs. Everyone knows that." She laid her pencil down and clasped her hands. "I'm not sure I believe Dewey doesn't agree with his uncle about your involvement in the murder. He was a little too eager to bring it up."

The assertion hung heavily in the air because Jax didn't believe it, either. He put one hand to his face and rubbed his jaw while considering the scant information about Dewey Fikeland. "Where has Dewey been since the war?"

"The last I heard, he was in New York City. I didn't ask him today," Bella replied. "Why?"

"Just wondering."

Silence descended for an endless moment. Only Bella, tapping her pencil on the notepad, broke the quiet until she spoke again. "Dewey is about your height, and he went to France in 1916. He could have a French army coat, and he could've met Celeste. For the first couple of years, the ambulance corps drivers ferried mostly French soldiers from the trenches to hospital camps."

Her astute observations came as no surprise. "It's possible, but is it probable?" He released a pent-up breath.

"I don't know. Even a slight chance is worth checking on his whereabouts lately and his movements since getting to town. He never liked you, and you chastised him for bothering me. Then, he made up the ridiculous story about you grabbing him, and his uncle wanted your dad to arrest you. So ludicrous."

"Both Dewey and Lyle were plenty worked up back then. Dewey said I'd be sorry for warning him away from you, but it was a long time ago." Lyle still disliked Jax. Maybe Dewey did, too. But were he and Celeste connected? Of course, the same question could apply to Gaspard, Collier, and Orlington.

A stricken look fell over Bella's fine features. "I never knew he threatened you."

The fear on her face made Jax hurry to offer reassurance. "He was a scrawny kid talking out of a hole in his head. I didn't take him seriously." Had that been a mistake?

"Being skinny and young aren't impediments to holding a grudge. It wouldn't stop him from blackmailing you or killing Celeste."

Jax ran a hand over his face. "All true. Even so, we know nothing about Dewey's time in France, and I'm not sure how we'd find out. No one else from around here served in the ambulance service, and he didn't have many friends growing up. Although he must've stayed in touch with his aunt and uncle, neither of them would answer questions. Especially if those questions were related to his guilt."

"No, they wouldn't," Bella agreed. "The cousin of one of my sister operators was a driver who went over in 1916. That was a fairly small group, so he could've known Dewey. I never met him, but I'll contact her."

To Jax, the idea seemed futile. "Victor Gaspard seems like the top suspect. Collier, Orlington, and Fikeland are farther down my list."

Her brow furrowed as a frown formed. "You and Richard always say we can't get stuck on any particular person until we know all the facts. Right now, we haven't got much information. Talking to my friend may help us decide if Dewey stays as a suspect or not."

She was right. "I agree."

"Good." Bella looked down at her notes. "We have four suspects. Two have personal reasons to target you. They could've all known Celeste and been smitten with her."

"Orlington isn't the type to be smitten, but he considered himself to be a ladies' man."

"I wonder if he saw Celeste after Alan died." Bella's forehead furrowed. "She would've been more vulnerable after losing Alan, especially if she was carrying his child. Maybe Patrick stayed in touch with her, even sent for her, after the war. From what I know about the Orlington family, they all traveled widely before hostilities broke out. He might've gone back for her. The Colliers aren't as well-to-do, but Smithson might've done the same thing. Gaspard stayed in France for a while, didn't he?"

"He did."

"Finding out if he and Celeste arrived in America around the same time would be helpful. Dewey said he stayed in Europe to help ferry supplies to stricken villages. Other than Gaspard, he'd have had the most contact with the French."

Jax considered the ideas. "All valid points."

"We'll look into everything. I'll do it carefully." As she spoke, Bella smiled.

"There's an awful lot for you, Richard, and Jenny to check out."

"Nolen and Newton will investigate thoroughly, and we'll all share what we learn. As far as Patrick, his younger sister was one of my students when I substituted at Boxmore, and she's chatty, so she might've talked about his travels at school. I'll ask Ida."

A laugh escaped him. "A great idea."

"Thank you." Her amusement slipped away. "It's the least I can do. That and call my friend. I'm sure Richard and Jenny will have more ideas."

He briefly bowed his head. When Jax looked back at Bella, he saw her intense expression. "You're such a good detective. I'm glad you're on my side."

"Always."

The single word resonated in his heart and soul. "Don't neglect your responsibilities at the resort. You have a lot of guests coming soon, so I know you're busy."

"Ida and Griff will shoulder extra work, and so will the others. Mac is eager to do more. He said finding the killer is most important of all."

"I appreciate that." He rubbed his temple. "I feel pretty helpless being stuck here."

"You can help by thinking about the four suspects and considering anyone else who might have motive and opportunity."

"I'll give it all serious thought."

"You can do that later today."

The comment reminded Jax of his plight. "Right. It's not like I'll be going any place for the foreseeable future."

"Not today, but soon, I hope." Bella offered a smile.

Jax scanned her face and found only sincerity. Their last discussion still bothered him, so he broached the subject again. "We haven't talked since the tree lighting. I know you and Ida went to see a friend yesterday."

"Due to the steady snow, we were delayed getting back. It was midnight before we reached Ballantyne. I planned to call, but that was too late. This morning, you weren't home."

Relief filled him. "I was probably already here. Anyhow, I hope it was a pleasant visit."

She shrugged. "It was good to see her on Tuesday. I got that information from the conductor, and Ida and I talked everything over."

"Everything?"

"Most everything about Alan. It turns out Ida was already suspicious." Bella leaned forward. "Remember how Alan said he couldn't get a day's leave to see her in the weeks before he died?"

Jax nodded. He remembered all too well.

"You must've known he was lying, and I wondered because other officers were off the line for a day or more. It turns out Ida was skeptical, too."

"She took Alan's death very hard."

"She did." Bella paused for a moment. "But she wasn't sure they'd actually get married. Now, Ida is thrilled about her engagement to Griff. She said she knows what genuine love is."

Surprise rippled through him. Although Biggins appeared to adore Ida, Jax hadn't been certain she returned the deep feelings. "She and Alan seemed smitten to me."

"To me, too. But they got engaged in a hurry. Maybe too much of a hurry. That's what Ida thinks. In France, she kept her doubts to herself because she didn't want to upset or distract Alan. Anyhow, if Alan is the father of Celeste's little boy, Ida won't be distraught. She's looking forward, not back."

Jax got to his feet and went to the front of his cell. Although he wanted to reach out to Bella, he grasped the bars until his knuckles showed white. "What about you? I know you had to be thinking about that day in France when you saw and heard Celeste the other evening. Are you looking forward or back?"

When Bella stood up and came to him, she laid her hands over his. "I remembered that day, and it affected me far more than it should have. You deserve my support, and I shouldn't have run for home. I let you down by not staying and listening."

"You've never let me down, Bella." He turned his hands to clasp hers. "And I never want to give you reason to doubt me again."

"After over twenty years, I know you well enough to realize you'd never walk away from a wife and child. Or anyone else close to you. I didn't stop and think logically. I felt and reacted on a purely emotional level."

"Completely understandable." His fingers tightened on hers. "If I hadn't promised Alan I'd cover up his indiscretion, I wouldn't have been able to be blackmailed. Celeste knew he asked Matt and me to lie for him. She must've told her partner in crime, whoever it is. Not that

I ever figured on her showing up with a fake marriage license and a photo of her child. I wish I had given her the money and said to get out of town and not come back."

"She could've come back anytime and probably would have."

"That's what Richard thought, but I could've gotten the license from her."

"Since it's not real, getting another one made wouldn't be difficult." Bella gently ran her thumbs over his fingers. "A printer had to do the work. If her child is in Cleveland with her relatives, maybe she got someone at a print shop there to create the license."

"Probably so. As far as a child, the photograph of a boy means very little."

Her eyebrows rose a fraction. "You don't think there's a Xavier."

Jax shrugged. "The youngster in the picture could be named Xavier. I'm not at all sure he's Celeste's son."

"I hope you're right, because I hate to think of a child being without his mother. If Alan was his father, he'd be an orphan."

"It's a sad situation, but why not bring the boy along to Moreley? Instead, she left him with her aunt and uncle in Cleveland? It doesn't ring true. Wouldn't a father feel more pressure after seeing his son?"

Bella's brow furrowed. "She planned to be back there before Christmas, didn't she?"

"I guess. Mostly, she wanted to get as much money as possible, as soon as possible."

"Which makes me wonder why the man would kill her. Especially if he needs funds."

"Richard and I discussed possibilities. Her partner might've wanted to escalate the threat to me. Maybe Celeste refused."

A puzzled expression blanketed her face. "Escalate how?"

For several moments, Jax considered whether to reveal Richard's supposition. Finally, he decided Bella needed to know. "Kidnapping you would've worked. I would've given them whatever they wanted."

"Whatever they wanted?" she echoed.

The emotion clouding her dark gaze had him swallowing hard over his own potent feelings. "You must know I'd give anything, including my life, to keep you safe."

With one hand, she reached between the bars to cup his jaw. "Oh, Jax."

He lightly clasped her wrist and moved her hand so that he could place a kiss on the palm. Because he had to press his face to the bars, Jax made the caress featherlight. Warm recollection spread through him. They had been discussing the case like they had gone over several others. But this investigation was different. Jax always had doubts about involving Bella in his work, and this time, the doubts were escalating into terror. What if the killer became her kidnapper? Or worse, killed again. "I'm not sure you should spend much time around me right now. Like I said, it might be better if you aren't actively involved in investigating Celeste's murder. Richard and Jenny can work on it together and keep you posted." Anxiety rode him hard. The last thing he wanted was for Bella to get caught in any crossfire—physical, emotional, or otherwise.

Her jaw dropped. "You will not get rid of me so easily. I already said so."

"I don't want to get rid of you. I want to protect you and the resort." He released his hold and stepped back.

"We won't lose Ballantyne. We have loyal guests who won't be bothered by a false allegation. I wouldn't turn my back on you, Jax. You should know that." She lifted her chin a fraction and put her hands on her hips. "You can refuse to see me while you're here, but you can't keep me from working on the case."

Jax grinned.

"What's so funny?" she asked in a tart tone.

"I've seen that stance before, frequently. The first time was when you wanted to go fishing with Matt and me. You were six, and your parents said you were too small. They were right, so Matt and I set out before dawn, but you followed. We didn't see you right away." Laughter rumbled out of him before he could repress it. "In fact, we heard you before you came into view."

Color flared in her cheeks. "It isn't gentlemanly of you to bring that up."

"I wasn't a gentleman then. I was an eight-year-old kid." Jax schooled his expression. "Besides, neither of us made fun of you. We were too worried when you tumbled into the water."

"I knew how to swim." Her tone was as defensive as her stance.

"Yes, but you were fully dressed with boots on. Heavy boots that might've pulled you under. Besides, you could've hit your head on a rock. We didn't know."

"And you jumped right in to save me."

"I was closer to you than Matt." All humor had left Jax as the memory washed over him. Both he and her brother had panicked when Bella, trailing them over wet rocks, had fallen into the river. Jax, fear driving him, had tossed down his pole to dive in after her.

"I'll admit I was relieved, because you're right. My boots and clothes made swimming hard." Her gaze narrowed on him. "You had little trouble, and you were fully clad."

"Adrenaline. I didn't know if you'd knocked yourself unconscious, so acting fast was important."

A smile played across her lips. "That's when my crush first started."

The statement caught Jax off-guard, but a question immediately arose. "It did?"

"Yes, it did. When you got bronchitis and ended up at home for a week, I thought you were very heroic to suffer on my behalf. You risked your life for me, even back then."

"I didn't think about it that way, but I suppose so." His voice sounded solemn, so Jax offered a smile. "I never wanted you to be hurt, if I could stop it. I never will."

"I don't want you hurt, either," Bella replied, "and I certainly don't want you being found guilty of a murder you didn't commit."

She didn't need to say, I certainly don't want you going to the electric chair, but the possibility hung silently and ominously in the air. He fought back a shudder.

"I'll stop and see the Jenkinses on my way home. I told Jenny they could stay at the resort, but they want to be in town."

"I know, and they can use my house." Jax bowed his head for a moment before again meeting her gaze.

"They ought to be home enjoying the holidays. You should be, too."

She returned to the stool, picked up her notepad, and grabbed a pencil. "I will when the killer is in here instead of you. Now, let's go over the last details, so I can put things together before meeting with the Jenkinses."

"I didn't think you'd ever be interviewing me as a suspect," he admitted.

Her eyebrows rose a fraction. "I don't think of you as a suspect, more like a witness."

"Good to know." A hint of humor was back in his voice.

Again, she rolled her eyes. "Let's go through the chronology of events."

"From when Celeste arrived here, or from when I first met her in France?"

"Let's talk about how you, Matt, and Alan all got acquainted with her. Even though you told me last spring, I didn't take notes. As things stand now, we need to explain the issues clearly and concisely as part of our undertaking. Going over details might jog your memory and expose someone else who could mean you harm."

Jax took a deep breath. "Celeste's brother Etienne was mortally wounded in September. He was found by an American platoon and taken to one of our field hospitals. Celeste heard and went to nurse him. She'd been volunteering at a French facility and wanted to have her brother moved there, but he was in rough shape. When she saw him, she realized as much."

Bella's pencil darted across the notepad. "How long did he live after she arrived?"

"About a week. Alan was in the bed next to him, which is how he and Celeste became acquainted. She leaned on him, especially after Etienne died. Alan was almost well by then, but Celeste stayed as a volunteer nurse when he went back to the line. She did an excellent job and spoke fluent English. You know how hospitals and clearing stations were always short-staffed." When Bella nodded, Jax continued. "Alan visited her every time he got leave."

Her gaze rose to meet his. "And lied to Ida."

"Both your brother and I urged him to break off with Ida if he was really in love with Celeste. It would've been fairer to my way of thinking."

"You knew Alan much better than I did. Do you think he ever loved Ida?" Bella asked.

"I've never thought much about that." For several moments, he gazed at his hands folded in front of him. "I remember when they were courting before the war, he seemed smitten. I was surprised when they became betrothed, though. On the troopship, he talked a lot about life after the war, and how he was glad to have someone waiting for him. From what he said, he wasn't close to his folks or his older sister."

"Which gives credence to Ida's supposition that he needed someone, more than loved her."

"It does," Jax agreed. "Alan wasn't a bad person, and I think he fell in love with Celeste. But he didn't want to hurt Ida. If he had lived and knew about a child, he might've broken the engagement. I don't know. My view is he should have anyhow."

"You're right. It would have been better for both Celeste and Ida. Hurtful for Ida, but she's found someone else."

"Someone better," Jax observed.

A chuckle left Bella. "You didn't think so when you first met Griff."

Unable to deny the truth, he nodded. "I was jealous of him then." Since Jax now knew he had no reason to envy Biggins, the admission was easy to make. "Ever since he started courting Ida, I've liked him fine."

Low laughter escaped her. "There was never a need for you to worry about Griff and me stepping out. Or about me stepping out with anyone other than you."

His heart constricted with gratitude and anxiety. With effort, Jax voiced his deepest, darkest apprehension. "If the worst happens and I'm found guilty…"

She cut him off. "That won't take place, Jax, so I won't entertain the possibility. You shouldn't, either."

Her belief in him buoyed Jax's flagging spirits. Even so, facing reality was important. With her parents and brother dead, Bella had only Mac, who was in his seventies. She was apt to outlive the old pro by decades. Jax didn't want her spending those years on her own. He wanted her to be happy, safe, and supported. "Let me put it this way, if anything ever happens to me, I don't want you to live your life alone."

A tremulous smile touched her lips, but her dark gaze was steady as it met his. "If something happens to me, would you court another woman?"

"Of course not." The assertion came from the depths of his heart and soul but, as soon as the words were out, Jax realized his error.

Her grin widened. "Good, because I won't, either." She put pencil to paper. "Let's continue."

Chapter Seven

After briefly reviewing Jax's two recent encounters with Celeste, and her body being found, Bella reluctantly took her leave. A last glance at him, sitting on the narrow cot in the dim cell, had her blinking back tears. He needed to be at home, resting and recuperating, not jailed for a crime he didn't commit. Her footsteps were slow as she went into the main office.

"You and Jax talked for quite a while. I'm sure he was glad to see you." Jillian, a pretty blonde in her early twenties, looked up from her desk.

As Bella leaned on the counter, she wondered what the clerk and Nolen had discussed. Since they were courting, probably everything about the murder, including town gossip. "He's in a tough position, but I assured him that Richard, Jenny, and I are in his corner."

Dismay flashed in Jillian's ice-blue gaze. "Newton, Nolen, and I wish we could do more, but Mayor Cawlings warned us to be careful and not favor Jax."

"Jax understands, and he wants a fair investigation. In the long run, it'll be better because people won't suspect Jax was set free due to favoritism."

"Folks like Lyle Fikeland." Jillian frowned. "He keeps spreading nasty gossip. I don't know why he doesn't like Jax."

The mention of the older Fikeland reminded Bella of her meeting with his nephew. She felt ambivalent about crossing paths with Dewey again, because he was a pest. But she needed to know more about his time in France. A telephone call to her sister operator would be the first step. Later, seeing Dewey again might be necessary. Bella moved her attention back to the conversation. "When we were growing up, Jax spent his free time at Ballantyne. His dream was to be a golf pro, and he always said he'd never follow in his father's footsteps as a lawman. Mr. Fikeland thinks golf is a foolish, useless game. He has a low opinion of those who play, especially professionals. Mac, Grampa Stewart, and Dad stopped patronizing his store years ago because he was so outspoken. They went to the hardware in Boxwood instead." Another issue had arisen between Mac and Lyle, but she didn't share it, since Jax hadn't been directly involved.

Jillian nodded. "Understandable, since they were all pros. Nolen told me about Jax working as an assistant golf pro before the war."

"He planned to resume his career, but his wounds made playing almost impossible. Playing well, at least."

"Important for a pro, but maybe the surgery will make a difference. I know it hasn't been long."

"I hope the operation was successful." Jax deserved to have his dreams come true. Finding Celeste's killer would be a big step in that direction. Before Bella could say more, the bell over the front door jingled, and the mayor stepped inside. Annoyance swept through her. Hadn't the man been here only a short time ago? Why wasn't he letting Nolen and Newton run the investigation? Why come back?

Cawlings swept his hat off as he glanced from one woman to the other. "Arabella. Jillian. I suppose you two are discussing the Hastings case."

Anger replaced annoyance, and Bella spun to face the mayor. "It's the Bouchard murder case. Jax isn't involved at all, except as a scapegoat. Hopefully, a temporary one."

Dull color rose in the man's lean cheeks. "A lot of evidence points to his guilt."

"Circumstantial evidence, and even that is scanty." Bella found it impossible to let the mayor's comments stand. Evidently, he wanted someone in jail, probably to ease visitors' minds. And to pacify some merchants. Surely, he knew Jax was not guilty.

Cawlings' nostrils flared with a sharp intake of breath. "I don't consider his threats to the victim or his presence near the crime scene to be circumstantial."

"Those are primary examples of circumstantial evidence," Bella said.

Dark color rose in the mayor's face. "But a green mitten was found. Jax admits he got a similar pair while in France."

Bella gritted her teeth to gain control. "Hundreds, probably thousands, of soldiers got knitted mittens."

"But they weren't all green." The mayor was insistent, if nothing else.

"He isn't the only one who had that color," Bella replied.

Cawlings shrugged. "Perhaps not, but Jax has a powerful motive. You can't deny that."

Since she couldn't, Bella took another tack. "You know Jax wouldn't kill anyone. It's preposterous."

The mayor had a quick response. "He killed people in France."

The sharp retort pierced Bella like a spear to her heart. "Is that what Lyle Fikeland is saying?" When Jillian bent her head and the mayor looked away, she knew Fikeland had made the ugly accusation. Harnessing her temper was a struggle. "Jax was a soldier fighting for his country. He defended all of us, and I'm disgusted with those who don't defend him. They should be ashamed." She nodded at Jillian, brushed past Cawlings, and hurried outside. Once there, tears sprang to her eyes. With the back of one hand, Bella brushed them away and blinked hard to keep more at bay. Giving in to fear and sadness wasn't an option.

Despite her reassurances to Jax, she felt sick with anxiety. People had overheard his arguments with Celeste, but no one had seen her with another man. Maybe better evidence would emerge soon. Bella planned to do her part in unearthing clues. Jax needed to be set free and labeled innocent.

The dim light of a late winter afternoon was descending as she walked to her Ford, got in, and turned the vehicle toward the Hastings house. Within moments of her tapping on the front door, Jenny answered. Richard was in Boxwood, so the two women only exchanged the briefest information. Bella returned home, talked to the staff, ate dinner, and called her friend. No one answered, so she put that task on the next morning's agenda and fell into bed.

Thursday morning, Bella finally reached her sister operator and asked about contacting the other woman's cousin. Her former colleague provided his location, but Bella could not speak to him since he was at work. His wife promised to have him call Bella after four o'clock. Immediately after hanging up from that call, Jenny telephoned to say Richard wanted a group meeting, so Bella hurried to get her tasks completed before heading back to town. Bella hoped the older couple had made more progress than she had.

After parking in front of the Hastings house, she rushed to the door. Before she knocked, it swung open. Surprise and delight filled Bella when she saw Jax.

"Good morning," he said with a grin.

"A very good morning." Before she said more, he swept her into his arms and held her close. Bella let her head rest on his chest. The steady beat of his heart provided solace and hope. He was free. For now. With luck, for always. Too soon, he stepped back. "Jenny and Richard are in the parlor." Jax took her hand and led the way.

Bella laced her fingers with his and held on tight. Had the charges been dropped? Or was he out on bail?

The Jenkinses greeted her warmly. Once they were seated, Jenny served coffee and biscuits before settling down herself. After a long swallow of the hot beverage, Bella turned to Jax. "When did you get home?"

He smiled. "I got out of jail an hour ago. Thanks to Richard and the local prosecutor."

"The man agrees your history should be considered. I wish we could've gotten the case dismissed, but we will soon," the older man observed. "Let's get down to business, because we need to find the killer before Cawlings gets itchy to have a suspect in jail again."

As murmurs of assent went around the room, Bella felt a chill ripple through her body. She couldn't bear having Jax back in a cell. Bail was better than nothing.

Richard nodded. "Yesterday, I asked if you knew who might hold a grudge against you going back to your time in France. I know it seems like a stab in the semi-darkness, but all of our current list was there."

"My husband has a gut feeling about the possibility," Jenny observed with a smile.

A low chuckle left Jax. "And we don't ignore those."

"We certainly don't," Bella agreed. Her spirit lifted a little as she joined in the teasing.

Dull color climbed in the older man's face. "Very funny."

"We weren't laughing at you, dear," his wife said. "We all agree about using intuition as guidance. It's been an excellent tool in the past."

"It has," Bella agreed. Her amusement ebbed as she pulled her notepad and pencil out. "I hate to think someone feels enough antipathy toward Jax to frame him for murder." During a restless night, she had reviewed the details about Smithson, Dewey, and Patrick. "I suppose Jax told you about our conversation yesterday." Both of the Jenkinses nodded.

"Did you call your friend?" Jenny asked.

"Last night, but no one answered. I reached her earlier, and I called her cousin. He's at work until four," Bella replied. "What about you two? Learn anything new?"

Richard shook his head. "I went to Boxwood yesterday afternoon. Talked to Gaspard's landlady, the diner owner, and Burton Cratton. I learned little more than Jax, but I got confirmation of Gaspard's failing business, forays out of town, the late night on Monday, and his current disappearance. The money issue could be a motive, but we need to know if he and Miss Bouchard were acquainted in France or here. Nolen and Newton already asked around town about someone driving an old Packard and found no one who had seen such a vehicle."

"I didn't know him well enough for him to want revenge, so money would have to be the motivation," Jax said.

"That has inspired a lot of killers," Richard said.

"What about Smithson Collier?" Jenny posed the question. "He's on the list, but I don't know much about him."

"He talked with Celeste on the train," Bella put in, "which is why I brought him up. Also, he came ahead of his family and stayed at the hotel for a couple of days instead of coming directly to the resort."

"Somewhat odd," Jenny observed.

"It is, but I never had a run-in with him. He was a quiet, pleasant guy." Jax ran one hand over his face. All lightness left his expression. "He ended up in Alan's platoon, so he had to know about Celeste."

"Did he get along with Brewster?" Richard posed another question.

Jax nodded. "To my knowledge, yeah. I never heard about any problems, and Smithson was a sergeant."

"Then, he definitely knew about Celeste and Alan," Bella observed. "I remember him being rather straight-laced before the war. I can't imagine he would've approved of them having a love affair."

Jax gave a shake of his head. "Your brother and I didn't approve, either, because Alan was engaged."

"But you and Matt were never so starchy," Bella said. "Smithson always seemed prudish. Did the war change him?"

With one hand, Jax rubbed his neck. "I only saw him a handful of times, and I can't say that he seemed a lot different. I remember some of the boys getting booze when we were away from the line for a few days. Smithson wanted no part of the demon rum, as he called the stuff. That doesn't mean he'd blackmail me. Or that he needs money."

While Bella couldn't disagree with the last assertion, she wanted to know more. "He seems like the type who would take up for a lady, so I'd like to find out what he might've said to some of the other veterans about Alan and Celeste. Since Nolen was also a sergeant, the two of them could've talked."

"They did from time-to-time." Jax paused as if in thought. "In fact, I remember the two of them refusing booze. Instead, they went off together to visit the Salvation Army Doughnut Dollies."

"I don't want to visit the constable's office, since the mayor is probably keeping track of who comes and goes," Bella said. "But I'll try to talk to Nolen about Smithson. He may have some useful details, and I can share what I've heard."

Jax leaned back and stuck his legs out in front of him. "I think it's a waste of time, but maybe I'm not thinking clearly. Or maybe I don't want to believe guys who served with me could commit murder and try to pin it on me."

"Collier doesn't seem to have as many warning indicators as the others on our list. At least, not from what we know at the moment," Richard observed. "Let's put him on a back burner but not forget him entirely. Arabella can speak with Nolen, and we can change our minds, if necessary. All right?"

Jax, Jenny, and Bella agreed.

"Let's go over what we've learned so far," Richard suggested. "Unless you've come up with a new suspect, Jax."

"No one else comes to mind, and I went over and over possibilities last night," Jax replied.

A quick glance at him revealed he looked as drained as Bella felt. "Maybe our discussion will spark an idea or highlight someone."

Jax offered a weary smile. "Maybe so."

"When I came back from Boxwood, I stopped at the train station," Richard said. "The stationmaster was gone, but I spoke with two porters. They both remembered a French woman and said several other folks got off the same train."

"Did any of them seem to be with her?" Bella asked. Probably a futile question, since any sensible accomplice would be cautious, but Smithson had openly spoken with Celeste on the train. If he was involved, he was foolish.

"They were too busy to be sure," Richard replied. "Dewey Fikeland arrived then. Jax and I haven't had much time to talk this morning, but he passed along some details about the young man. Jenny and I agree the younger Fikeland is a suspect."

Bella agreed. "What about Celeste's aunt and uncle? I've been wondering if they're coming to get her body."

"When I first talked with Nolen, he'd already spoken with the uncle, who was distraught and unable to answer questions. About all Nolen learned was that Celeste left their home alone, ostensibly to visit a friend from the war. No name, although the person supposedly lived in Sandusky. She planned to return to Cleveland tomorrow."

"What about Xavier?" Jax asked.

"There is or was a child," Richard said. "Nolen asked about the boy's father, and the uncle said he was a doughboy. When Nolen tried to find out where Xavier is, the uncle started sobbing. Nolen couldn't tell if Xavier was in Cleveland or not."

"There are so many childhood illnesses," Jenny said in a solemn tone. "I hope the youngster didn't succumb to one."

"Conditions in France were terrible after the war, and they were also hard hit by the Spanish flu," Bella observed.

Richard nodded. "Nolen will try to get more information when the uncle calls to make final arrangements.

141

I advised Nolen to give them a couple of days. If they don't call back, he'll need to contact them again."

Sorrow squeezed hard on Bella's heart as she thought about the youngster who might be left in the wake of Celeste's murder. "Understandable that the family needs time." When Jax laid his hand over hers, she knew he was offering silent support for her own grief and losses.

"It's such a tragedy," Jenny said. "But we need to get back to the case. What else should we discuss?"

"I found out Patrick is driving a Pierce Arrow." Bella turned to Jax. "Did you see one when you were walking around after the tree lighting?"

He released her hand and settled into the corner of the sofa. "No, I didn't."

"We need to see if anyone else did," Bella commented.

"Nolen and Newton need to know a lot of these details, in case they haven't gotten them," Richard commented.

Jenny picked up a pad of paper and a pencil from the stand next to her. "I can note anything new, and you can give the list to them, dear."

"Wonderful," her husband replied. "They've spoken with the night desk clerk, but I want to do that, too."

"I saw him when I went looking for Celeste and her accomplice the night of her murder," Jax said. "He wasn't helpful. In fact, I had the distinct impression he believed her lies and disliked me based on that."

"Korbert Lannigan and Lyle Fikeland are friendly," Bella replied.

A grimace darkened Jax's face. "That explains his attitude toward me."

"Can I go along to take notes?" Bella glanced at Jenny. "I know you usually go with Richard."

"I don't mind if you go," the older woman said. "One of us should stay here with Jax, just in case something else happens."

Jax shifted restlessly, which made Bella turn toward him. "We'll always discuss what we learn with you, so you aren't being left out."

With the heels of his hands, Jax rubbed his eyes. "I know." His voice sounded rough and raspy.

"You need to get some rest," Bella told him. Celeste's threats and murder, followed by his arrest, were taking a heavy toll. "You probably haven't slept well since Celeste came to town."

He shook his head. "No, I haven't."

"After we finish talking, you can head upstairs and sleep," Jenny put in. Concern etched her face as she studied Jax.

"Good idea," her husband added. "You'll think better after a nap."

"I hope so," Jax murmured. "But what about Edgar Geneve? As stationmaster, he might've seen more than the porters, who would've been busy with bags."

"He'll be a big help, I'm sure. He doesn't miss a thing, and he's always out and about with departures and arrivals," Bella said.

Jenny scanned her notepad before looking from Bella to Jax. "Before Bella got here, you said you saw someone in what might've been a French army greatcoat. Those aren't fitted like a trench coat or Chesterfield, are they?"

"It definitely wasn't fitted, and I couldn't tell the color. Only the shape," Jax replied. "I saw quite a few of them overseas."

The revelation scraped Bella's memory. "I did, too, and they weren't at all like current American styles. Mr. Geneve has a good eye, so I'm sure he'd note something different. If he saw the coat in daylight, he could describe the color, which would help. The French coats were a particular shade of blue."

"They were, and he'd remember the hue." Jax looked at Richard. "When we spoke at the jail, everything was a blur to me. Since then, I've thought and thought about exactly what I witnessed. I still can't be positive. I'm sure about the general look of the coat and the man's height. That's about it."

"Not surprising," the retired constable said. "You're exhausted and frazzled. But the description of the coat could help us hone in on the killer. I haven't seen any outerwear like you've described."

"Neither have I. Victor Gaspard probably kept his greatcoat," Jenny said. "Could Americans have gotten one in some other way?"

Jax put the heel of his hand against his forehead. "Celeste kept her brother's coat. He had a head wound, so the garment had no holes. Just a little blood, which she cleaned up. I suppose it comforted her to have a link to him and his service."

A brief silence fell before Richard made an observation. "She could've given the coat to anyone. Even an American."

"You're right," Jax said. "But how would she get the coat to Orlington or Fikeland or Collier?"

144

"That's a good question, but any of them could've gotten a similar coat while still in France," Bella pointed out. "Dewey was there the longest, so he had to meet more Frenchmen."

"Do we know where Dewey worked in 1918?" Richard asked. "What part of the line?"

"Not yet. I'm hoping my friend's cousin will have information," Bella responded.

"Even if you talk to him, the cousin may not know Dewey, and he's even less likely to have met Celeste." Frustration echoed in Jax's voice. "In fact, it seems pretty unlikely."

Bella shifted toward him. "My friend said the ambulance drivers are a close-knit group, and they stay in touch. I don't know if her cousin and Dewey are acquainted, but it can't hurt to find out." She would pursue any line of inquiry, even if the chance of finding solid evidence was slim. With Jax's life on the line, all avenues of exploration were crucial.

"I agree," Richard said. "Building a case is important. We all know that. I don't want to talk to young Fikeland yet. His uncle is on the warpath, and revealing his nephew is a suspect isn't a wise strategy." He pulled out his pocket watch. "I'm calling a friend in Cleveland to see what he can discover about Patrick Orlington. He should be in his office in an hour. Orlington's comments to Bella about maybe being caught in a speakeasy raid interests me."

"Me, too," Jax said. "Orlington liked to gamble, period. On cards, or golf, or horse racing. Anything that could be bet on, he'd try. If he got in too deep, his father bailed him out." Jax took a long swallow of coffee before going on. "If he goes to speakeasies, I'm guessing they're ones with illegal gambling operations."

Since selling bootlegged booze often went together with illicit gaming, Bella figured Jax was right. Imagining Patrick Orlington running with a fast crowd was easy. He was exactly the type to drink and gamble in illicit establishments. As Bella considered the leads, she felt a sliver of relief that Richard and Jenny had come to help. Richard was also willing to follow an array of hints. Surely, one would pan out.

"What if the killer is someone else entirely?" Jax asked. "And what if he left town already?"

Both questions revealed the depth of Jax's anxiety. And they made sense, but Bella had no reassuring answers. She glanced back at Richard, who looked uneasy as he focused on Jax.

With one hand, Richard rubbed his jaw. "If the killer's desire for revenge is strong enough, he may stick around to see you suffer, son. It's not a pretty picture, but I've had a couple cases where a blackmailer stayed to observe his victim's misery. And that's how both got caught."

For a long moment, no one spoke. Finally, Jax nodded. "Even after being a lawman for going on three years, I hate thinking someone tried to extort money from me before committing a murder and wanting me to take the blame."

"We can't be sure this man killed Celeste Bouchard, intending to pin it on you," Jenny put in.

"I agree," her husband added. "A rock is a weapon of opportunity, which means he may not have planned to kill her. They might've argued, and he lost control."

"It's still awful," Bella murmured.

"It is," Jenny added. "We'll make sure the killer is caught, even if he didn't plot to murder her."

"We will," her husband agreed. "At least not too many tourists have arrived yet. That'll help in checking on them, but the four on our list are strong suspects. We may turn up others, but I have a hunch we have the killer's name already."

"There's a lot of legwork to do, and I'm stuck here in the house." Jax bowed his head and rubbed the back of his neck.

Bella laid a hand on his forearm. "It has to be hard, but you need to be careful. If the killer has it in for you, and he's still here, you could be in danger."

His expression grim, Jax shifted to face her. "You could be, too." His gaze went to Jenny and Richard. "All of you could be."

The older man held up both hands. "We'll be fine. I think we'll wrap the case up quickly, even without you being in the thick of it, Jax. I know you want to dig in and prove your innocence, but have faith in us." Richard offered a reassuring smile.

"I do. Believe me, I do," Jax said.

The avowal was sincere, yet Bella's heart went out to him. Jax didn't deserve to be wrongly accused, let alone be put behind bars. "At least you're home, where we can talk freely and often."

"I'm relieved about that," Richard put in. "Yesterday, when I spoke with Mayor Cawlings, he was clear about Nolen needing to limit the number of visitors and the length of visits."

Bella's stomach clenched. The mayor's attitude disturbed Bella because a rush to judgment would be bad for Jax. She wasn't sure about the consensus among the townsfolk. Once the killer was found, Cawlings and others would have to face facts, which couldn't happen a moment too soon. "That's unfair of the mayor."

Richard shrugged. "Prisoners rarely get unlimited visits. I think Cawlings primarily wants to avoid the appearance of impropriety, but we don't need to worry about curbing our conversations. We can speak as long and as often as we want now."

"In any case, we need to move forward. What's our plan for today?" Bella asked.

"Yes, let's get down to brass tacks," Jenny agreed with a smile.

A deep chuckle rumbled out from Richard. "Arabella, why don't you go to the train station on your way back to Ballantyne, and I'll talk to my friend in Cleveland. We should go back to the hotel, since we haven't spoken with the night clerk or the proprietor. Both were out when I stopped. Other than that, I'm open to ideas, ladies. And Jax."

"I'd like to hear what Bella and Jenny suggest," Jax said.

Bella didn't need to look at him to know he was smiling. Good humor was in his voice. Thank heaven. For the most part, he looked grim and beaten—and who could blame him? She turned to Jenny. "What do you think? I know one of us will stay here."

"I can do that. After you dropped me off yesterday, I ran into a couple of ladies aid members. There's a bake sale this weekend, and I promised to contribute, so I'll get my supplies in order," the older woman replied. "The case is my top priority, of course."

"But you'll have time to bake while you babysit me." A rueful edge was in Jax's statement.

A chuckle left Richard. "Son, I'd trade places if I could. One of my favorite holiday activities is sampling my wife's special concoctions."

"That sounds good," Jax said.

Relief spread through Bella. Jax sounded and looked more at ease. She wasn't sure about the way to a man's heart being through his stomach, but Jax enjoyed sweets. As soon as the case ended, she would bake some for him. "I can go to the train station and talk to Mr. Geneve." Her gaze went to the senior constable. "What do you think about talking with Lyle Fikeland again? I haven't set foot in his store in years."

"No need for you to subject yourself to the man's rudeness," Richard replied. "I may stop at the hardware store to pick up some nails or such. Any excuse that won't put Fikeland on immediate alert. I'm sure Lyle will have plenty to say without me asking questions."

"All bad about me," Jax said with a grimace.

"If he gets worked up, he may reveal something useful," Jenny pointed out before turning to Bella. "What about Dewey? Might he be in the store?"

"Probably so. He started working there when he first came here as a little boy. Mr. Fikeland will likely get him to pitch in while he's home," Bella replied.

"I hope Dewey is working. I'd like to get an impression of him. We have a sound plan for today." Richard turned to Bella. "When you get back to Ballantyne, you may see Collier and Orlington. Don't interrogate them, but some general conversation may bring out details. If you get any, I want to know. We can't formally interrogate suspects, but I'll pass everything on to Nolen and Newton, who can. I'll stop by the constable's office later and share what I learn with them. I can also find out how they're doing. They're hampered by regular duties, so they don't have as much time as we do."

"Or many leads, from what I overheard earlier today when Nolen and Newton were discussing the case," Jax added. "Newton went to Boxwood. I mentioned Orlington to them last night. Nolen knows him and Collier, so he may be out at the resort today."

"Good," Bella said. "I'm ready to go, if you are, Richard. I'll head to the station after the hotel."

The older man's reply was getting to his feet.

"Will you have enough time for your work at Ballantyne?" Jenny's face held a look of concern.

"Everyone is pitching in, so my tasks are fewer until next week." Nothing was as important as proving Jax's innocence.

Chapter Eight

R ichard drove his Winton, while Bella took her Ford. The pair met outside the hotel's front door.

"I hope Mr. Cooper has some sort of helpful information," Bella said, "and Lannigan, too."

A frown furrowed the older man's forehead. "I didn't want to say too much in front of Jax, other than Lannigan being friendly with Fikeland." He shifted from one foot to the other. "Lannigan has spread Lyle's vile gossip, so he may not be cooperative."

"And he won't have to talk with us, since we have no formal standing."

"Exactly, but we'll try to get whatever information the man has." Richard ushered her inside and headed to the counter where Korbert Lannigan, a gaunt figure of medium height—stood. His dark hair was swept away from his face, and half-spectacles perched on his long, narrow nose. "Good day. We want to speak with Thad Cooper. And you, since you're here. I thought we'd need to return later. Don't you usually work nights?" Richard asked.

"I do, but I switched for a couple of days." Lannigan glanced from Richard to Bella and back. "He's working, and I am, too. Besides, I don't know why you want to talk with me."

Annoyance filled Bella. Lannigan had been telling tales throughout town, but he didn't want to be interviewed? She opened her mouth to berate the man. Richard spoke first. "Just a few questions. I'm sure Thad will cover the desk while the three of us chat in his office."

Lannigan gave a slight nod before turning toward the back of the hotel. While he was gone, Bella sighed and said, "He's often brusque, but he was worse than usual."

"He's not curt when he's gossiping. Lannigan loves gossip. Especially, if it's bad. But he knows we won't listen to it."

"I don't understand why some people like to spread nasty hearsay."

"Nor do I," Richard said, "but I've run into a few over the years. Usually, they're folks who are unhappy with themselves."

Since Bella couldn't deny the assertion, she fell silent. Within a few moments, Thaddeus Cooper appeared. He welcomed them with a wide smile. "Come in, come in." Cooper gestured down the narrow hall to where a door stood open. "You both know the way."

"I thought you wanted to talk to me," Lannigan said.

"We do," Richard replied. "Next."

Bella preceded the two men and sat down when Cooper gestured to the other chair facing his desk before taking a seat himself. She immediately pulled off her gloves and retrieved her pencil and notepad.

"We only want to ask a few questions, since you weren't around when I chatted with your other clerk," Richard said. "We aren't here in any formal capacity, just as interested parties who want to help Jax."

"Good, because the mayor already told me not to let you see Miss Bouchard's room." Cooper leaned back in his chair. "You know about the marriage license that was found?"

"We do," Richard said.

Bella studied the hotel owner's face. Was his expression sympathetic, or was she engaging in wishful thinking? Her doubts were dashed when the proprietor spoke again.

"I don't think for one minute that the document is genuine," Cooper said, "and I'm sure Jax didn't kill the girl. I wish I had more than personal beliefs to give you, but I'll answer all your questions."

Relief allowed Bella to breathe more easily. Evidently, the man was on Jax's side. While individual support wouldn't prove his innocence, it was welcome.

"Glad to hear you aren't listening to Lyle Fikeland's lies," Richard put in.

Cooper took off his spectacles and cleaned them with the end of his tie. He slid them back on before responding. "Lyle never liked Jax." His gaze moved to Bella. "You know, he thinks golf is a foolish game, and he has a vendetta against Mac."

She nodded. "I know. He and Mac had a run-in years ago."

"Do you know what it was about?" Richard asked.

153

"Mr. Fikeland sold Mac and Grampa Stewart some shoddy materials when they were building the cottages. Mac wanted a refund. When Fikeland refused, he went to the town council with the complaint. Ballantyne was already a big draw for the area, so they backed Mac and Grampa," Bella explained.

Cooper nodded. "I was just coming up then, but I recall a little about the dispute. Jax being associated with the resort probably adds fuel to the fire, but there's the time Jax told Dewey to stay away from you. Even though there was no evidence of a physical confrontation, Lyle insists Jax grabbed Dewey by the neck and threatened to box his ears, which is something Jax would never do. Lyle would look for any reason to find fault with Jax. Back then, Jax's father was constable. Lyle went to him, insisting Jax be charged with assault. There was no assault, so there was no charge. But there was a big stink for a long time."

"Which only made Mr. Fikeland angrier." Bella remembered the man's reaction all too well.

The hotel owner nodded. "I've told him it's foolish to hold a grudge. He doesn't listen."

Richard rested his elbows on the chair arms. "We can't concern ourselves with Lyle or others who spread malicious rumors."

Cooper shrugged. "I agree with you, but the rumors are plentiful. I don't spread them, and I won't repeat anything you reveal in your questions. Made the same promise to Nolen." He laid his clasped hands on his chest. "He inquired about seeing a man with Miss Bouchard. Someone about Jax's height with a greatcoat. Nolen asked Korbert, too, although he didn't mention size or attire in their exchange."

"Very sensible, since giving out too much information can create problems," Richard replied. "We don't want the killer learning too much."

Briefly, Bella considered the revelations before commenting. "I'm sure Nolen knows you're trustworthy and circumspect."

The hotel owner smiled. "I've always tried to be both, and I won't do or say anything to hurt Jax."

"Thank you," she murmured over the lump of emotion clogging her throat.

"No thanks needed. He's a fine young man, and he deserves to have good things happen." The man's grin widened. "You both do."

When warmth rose in her cheeks, Bella put pencil to paper. They needed to focus on proving Jax's innocence. Unless they did…she didn't allow the thought to develop.

"To that end," Richard began, "we want to get details about anyone who might have known the victim. Did she talk with another guest?"

"Not that I saw." Thad Cooper's brow furrowed. "She spoke very little to me and my wife. The girl seemed private. The missus asked what brought her to Moreley all alone. Miss Bouchard acted uneasy and confused, like she wasn't sure why she was here. Strange. Finally, she mentioned knowing folks from during the war, although she didn't say who. She mumbled something about field hospitals and a facility in Nantes, where she was a nurse. When we mentioned names of some veterans, she had to hurry off."

As Bella and Richard exchanged a long look, she scribbled more notes.

"We'd like to speak with your wife and Lannigan," Richard said.

"The missus is at the church preparing for this weekend's bake sale, but I'll stay at the front desk and you can interview Korbert here," Cooper replied. "Do you have other questions for me?"

Richard nodded. "Only one. Korbert snoozes in the little room off the lobby. If guests return late, would he have to let them in? Or can they take a key to the outer door, if they plan to come back after the front desk closes? I know you have bells at both doors."

"We do," Cooper responded, "because we've found that giving out keys to our main doors can be a problem. People lose them or don't return them. Now, we ask that they ring. Very few come in after midnight, unless there's a big function in town. Then, we keep the lobby open until later."

"But this week, you didn't." Richard made the comment.

"No, there was no need to. We will this weekend and next week. The annual play, the big dance. All those nights, folks stay out after midnight. At least, that's how it was before the war and influenza. We're booked up for the first time in a few years." Cooper grinned at Bella. "I hear your place is, too."

His enthusiasm resonated with Bella, but at a low pitch. She couldn't completely enjoy the holiday season as long as a cloud hung over Jax. With effort, she smiled in return. "We're expecting an influx of guests over the next few days, so the inn and cottages will be filled."

"Good for us all." Cooper looked back at Richard. "If you don't have more questions for me, I'll send Korbert back."

"Thanks," the retired constable replied.

When they were alone in the office, Bella addressed Richard. "Around the Armistice, Celeste took patients to the hospital in Nantes and stayed there, as far as I know. Any of the suspects might've been in that facility."

"True." He ran one hand over his face. "I don't want to dismiss anyone yet."

A tap on the door interrupted. "I'm here." Lannigan looked and sounded put out.

"Come in and sit down." Richard gestured to the third chair on the door side of the desk.

Lannigan pulled the seat a foot away from Bella before settling in it. After folding his arms across his chest, he sat back and thrust his legs out. A scowl darkened his expression.

Could the man be more obvious about not wanting to cooperate? Bella didn't think so.

"We only have a few questions," Richard said. "Just to confirm, you worked the front desk the night of Miss Bouchard's murder, right?"

"Yep," Lannigan replied.

"What time did you leave the front desk to lie down?" Richard asked.

"Around one in the morning. We don't have a lot of guests, but they all went out. Probably to the tree lighting. I didn't ask. Most were back here before midnight, I think."

The senior constable nodded. "So, you laid down shortly after Jax Hastings came in looking for Miss Bouchard and her friend?"

157

"Never saw her with a friend," Lannigan said. "I'm guessing Hastings was setting up an alibi for himself. But it didn't work."

Bella's fingers tightened on her pencil until her knuckles went white. The man's suggestion that Jax had been plotting murder when he stopped at the hotel infuriated her. And he hadn't directly answered Richard's question. "Is that what Lyle Fikeland is saying?"

Lannigan's lips twitched into something akin to a sneer. "I don't need no one to figure that out for me. Pretty obvious."

"Drawing conclusions comes after we gather facts." Richard kept his tone even, but anger flashed in his gaze.

A humorless laugh left the desk clerk. "I know how you coppers work. You only use the facts that back up your opinion. Sometimes, you lie to protect your own."

Richard's jaw tightened. "I don't know what your experience with policemen is, but I've never manufactured information or ignored clues, and I won't be starting now."

The retired lawman's implacable tone fell like ice shards and was just as chilling. Bella watched Lannigan shift restlessly in his chair while color climbed into the man's narrow face.

"Maybe so. Maybe not, but my pa was railroaded by coppers in our town. Went to prison and left my ma with five little ones to raise. Even though I left school at ten to help, we went hungry a lot."

Richard's expression softened. "I'm sorry. Such things should never happen, although I know they sometimes do." He allowed several seconds of silence before he continued. "I only want the truth, and you can help by providing whatever you know."

After a long moment, Lannigan nodded. "All right."

"So, you rested after one in the morning, and no one else came or went?" Richard inquired.

"Folks need to ring the bell to get in. I suppose someone could leave without me knowing." He braced his elbows on the chair arms. "Few guests at present, so that don't seem likely."

"You said Miss Bouchard wasn't with a friend," Richard continued. "Did she speak with other guests?"

"She exchanged pleasantries in passing with a few folks and did the same with me. Otherwise, she went in and out quickly." Lannigan kept his focus on Richard.

"You must have seen her leave to meet Constable Hastings," Richard suggested.

A grimace marred the clerk's face. "He's not the constable now."

Once again, Richard's jaw set hard. An internal battle seemed to ensue before he finally spoke again. "Did you see her leave?"

Lannigan nodded. "Yep. Took off around eleven."

As Bella logged the information, she mentally noted the Frenchwoman had left well before her meeting with Jax, probably to join forces with her accomplice. "Was she alone?"

"I thought you were a notetaker," the clerk said, his tone dismissive and his gaze hooded.

"Miss Stewart is an important part of our team, and she has more than clerical duties." Richard spoke in a firm voice. "Please answer her."

Lannigan shrugged. "All alone."

"Were you worried when she didn't come back by one o'clock?" Bella posed the query.

The clerk started, as if in surprise. "Uh. Well, no. Not really."

His reaction further intrigued Bella. "She must've known the doors would be locked. You warned her, didn't you?"

His gaze moved to the floor. "She knew."

Bella exchanged a long look with Richard, who seemed puzzled. "Did she say she wasn't coming back that night?"

With one hand, Lannigan finger-combed his sparse hair. "Not exactly." He cleared his throat. "I told her I doze in the little alcove off the lobby, so I'd hear if she rang the front door bell. She was very sweet, said she didn't want to wake me up. Not all the guests are so kind. Most don't care if I don't get my rest. I appreciated the concern and said I'd leave the back door open." He kept his attention on some point beyond Bella and Richard.

"She planned to be out all night?" Bella asked. Had the woman suggested she would spend her time with her supposed husband? In reality, Celeste must have planned to be with her accomplice. Did Lannigan know any details? If he did, would he provide them?

"Of course not. She was a lady." Lannigan looked back at them.

Fresh dismay filled Bella. The man definitely wasn't on Jax's side. She hoped he didn't lie to protect the Frenchwoman's reputation. "Did you know where she was going?"

"She told me about meeting someone at the café. I said it was probably closing. I know Push stayed open a little longer than normal. Even with the school potluck, he expected some late business. Anyhow, she'd made some sort of arrangements. I warned her to be careful. Even though Moreley is a safe place, no lady should be out alone late at night. Miss Bouchard assured me she'd be fine." Lannigan hung his head. "But she wasn't."

Several moments of silence ticked away. Finally, Richard spoke. "So, you left the back door open and went to sleep?"

When the clerk's head came up, his face was a mask of misery. "Even though I said I'd leave the back door unlocked for her, I planned to stay up and make sure she got in all right. But I was so tired…" His voice trailed off.

"It was unlocked all night?" Bella asked for confirmation.

"Until I woke around five in the morning." He shook his head. "I'm sorry I didn't keep watch for her. I should have."

"It wouldn't have made any difference, since she never came back here." Richard drummed his fingers on the chair arm. "Someone else could've come in or left late without you hearing."

Lannigan released a long exhalation. "From the front desk, we can't see or hear comings and goings out back. It's usually not a problem."

Although Bella didn't doubt the assertion, she thought it might have been an issue the night of Celeste's murder. Had her killer been in the hotel?

"Thanks for your help," Richard said. "It's appreciated."

The clerk got to his feet. "Can't see how I helped at all, unless you plan to give up trying to clear Hastings. The right man was arrested. All the evidence points to him." With that, he left the room.

While Bella knew his belief was wrong, she felt her fear escalate. She knew her anxiety must be obvious when Richard spoke. "We're still at the start of our investigation, Arabella. We have more leads to follow. A lot more."

"I know," she murmured.

"Let's get going on them. That'll make us both feel better."

Bella tucked her notepad and pencil away. She hoped Richard was right. At the moment, her spirits were low.

Outside the hotel, Bella and Richard parted ways. Since the train station wasn't far, she left her vehicle and walked. The town looked as festive as the night Celeste died, but Bella felt little holiday enthusiasm.

She arrived at the train station to find it nearly empty. A glance at the arrival and departure board indicated the place would stay that way for another hour, so she headed to the office next to the ticket booth. Her tap on the door was answered by a male voice.

"Come on in."

Bella stepped inside and looked around the cramped room before focusing on the man at the rolltop desk in the corner. Edgar Geneve had been the stationmaster as far back as she could remember. Years ago, his hair had been dark. Now, it was gray. But he still had the same welcoming smile. "Arabella. How lovely to see you! Sit down." He gestured to the chair at a right angle to him. "What brings you here? We won't have another arrival for a while."

"I'm not picking up guests." Bella took a seat. "I wanted to talk."

"Before you do, how about a piece of rock candy? It was your favorite as a little girl." Geneve opened the glass jar on the corner of his desk and tipped it toward Bella, who took one chunk. He helped himself before setting the container aside.

Unable to postpone the special treat, Bella popped a bit into her mouth. The sugary concoction still tasted incredible. "Your wife makes the very best rock candy."

"I'll tell her you said so." Geneve's smile faltered. "Since you didn't come to fetch guests, I imagine you're probing the murder of that poor girl."

Bella licked the stickiness from her fingers and nodded. "I am. Richard and Jenny Jenkins are helping. Of course, Nolen and Newton are running the official investigation."

"One porter told me about Richard stopping. I'm really glad he's back in town and working on the case. Nolen and Newton are hard workers, but it's a tricky situation. I've heard the town talk about Jax killing the young woman. Anyone with sense knows he'd never commit a murder. Not for any reason."

The residual tension she had been carrying since Jax's arrest, which had only escalated after talking with Lannigan, eased a little. "No. He wouldn't."

"Mayor Cawlings was here earlier, picking up his aunt. I told him he ought not contribute to foul gossip or pressure Nolen. Jax is a good man. He deserves the benefit of the doubt."

Gratitude filled Bella. Geneve and Cawlings were lifelong friends, so the stationmaster probably held more sway with the mayor than most townsfolk. "I'm sure Jax will appreciate you taking up for him. I surely do."

The older man's expression softened. "The wife and I were happy to see the two of you finally courting. None of our business why you didn't sooner, but we're real sorry this mess has affected that. I hope you find the killer before Christmas. Otherwise, it's bound to put a damper on your holiday."

Mr. Geneve's observations reinforced her worry about the holidays being far from festive while Jax was under suspicion. As a little girl, Bella had found Christmas to be a magical time. She had loved helping her mother decorate the inn. And it wasn't only looking forward to gifts under the tree. Bella had savored the activities at the resort and in town. Ice skating, sledding, and caroling were all highlights. So were the town play, the big dance, and the tree lighting.

For a moment, Bella looked out the door to the station platform. Five years ago, she had come home from college and Jax had met her train. The memory made her smile, although what followed didn't. It was then that the shadow of impending war fell over them and altered the future. With effort, Bella jerked herself back to the present. A pall fell over this season, too, but she needed useful information, so she stated her purpose. "I'm here because I hoped you might've noticed Miss

Bouchard with someone when she got off the train. Or even how many folks got off at the same time. As you know, Richard spoke with the porters, but they were busy and didn't have helpful details."

"Let me think." Geneve's brow furrowed. "Four got off, including her. The others were all men. One helped her with her bag, and they spoke a bit, from what I could tell. As you said, the porters had their hands full as trunks were unloaded. Plus, some freight came in."

As Bella retrieved a pencil and notepad from her pocketbook, her heart raced. "Did you recognize him? The one who helped Miss Bouchard?"

"No, he looked a little familiar, but neither of them came over to the ticket booth. Most folks don't when they arrive."

"Can you describe him?"

"Fairly tall. Brown hair cut close. No hat." Geneve put one hand to his head as if trying to picture the person. "They were at least a hundred feet from me, so I didn't get the eye color and such."

"Understandable," Bella replied. Smithson fit the description. "Was he wearing or carrying a coat?"

"Not that I could see. Coulda had it in his bag, which was a big one. The weather was mild that day. Mild for December anyhow. Luckily, it's turned colder again, since we need snow for sledding and such." He leaned back in his chair. "But I'm getting off topic. No outerwear on the man."

An interesting detail, but was it a pertinent one? Time would tell. "Did they leave the station together?"

"They did." Geneve paused for a moment. "I'm sorry the porters were tied up and saw little that's helpful."

"They spoke freely, which is important. As far as the man with Miss Bouchard. You said he was fairly tall. About the same height as Jax?"

"About the same height, with a similar build."

"Did any other recent male passengers fit the same description? Ones who came the day before Miss Bouchard?"

The stationmaster braced his elbows on the desk and put his chin in his hands. "No one I recall.

You know how it is with arrivals. We're pretty busy at the station nowadays. Thank goodness. We had some slim years, but things have turned around."

"At the resort, too." While happy both Moreley and Ballantyne were again prospering, Bella was focused on clearing Jax. "

Anyone else about the same build and height of Jax come in?"

Geneve furrowed his brow, as if in deep thought. "Dewey Fikeland was on the same train, but you know him. He had a small valise, but a big box with gifts for his aunt and uncle. She was so pleased to have him come home. Lyle was, too, I think. They stopped to chat before the train arrived. I'm not sure I would've known Dewey if they hadn't met him. He's filled out since he left for France.

Since Dewey was on the suspect list, Bella took careful note of Geneve's observations. She already knew his height and weight were like Jax. "Was Dewey wearing a coat?"

Geneve furrowed his brow as if in thought. "I believe he had one slung over his shoulder, but I can't be certain."

"Could you tell the color?"

"Not sure of the color, not really dark. But I don't know the exact shade. It was hectic right then. People coming and going. Otherwise, I would've greeted young Fikeland myself." He sighed. "We've got two porters on each shift again. Both were busy, since folks from here were boarding and visitors got off." For a moment, the stationmaster studied her face. "You're not thinking Dewey was involved in the murder of that girl?"

Because she didn't want to send any signals about who might be under suspicion, Bella smiled. "I need to find out about anyone who came into town around the same time as Miss Bouchard. We'll be speaking with a lot of folks over the next few days." She hesitated to mention Jax seeing Celeste with another man. Edgar Geneve wasn't as gossipy as a lot of other townsfolk, but he chatted with people all day, every day, at his job. Would he let something slip to the wrong person? Bella would not risk it.

"Understood." A rueful smile lifted his lips.

"Thank you so much for talking with me, Mr. Geneve. I know this is a busy time, so I won't keep you." As Bella got ready to leave, the stationmaster rose, too.

"Happy to help in any way I can." He stroked his chin. "I'm guessing you think the killer knew the girl before they got here."

"We do." Bella smiled. "I can't reveal details. I'm sorry."

Geneve put up both hands. "I understand. Like I said, there's gossip about the murder. And about the girl making her outrageous claims at the tree lighting. Some other nonsense is going around, too." He hesitated briefly, as if weighing his next words. "Most of us don't believe Jax was married to her. Or had anything to do with her, except in passing. Maybe she was involved with one of his men, and maybe he's dead. So she looked for Jax. We all know he's one to help people in distress. Always has been. The trouble is, she came a long way, which has stirred some folks up. Leaving her country and her folks. To some, it seems odd."

The stationmaster's revelations brought realization. People in town didn't have some of the fundamental details. "Miss Bouchard has no family left in France. She has an aunt and uncle in Cleveland, though. As for her involvement with an American, I believe that was the case. But you're right. Jax wasn't the one."

Geneve's expression lightened. "That makes sense. I'll put the word out. The wife will, too. It won't convince those like Lyle Fikeland, but he's almost a one-man band."

Almost was a key word, since Lannigan was among the anti-Jax players. But she couldn't focus on the naysayers. "Thank you." His willingness to support Jax boosted Bella's spirit. "I better get going."

The older man grinned. "It's good the big crowd won't be here until Saturday. That gives you fewer people to check on."

"It does." Fewer people, but little time. Bella tucked away her pad and pencil. "Thank you for your help." As she headed to the Ford, Bella reviewed what they had learned. Next on her agenda was learning more about Smithson Collier and, with luck, talking to him and Patrick Orlington.

Chapter Nine

As she walked toward where she had parked, Bella heard a familiar voice call out. She pivoted to see Nolen approaching her.

"Bella, what brings you to town?"

"Some errands." Bella kept her reply brief and benign due to other folks going by them. Revealing her real purpose would provide fodder for the town gossip mill, which she wanted to avoid.

Nolen glanced up and down the street. When people were out of earshot, he spoke again. "I saw your vehicle in front of the hotel, but you're coming from the station."

"We're speaking with people who might've seen something important." There was no need to say important about the case, since Nolen knew.

Again, his gaze went around the area before resting on her. "Good. I suppose Richard shared the latest from our talk."

"He did. We all had a long chat, and another suspect came up. You know about Gaspard, Collier, and Orlington."

He nodded. "Orlington definitely has an axe to grind with Jax. Do you know about that?"

"I do. A little." Bella provided the rest of her information. "What do you think about the four suspects?"

"Let's walk and talk."

After falling into step beside him, Bella waited for an answer.

When Nolen provided one, his voice was a whisper. "Smith, which is what the boys called him, met Celeste when he had a minor wound. He was taken with her. When he got a day off the line, he visited the field hospital. Somehow, he got candy to take. By the time he got there, Lieutenant Brewster was already involved with Celeste. Smith was upset. We all knew the lieutenant was betrothed, and Smith was angry about the whole thing."

"Did he see Celeste after Alan died?" Bella asked.

"Not until after the Armistice. I heard he was among the patients she escorted to the hospital in Nantes. I haven't seen him since then, so I don't know how long he was there."

"Maybe I can find out by chatting with him. If he had a lengthy stay, they could've gotten much better acquainted, if she was there the entire time. On the night of the tree lighting, Celeste mentioned working in Nantes, but nothing about going with wounded soldiers."

"Smith was gassed right before the Armistice and came back to the line too soon and ended up in a field hospital again. Celeste was nursing there. I'm not sure exactly when the transport left, but Celeste was with it. I don't know if he's recuperated from the gassing. Some fellows do better than others."

Dismay assailed Bella. "I see." Could Smithson's condition affect his ability to commit murder?

"Then, a bunch of us got shipped back pretty quickly. I only heard about her escorting some patients to Nantes because I was near the collection point when the caravan went through."

"It could be important, but I'm not sure how we'll find out who else might've been in the Nantes hospital."

"I'm going to go to Ballantyne to talk with Patrick, and I can casually catch up with Smith."

Bella sent him a sidelong glance. "Good. If I talk with him or Patrick, I won't be direct."

"All right. You're a fine detective and, heaven knows, Newton and I need all the help we can get." He took his cap and ran a hand over his head. "We're working eighteen-hour days with regular routines and the murder case. As far as Dewey, I'll let Richard stop at the hardware. Lyle will have his back up if I go. Same with Newton."

"I'll let you know if I discover anything important. If you come out later, we can talk in private."

"Good idea, since our mayor is headed this way."

Annoyance filled Bella, but she managed a smile and a greeting. "Hello, Mayor Cawlings." She looked at Nolen. "Please tell Jillian that she and her aunt are both welcome for Christmas Eve and Day. Now, I must be on my way." With that, Bella hurried to her vehicle and headed home.

Ten minutes later, she entered the inn's kitchen in time to see Mrs. Rogers and Ida carrying empty dishes from the dining room. Their young maid was helping. "I thought I'd be back to help sooner. I'm sorry." Although she wanted to talk with Smithson and Patrick, Bella felt the press of resort duties.

Her best friend shook her head. "We didn't expect you this early. Clearing Jax comes first."

"It does," Mrs. Rogers agreed. "I'm glad you're working on the case. Of course, it's Nolen's top priority, but he's under a lot of pressure from the mayor." She tsked, tsked. "No one with a lick of sense believes Jax is guilty. I doubt if Cawlings does himself. He just wants someone charged, so holiday business isn't affected. Once visitors leave, he'll undoubtedly tell Nolen to clear Jax."

As the acting constable's mother, Mrs. Rogers was in a tough position, which made her observations even more interesting. The comment about the mayor was new to Bella, but it could be true. Unfortunately, the idea didn't ease Bella's mind because she wanted Jax to be completely exonerated. "Nolen is in a difficult position, but we all want to find the killer."

"You will." Mrs. Rogers offered a reassuring smile. "Now, we need to get the kitchen cleaned up before I bake." She looked from Ida to Bella. "The two of you have plenty of other things to do, so run along."

"If you're sure." Bella shifted from one foot to the other.

"I am," the older woman said. She gestured with one hand. "Go on. I know Ida hasn't eaten, so take some food with you and relax for a bit. I made extra sandwiches."

"Before we do that, I want to pass my information on to Jenny and Richard." Bella telephoned the Hastings house, but talked to Jenny, since Jax was sleeping. Although he needed rest, Bella felt the sting of disappointment. She quickly relayed the details and joined Ida in the family suite. They settled on the sofa facing the fireplace.

"Help yourself to a plate." Ida pointed to the coffee table.

"Thank you, I will, and the warmth feels good. Someone got a fire going. How lovely."

"I asked Griff to do it," Ida said. "I knew you'd be tired and hungry and maybe cold after running around all morning and into the afternoon."

Bella sipped her coffee. "How did you know I'd be out-and-about a lot?"

A grin tipped up the corners of Ida's mouth. "Because I know you. Once you talked with Richard and Jenny, you must've set a plan to investigate."

Laughter left Bella. "You're right, but I didn't just meet with the Jenkinses. Jax was there, too."

Ida's eyes rounded. "He was released?"

"Yes, early this morning. I was surprised when he opened the door."

"Happily surprised," Ida said.

"Absolutely." Bella briefly relived when Jax had held her close before uncertainty descended. "But he isn't in the clear. We still need to find the killer."

"Of course, but your mayor may not believe Jax is guilty, which means charges will probably be dropped soon. At least, that's how Mrs. Rogers made it sound."

"She did, and that may be what happens." Bella let the plate rest in her lap.

"You and Jax can go to the dance on Saturday."

"Not unless he's absolved by then. Richard wants Jax to stay home, partly because we don't know if the killer has a grudge again him or simply wanted money." Bella revealed the suspects and their backgrounds. "Nolen will be out yet this afternoon to talk with Patrick and Smithson. I'd like to chat with both of them, too."

"Not interrogate them."

"Of course not. I'll make the conversations casual." Bella laid her food aside but took a swallow of coffee.

"You're very good at that."

Ida's vote of confidence made Bella smile. In the current case, Jax's case, good wasn't enough. She needed to be great. And thorough. And quick.

After a brief respite, Bella went to the front desk. The wide lobby was already decked out for the holiday. Pine roping was wound around the polished handrails on both sides of the wide staircase leading to the guest rooms, while red ribbons festooned the newel posts at the bottom. An arrangement of evergreen, pine cones, and more ribbons sat on the fireplace mantel. Only a tree was needed to put a finishing touch on the space. Most of the cottages also had festive touches. The rooms and upper hallways still needed to be decorated, which Ida would handle. Bella just wished she felt as merry as the inn would look. Perhaps soon. Her thoughts were interrupted when, much to her surprise, Smithson Collier walked in. Although he wasn't a top suspect, Smithson remained on the list. Maybe a brief talk would change his position. Or remove him entirely. They exchanged greetings before Bella asked about his accommodations, something she would do with any guest. "Are you comfortable in the cottage?"

"Very much so. My mother and sister will love the decorations. Very festive. I'm glad the resort is open for Christmas again. It's a nice family tradition for us," he said with a grin.

"On this end, too."

His smile faded. "I was so sorry to hear about your parents, and I haven't seen you since Matt died, either. A lot of losses for you."

"I miss them all," she admitted. As always, emotion formed a knot in her throat, but Bella swallowed it down. "I'm lucky to still have Mac as my partner."

"I spoke briefly with him." Smithson hesitated a moment. "You and Jax are stepping out."

Bella's pulse sped up. "We are."

"I heard he was arrested for Celeste Bouchard's murder. I can't believe it."

Since Smithson seemed sincerely shocked, Bella accepted the words at face value. "He didn't kill her."

"I never thought he had."

"Did you know Celeste in France?" Bella knew the answer to her question but getting his reaction could be important.

"I did. Most of us in Lieutenant Brewster's platoon either met her or were aware of her."

"Due to their relationship."

For a moment, Smithson glanced away. When he looked back, he nodded. "It wasn't a secret."

Only to Ida, Bella thought with dismay. "I suppose not." In order to keep the conversation casual, she moved to another topic. "I know you wanted to be a policeman. Is that what you do now?"

"I wanted to, but I couldn't handle the physical stuff. Got gassed toward the end and was in a hospital for weeks afterward. On top of that, I caught influenza."

"I'm so sorry." Many soldiers had suffered the same fate, but Bella focused on his last revelation. "Did you have to stay in France, or were you sent home to a facility?"

"I had to stay in Nantes for almost two months."

Which was plenty of time to get better acquainted with Celeste. With Alan gone, had Smithson cornered Celeste's affections? Or had she sought and found a protector? The man's voice broke into her thoughts.

"If you'll excuse me, I'd like to take a short walk. The weather is fine, which is what I need with my bad lungs. Cold, damp air still makes it hard to breathe. I'll see you later."

Calling him back wasn't wise, so Bella reluctantly let him go. Smithson was barely out the front door when Ida came into the lobby. "Mac told me about some old ornaments in the attic. I didn't want to dig through them alone, but I thought they might be pretty in the big crystal bowls in the butler's pantry. Maybe one on the dining room buffet, another in the lobby, and so on. Could you spend a little time up there with me?"

"Of course. It'd be a pleasant change, and using those bowls is a superb idea." Bella glanced at the grandfather clock. "The cousin won't call for about an hour, so let's go."

Sorting through decorations proved to be a lovely way to distract herself. When her watch read three-thirty, Bella made her way back downstairs, leaving Ida behind to go through the last box. As she reached the bottom of the staircase, Mrs. Rogers stepped into the lobby. "Nolen is here talking to Patrick Orlington and Smithson Collier. He'll stop in the kitchen before leaving. He'd like to talk with you, and I want to get some food into him."

Bella nodded. "As you said, he and Newton have their hands full. A good meal will help him. And maybe send a basket for Newton. I'll see Nolen, since I have some information to share with him." And she hoped the opposite would be true.

Mrs. Rogers smoothed her apron. "I hope one of you gets some big news soon. News that reveals the actual killer. Now, I'll get back to work."

Bella followed the older woman into the kitchen and waited. Nolen appeared within moments.

"Hi, Bella."

"I'm sorry I missed you when you first got here, but Ida and I were getting some things in order," Bella replied.

He nodded before taking a seat across from her. "After Mayor Cawlings saw the two of us earlier, I have to be even more careful about talking to you and Richard in town. He stops by the house or the office once a day, which is all right. We share what we've learned, so I wanted to do that with you."

Some of her tension drained away. "I've uncovered some information today, so why don't I begin? I couldn't share it all when we met in town." After Nolen nodded, Bella fully reviewed the interviews at the hotel and train station before going over her chat with Smithson. "I kept my conversation as casual as possible, since I'm not part of the official investigation."

Nolen rested his elbows on the chair arms. "The information is important, especially since Smith and Celeste were both in Nantes for weeks. Patrick told me more, which is surprising. Anyhow, as soon as I explained why I wanted to talk with them, they also realized you must've been looking for clues. I interviewed them separately, of course, but they had similar reactions. Both mentioned being guests here, like that made them innocent of any wrongdoing. Orlington made it more of a threat. I don't think they'll cause trouble for you, but be aware they weren't happy about being questioned."

Bella clasped her hands together and laid them in her lap. "We'll deal with whatever happens. I know Jax isn't guilty, and he's my primary concern."

Nolen smiled. "I feel the same way. I asked Orlington where he was on Monday night. He claimed to be at his grandmother's house, which seemed strange since he arrived here Tuesday and went to visit her then. Why go back and forth? When I said I'd call and check, he changed his story and said he was visiting a friend in Sandusky over the weekend and into Tuesday. A female friend. He declined to share her name because he doesn't want to harm her reputation. His words. I promised to be circumspect, so he'll think about it. Maybe."

"Which means he can contact some woman and get her to vouch for him, if he is the killer and needs an alibi."

"Exactly." Nolen pulled out a notepad and flipped through it. "You already know he was acquainted with Celeste in France. Smithson was, too, of course. I hadn't realized he was in Nantes for two months. They might've gotten well acquainted then. I asked if he saw Celeste there. He was hesitant to respond but finally admitted she escorted his group and often stopped in his ward. He claimed he hadn't seen or heard from her after leaving France, and she left the hospital before he did."

Bella chewed on her lower lip. "Probably because her condition became obvious."

"Probably so."

"Did you believe that the two of them weren't in touch after she left?"

Nolen shook his head. "I'm not sure, but Smith had trouble looking me in the eye."

"Did you have a feeling about either Patrick or Smithson?"

With one hand, Nolen rubbed the back of his neck. "They both knew her, but only Orlington seems to need money. Smithson has a good job, and he didn't admit to spending time in speakeasies, which is likely the truth. He never drank when we were in France, and it was perfectly legal. Then, there's the damage to his lungs. Being out late at night in cold, damp air is a problem for him."

"He told me the same thing. You don't rank him as high as Patrick as a suspect."

"I don't, partly because he has no apparent motive to extort Jax. What do you think?"

"I agree on the lack of motive. As Richard will probably say, I'd move him to the back burner."

Nolen grinned. "The best place for now. Down the list, but not off it."

Bella wished they could erase a suspect or two. Until the field was narrowed, a lot more investigation needed to take place. "I wonder if Gaspard is back."

"When Newton talked to his landlady again today, she mentioned Gaspard coming from the same town as Celeste. I'm trying to find out what the population was before the war. If it was small, they surely knew each other."

Surprise hit Bella. "Jax didn't mention that."

"Evidently, the landlady didn't tell him. From what Newton said, she was reluctant to say much. He believes his badge made a difference in getting details."

"I'm glad you're sharing what you and Newton have uncovered. Without formal status ourselves, Richard and I are limited in how we can proceed."

"I'm happy to pass clues along. I just have to be careful doing it."

"I understand. As far as the landlady, she must now realize a murder took place here. Maybe she fears Gaspard is guilty and doesn't want to put us on his track. Jax thought she felt sorry for him."

Nolen drummed a thumb on the notepad. "That's a possibility. I wish we had some clue about where he went."

"I do, too." Gaspard ranked with Orlington as a top suspect to Bella, which brought another candidate to mind. "Have you spoken with Dewey Fikeland?"

"I hadn't planned to, but we crossed paths. I couched the conversation in terms of him possibly knowing Gaspard in France. That mollified him a little." Nolen leaned back in the chair. "Dewey didn't know Victor, or so he said."

"You didn't believe him?"

A long exhalation left Nolen. "I'm not sure I do. I was younger, but I remember him falsely claiming Jax hit him. His uncle went to Jax's dad and insisted Jax be arrested for assault. It was crazy. Dewey had a slight bruise, but it wasn't from being hit. Anyone could see that."

"Mr. Fikeland seems to continue holding a grudge. Dewey claims he doesn't agree with his uncle about Jax killing Celeste, but I'm not sure. He may have only said that to mollify me."

Nolen grinned. "Is he still sweet on you? I recall that, too."

Warmth rose in Bella's face. Although her first urge was to deny the assertion, Bella knew better than to hide even the most obscure detail. "Maybe a little."

"Richard mentioned you speaking with one of the ambulance drivers in Dewey's group."

"If he doesn't call, I'll try again since he should be home from work." Bella chewed on her lower lip. "I'll do it before you leave."

"Great. I'd like to know what he says."

"Then, I'll definitely put in a call. You're planning to eat here before you go home, right?"

"Mother suggested I do that, since I missed lunch."

"Good." Bella glanced at the clock on the mantel. "While you eat, I'll contact our operator to make my call. What else do we need to discuss in private? You and I haven't chatted much since the murder. I know it's been hard on you."

A rueful smile tugged at one corner of Nolen's mouth. "Newton and I both hated arresting Jax because we know he isn't guilty. I think the mayor knows, too, but he's worried about Christmas business. He's afraid having an unsolved murder will keep visitors away, and maybe he's right. But putting the wrong man in jail won't help in the long run. I told him as much."

"What did he say?"

"Basically, that I'm wet behind the ears and biased to boot. I don't deny believing in Jax's innocence, but it's not favoritism. It's knowing him well. As for being an inexperienced kid, I said being in France forced me to grow up fast."

Nolen's firm, forthright statements resonated deep within Bella because she knew they were valid. "Good for you. How did Cawlings respond?"

"He insisted he meant no criticism. That's when he admitted to fretting about holiday business. He sees this year as a turning point. If Moreley doesn't do well now, it's apt to lose its status as a great place for visitors." He ran one hand over his face. "I understand, and I don't want things to go back like they were a couple of years ago when no one came for Christmas, and few were here in the summer."

"Neither do I." Anxiety crept through Bella as she considered Jax's concern about her involvement in the case, and its effect on Ballantyne. For the most part, she didn't see it as an issue. But a tiny corner of her mind harbored doubt. One issue was sentiment among the townspeople. Nolen surely had a handle on that. She had gotten some encouraging words from Edgar Geneve and Thad Cooper. More reassurance was welcome, so she asked and held her breath. "Do many folks suspect Jax? I've only heard about Mr. Fikeland and Korbert Lannigan and others with general gossip. I haven't been in town much, though."

"Lyle and Korbert have been vocal. I'm sure Lyle's friends believe him, but none has said much. I've talked to a bunch of other people, and they all support Jax. All the boys who went to France with us do, too."

Bella's shoulders slumped in relief. "As they should, and he'll be glad to know."

"I wish I could talk with Jax, but I'm trying to maintain a professional stance."

"Which is best for everyone, including Jax." When Nolen's stomach rumbled, Bella laughed. "You better eat soon. Why don't you go ahead, while I make my call?"

"Good idea."

After leaving the young constable, Bella headed to the front desk. She exchanged a few words with the local operator before asking the woman to place the call. Bella sorted through paperwork, but listened for the telephone. When it finally rang, she jumped up and grabbed it. As soon as the voice of her colleague's cousin came on the line, Bella's pulse raced. The man answered her questions thoroughly, which had her putting shorthand to good use. After thanking him, she hurried to the kitchen. Nolen was eating a piece of apple pie but laid down his fork when he saw her expression.

"What did you find out?" he asked.

Since only Mrs. Rogers was in the room with them, Bella didn't hesitate to be honest. "Quite a lot. Mr. Worthing, Tad, sailed with Dewey and they were based near each other for over a year." When Nolen retrieved his notepad, she stopped him. "I took notes in shorthand, but I'll type them up for you and bring them to the office tomorrow."

"Thanks." Nolen went back to his pie but kept his attention on Bella. "From what I know, the ambulance corps drivers ferried mostly French soldiers in the beginning."

"Tad confirmed that," Bella said. "He also said a bunch of them met Celeste at one of the French hospitals shortly after their arrival. Dewey included. The nurses usually met the ambulances and helped unload patients, so friendships were formed."

"Interesting," Nolen put in between bites of pie.

"It gets better. Dewey requested all the runs to that hospital, and Tad saw Dewey with Celeste frequently."

Nolen's hand froze midway to his mouth. "They were friendly or more?"

"Tad's view is that Dewey was smitten with Celeste. Very smitten."

"Did she return the sentiment?"

"She was pleasant to all the drivers but noticeably more to Dewey. At least, Tad didn't observe close connections with other men."

After finishing the pie, Nolen pushed the plate away. "You said Mr. Worthing and Dewey were in the same area for a year. Did they get transferred after America entered the war?"

"They did. Tad was sent farther up west. Dewey stayed in the same general area, where he would've been close to Celeste until her brother was wounded. After that, it's hard to say." Bella skimmed her notes. "Tad says the drivers stay in touch and even get together. Dewey has responded with brief notes, but none of them know much about where he's been living since the war."

Nolen ran a hand over his face. "Dewey couldn't have seen much of Celeste during those last few months, or some of us would've run into him. None of the boys mentioned him. I'll ask around more and see."

"I'm sure Jax never saw Dewey in France, or he would've said so."

"He would have," Nolen agreed. "Then, and since we got home."

Another piece of information resurfaced. "Dewey stayed in France for months after the war."

"I've heard as much." Nolen's eyes narrowed on Bella. "You and Ida stayed, too."

"We did stay, along with a few other operators. I didn't know Dewey was still there."

"And you never saw Celeste then." Nolen made it a statement.

"I didn't." Not that she had wanted to see the French nurse. "Did you ask Patrick about being wounded toward the end of the war?"

"I did, and he was wounded once in September, which we knew."

"Then, Patrick Orlington was never in Nantes. Smithson was, and Dewey might've taken patients there."

"Maybe Smith shouldn't be on the back burner. Maybe he and Dewey are top drawer suspects. Victor, too."

"I don't know," Bella murmured. "Maybe, but his weak lungs make me wonder about him being out at night and not coughing."

"I want to talk with Richard and get his thoughts."

"There's no time like the present." A familiar male voice broke in.

Bella turned to see the retired senior constable entering through the door from the lobby. "I'm glad you're here," she said. "Join us."

After Richard took a seat at the table, Mrs. Rogers brought coffee and pie for him. He expressed his thanks before she returned to her chores. While he ate, the trio shared their findings.

"You two learned a lot," the older man said.

"We had put Smithson Collier down the list. Nolen and I wonder about his physical condition."

"I agree it could hamper him, so Collier being in fourth place makes sense." Richard took another bite of pie. "We have a ways to go in solving this case. I'm going to stop by the café and have a late dinner with Sam Push. We know what he heard and saw the night of the murder, but I want to find out if he's gotten additional information from customers. Gossip sometimes contains facts. I stopped at the hardware, but Lyle didn't have much to say. Dewey was there, but left almost as soon as I walked in."

"Interesting," Nolen commented before sharing his exchange with young Fikeland.

"We've got several folks vying for first place." Richard finished his pie and laid down the fork. "I'll have supper with Sam, but I want to see Jax before then. Jenny went to Karston to pick up her mother. It looks like we may spend the holidays here, so we don't want to leave her Mama at our place."

"Is Jax alone now?" Bella asked.

"He is, since Jenny planned to leave an hour ago and spend the night. She left food for Jax, but I'm sure he'd like company and dessert. I should wrap up by ten o'clock. You wouldn't need to stay the entire time." Richard finished his pie and drank more coffee.

"Of course, I can go," Bella replied. And she would stay as long as necessary. Time with Jax was more valuable than ever. "I can tell Jax what we've found out since this morning, and you won't need to make another stop."

Richard smiled. "A great idea. He's apt to have insights that will help." He turned to Nolen. "Anything else of significance come up?"

"Since a mitten was found close to the body, I asked Patrick and Smithson if they got pairs during the war. Most of us did. Patrick said his folks sent him leather ones, so he had no use for homemade stuff." Nolen rolled his eyes. "Smithson admitted getting a couple of pairs. Khaki in color."

"Do you remember what shade yours were?" Bella made the inquiry.

Nolen grinned. "Sure. I got two pairs of brown ones. The only reason the lieutenant had bright green was a lot of boys didn't like the brilliant colors. They were afraid of being better targets with those, but we couldn't keep them on when we were firing our guns, so I didn't think it was a big worry. I would've taken them, but the lieutenant did."

Although Bella noticed how easily Nolen had slipped back into using Jax's army rank, she did not point it out. Nor did she comment on Jax taking mittens not wanted by his men, but the gesture revealed his character. While it was highly unlikely the bright green hand coverings would have been more noticeable than a blander color, he would have taken the risk or suffered the cold himself. "Do you think Victor Gaspard might've gotten mittens, too?"

"It's possible," Nolen replied. "Some units got more than they could use, so they passed them on to French and British soldiers. And even to civilians. Newton looked through Victor's room. No mittens, but if he's the killer, he lost one in the park and took the other one with him. Ambulance drivers definitely got them, too, but Dewey didn't admit to having a pair. Newton is making the regular rounds, but we'll speak this evening. Tomorrow, we'll circle back with all the suspects and witnesses. If you stop by the office around noon, we can exchange details."

"Good ideas." Richard looked at Bella. "Let's meet in the morning at Jax's house. If I get any news, I'll call you tonight. Otherwise, we'll review what we know then and set new plans."

"I hope we get a big break soon," Bella said.

"As do I. Solving the case hinges on a critical puzzle piece. A piece that's hidden from view right now," the senior constable observed as he looked at Nolen.

"And one that will pull the other elements together." Even as Bella spoke, she pictured the current puzzle with its gaping hole. Who or what would fill it in? She considered the question as she got ready to leave. On her way to the Hastings house, she needed to make another stop. After telling Ida about her plans, she left for town.

Bella pulled up to the front of the newspaper office. Mr. Yarken, the editor and publisher, had promised to send a photographer to Ballantyne for two special events. As part of her duties, Bella was to arrange the exact times but, since the tree lighting, she had been distracted. Because she didn't want Jax to be alone much longer, Bella hurried into the front door and ran smack into Dewey Fikeland, who put his hands out to steady her.

"We meet again," the man said with a grin.

The urge to smack his hands away was strong, but Bella merely stepped back. "Good afternoon."

"What brings you to the Moreley Monitor?" Dewey asked in a cheerful tone, as if she hadn't put distance between them.

Bella wanted to say it was none of his business, but she strove for civility. "Ballantyne business. What about you?"

His smile disappeared, while he shifted from one foot to the other. "Business, too," he said at last. "My uncle always runs a big ad around the holidays, and I had to make sure the copy is right."

"It's a busy time for all of us, which is wonderful. Now, if you'll excuse me, I need to talk with Mr. Yarken."

"And get back to Ballantyne."

Bella did not respond to his supposition. Instead, she gave a slight nod and bid Dewey farewell.

Chapter Ten

Thursday, as dusk fell, Jax paced the front parlor again and again, but the activity did nothing to quell his restlessness. Time hung heavily on his hands, and he felt frustrated and useless. Although he was out of jail, his freedom was limited. Since Jenny had left to pick up her mother hours earlier, he had been alone. Alone and tempted to leave the house and poke around town. But Jenny had asked him about Christmas decorations, so Jax had gone to the attic and brought a crate down. He was not enthusiastic about sorting through them, but Jenny was always kind to him, and handling this small task was the least Jax could do. He took some ornaments out before stashing the newspaper wrappings off to one side. Briefly, he glanced through the old issues. When nothing grabbed his attention, he resumed walking across the room until he feared he was wearing a path on the wool rug his mother had treasured. Resignation filled him as he sank into a chair. Unfortunately, sitting still only seemed to stoke his pent-up energy.

A knock at the door drew his attention, and he hurried to respond. When he opened it to find Bella on the porch, Jax grinned. "Welcome."

A smile touched her lips. "Richard stopped at Ballantyne and said Jenny went to Karston and won't be back until tomorrow. She felt bad about leaving you alone, but they'll probably be staying here for Christmas, and they want her mother with them."

"So, she said." Some of his enthusiasm abated. "And you're my designated babysitter."

She rolled her eyes. "No, I came to share what we've found out." Bella lifted the basket in her hands to his eye-level. "I brought a cake for us, too. Richard said Jenny left a meal, but dessert would be welcome."

"It is, and so are you." Jax stepped back and gave a slight bow. "Please come in."

"Thank you. Have you eaten supper?"

"I didn't feel hungry, but I could have some cake."

"I'm sure you could. We can talk during or after."

Jax let her lead the way to the kitchen. While Bella unloaded the basket, he got out plates and cutlery. "I could make cocoa for us."

"Sounds wonderful."

"How about having our treat in the parlor in front of the fireplace?" he asked.

"That's a lovely idea." Bella put the plates and mugs on a tray, and Jax carried it in. He stirred up the fire, before they sat in the pair of chairs flanking the hearth. He took a long swallow of the warm drink before digging into the cake. "Delicious."

"How is your arm?"

"Doing well." The statement was accurate. His recovery was going better than he had hoped. If his arm got back to normal, he might resurrect his dream of being a golf pro. But it was too soon to tell.

"I'm glad to hear it. Then, you don't regret having the operation?"

"Not at all. I should've followed your advice and done it sooner." Jax continued his snack but watched her expression, which became triumphant. He didn't repress another grin. "Say you told me so."

Low laughter left her. "I'm just happy it went well and you're healing fast. It's good news."

"About the only good news."

"Not necessarily. At the hotel, Richard and I found out Korbert left the back door unlocked so Celeste could come in if he was asleep." Jax laid his fork on the plate. "Which means anyone could've gone in and out."

"Unfortunately, yes, but I'm not sure that's an issue. Especially after what Nolen said this evening."

"You talked to Nolen?"

"He came out to interview Patrick Orlington and Smithson Collier. I spoke with Smithson beforehand, ostensibly as a casual conversation. I made my notes afterward. Same with when I talked to Patrick yesterday in passing, so they didn't know I was investigating."

"Very wise, as always." Jax smiled. Bella really was an excellent amateur sleuth. If he didn't return to his job as constable, would she miss investigating crimes? The question hovered on the tip of his tongue, but he bit it back. Time would tell about his future job prospects. And his future with her. "Did Smithson have much to say about Celeste? Or did Nolen know anything important?"

"Nolen had some pertinent information." She continued by revealing what the acting constable now knew. Bella ended by saying, "Smithson was among the men Celeste helped transport to Nantes, but he was gassed and had influenza. Richard, Nolen, and I moved him into fourth place. He probably still suffers after-effects, which would make it hard for him to attack someone, even a small woman."

"I agree, and he has no reason to target me. He had a crush on Celeste, but that's not much motive, either."

A grin curved Bella's lips. "Richard said you'd probably have insights into the information, and you do."

Her praise bolstered his low spirits. "We can keep him on the list, but not near the top, like the three of you agreed."

"What do you think about Patrick?"

"He's a more likely candidate to want to get even with me, and his shaky alibi reinforces him as a top suspect. He knew Celeste and probably flirted with her, since he's always considered himself as a ladies' man." Worry filled him. "Be careful, Bella. Remember, Richard thought Celeste's accomplice might've gotten angry when she refused to take the next step in getting money from me. A step that could've been abducting you. Don't go to any remote areas of the resort alone, and be careful when you get back tonight. In fact, call before you leave and have Mac or Griff watch for you to pull in. I'd follow you in the Chummy, but Jenny borrowed it."

Only a few seconds passed before she agreed. "I doubt if the killer will come after me at this point. In fact, it seems like he would want to get away from here as soon as possible. Unless, as Richard also said, the person wants to see you twist in the wind."

"Anyone set on extorting me could fall into that category, but I agree about the murderer escaping. Only Gaspard has. And he might be back." As Jax went over the key points, he felt fresh frustration. "I'd sure like to eliminate another suspect. In fact, eliminating everyone except the killer would be great."

"Richard wants all of us to meet again tomorrow morning, but you and I could rank the current slate of suspects."

"How about if we compare lists of where we rank everyone?"

"Sounds fine," Bella replied. "We can give brief reasons, too. You go first with your top suspect, and I'll give my rating."

Jax quickly finished his cake and picked up his cup. "Orlington is at the top because he has a major problem with me. In your summary, you mentioned his father wanting him to get promoted, and it could've been a big issue when Patrick wasn't. Also, if he's going to speakeasies and gambling, money is a concern—especially since he's not working and old Orlington isn't supporting him, either. He was never in the Nantes hospital, but he could've visited a fellow soldier there and seen Celeste. Or maybe they met in Cleveland. You've talked with him, and so has Nolen. Do you agree with me?"

Bella chewed on her lower lip, as if in contemplation. "I don't disagree. His weak alibi and grudge toward you support him being near the top."

"But not at the top?"

A half-shrug lifted one of Bella's slender shoulders. "No. Something makes me lean toward Dewey being in first place. I just saw him in town, since I had to stop at the newspaper, and he was coming out. Our exchange was very brief, but he seemed edgy. He also told me that his uncle always runs a special holiday advertisement. Dewey hasn't been home for six years. How would he know that?"

"He probably corresponds with them."

"Why would his aunt or uncle put information about advertising in a letter? Besides, he also has a grudge against you, and it goes way back."

Her assertion was food for thought. "Lyle used to run special advertisements around the holidays, since he stocks ice skates and sleds. He hasn't the last couple of years, but business was bad in town. He probably sent Dewey to check. Why else would Dewey be at the newspaper?"

"Maybe you're right, and I'm too suspicious."

Jax grinned. "I'm afraid sleuthing has influenced you to be skeptical. A desirable trait for a detective."

"I wish we had certainty instead of suppositions, because there are too many of those. My friend's cousin, Tad Worthing, said Dewey wanted to make all the runs to Celeste's hospital posting. Tad doesn't know if Dewey kept doing that after they were stationed in different areas, but I'm guessing he did. Not only that, Dewey stayed in France for months after the Armistice. So far, we don't know when Celeste left. They could've reconnected. You think his boyhood boast about getting even means little, but some people hold grudges for years. We've seen as much in past cases."

"I can't argue about that point, so you may be right. Dewey knowing Celeste over a long period is compelling." Jax let his head fall back against the chair. "Nolen will call her aunt and uncle back, if they don't contact him tomorrow. Finding out when Celeste got to Cleveland would help, and they might have information on Orlington. A chance meeting at the bakery could explain how he reconnected with Celeste. If they reconnected."

"Her uncle didn't reveal much, probably due to shock and grief. When Nolen talks to him again, he can ask more questions."

"He has to be sensitive. Grilling folks who've just lost a loved one isn't kind or productive."

"I understand, but they should want the murder solved quickly."

The worry darkening Bella's gaze telegraphed her concern. Although Jax wanted to offer reassurance about the ultimate outcome, how could he? "I'm sure they do, but you know people need time to come to grips with loss, especially sudden loss as the result of a crime."

She put both hands to her face. "You're right. They'll probably be willing to share more when Nolen talks to them again, which I hope is early tomorrow. As for our rankings, right now I'd put Dewey and Patrick tied for first place."

Jax pondered what Bella had told him and what he had already known. "I can't disagree."

"Where do you rank Gaspard?"

With one hand, Jax rubbed his forehead. "That's harder. Discovering Gaspard and Celeste are from the same town might be significant. Or not. He has no personal vendetta against me."

"He might resent American soldiers. Some French-men do."

Jax leveled his gaze on her. "He moved to Boxwood because he was friends with Bill Addison and Burton Cratton. He even lived with Mrs. Addison until she died. Not only that, he eats with some boys at the diner from time-to-time. When I talked to Burton, he indicated Victor was friendly with all the veterans over there. Just quiet."

"But Gaspard was out late the night of Celeste's murder and, shortly afterward, he left town for parts unknown. Plus. he was in Cleveland a few weeks ago."

"True." Jax sat forward and took another sip of hot chocolate. "He seemed like a pleasant person when I crossed paths with him in France."

"How well acquainted were the two of you? Other than him recommending his aunt's pension in Paris to you and Matt, how often did you encounter him?"

The pointed question had Jax shifting restlessly. "I didn't have other interactions with him. Someone told Gaspard about Matt and me going to Paris to see you, and he sought me out." Another memory surfaced. "Later, one of the boys said Gaspard wanted Americans to know about the lodgings because we had plenty of money."

A rueful smile turned up Bella's lips. "After several years of the war, the French were worn down physi-cally, emotionally, and financially. I'm sure we seemed rich to them."

"I understand his desire to ensure his aunt could make a living. His uncle died before the war, and their two sons perished at Verdun. So many French soldiers did." Jax gazed into the blazing fire, but he felt a chill deep inside him. Did Victor Gaspard harbor resentment toward him and other Americans? Was that, along with a failing business, enough to make the man turn to extortion?

"Envy can be a powerful motivator," Bella pointed out. "The accomplice wouldn't necessarily need to have a grudge against you. Maybe Gaspard found out Celeste was with child. If they were from the same town, he might've heard about it from mutual acquaintances."

"She must've hidden her condition as long as possible, and it's unlikely she confided in anyone."

"Perhaps not, but she couldn't conceal it for long. If she and Gaspard knew each other all along, which is possible, he could've known. Another new bit is the landlady in Boxwood told Newton that Celeste and Gaspard were from the same town."

Jax's fingers tightened on his cup and saucer. "It adds another clue, but how closely were they connected? Surely, they weren't married or Celeste would've moved to Boxwood, too."

"She might've told him about being with child. Maybe she even made up a story about being married to an American. If she told him after Alan died, she might've named you as the father and her husband. He would've recognized your name, I'm sure. Maybe he was angry when you shipped out."

"That's a lot of mights and maybes."

Delicate color climbed into her cheeks. "I suppose, but you have to admit, any or all of it is possible."

A low laugh left him. "I'll admit that much."

"Where do you rank him?"

"Behind Fikeland and Orlington."

She gave a slight nod. After finishing her cake and chocolate, Bella laid the plate and cup on the table next to her chair. She glanced at the notepad on the floor by Jax. "Can I use that to take notes?"

"Of course." He handed it to her, along with a pencil. "I was going over things when you got here. All it did was make me more restless, so I paced as much as I wrote."

After taking the paper from him, she studied it. "Your handwriting is better."

Her comment caught Jax off-guard. "I guess it is."

Bella met his gaze. "And you don't have as much pain?"

"No, I don't." Since he was not ready to express his guarded optimism about getting back to normal, or almost normal, Jax returned to matters at hand. "We have the four suspects ranked in order. Three, really. Now, I think Smithson is out of the running."

Bella ran one finger across his notes before looking back at Jax. "We can review our discussion in the morning. Richard should have additional details, and Jenny will lend her perspective. For now, we've covered all the suspects."

"Not really. If I was still constable, I probably would've arrested myself." He chuckled, although it lacked genuine amusement. "That sounds strange, but there's a lot of evidence against me, which we haven't gone over."

"Of course, we haven't. You didn't kill Celeste."

Her response indicated she hadn't considered the indicators of his guilt. Had Richard and Jenny? Surely, Nolen and Newton had done so before arresting him.

Otherwise, they would have resisted the action. "No, but maybe we should list the reasons I was arrested. Nolen must have already, and we can be sure the mayor has. The prosecutor will have to do that and also weigh all the evidence in order to make a case against someone else. Right now, the murder charge still stands."

Color leeched from her face as Bella ran the tip of one forefinger along the edge of the notepad. "I hadn't considered that, and I don't know if Richard has, either."

"He and Jenny could've discussed everything. I'm not sure they want to bring it all up in front of me." Or with Bella. Her distraught expression revealed the depth of her anxiety. Jax hated to add to it, but facts were facts and had to be faced. "I'd like to go over my status. Will you make notes?" When she didn't reply, he continued. "We've always discussed why each suspect is on our list."

"You aren't on the list."

"But it'd help identify the amount and weight of evidence."

"We know more about you. We're still gathering clues about the others."

Her resistance further amplified her emotional turmoil, which shone in her dark eyes. Jax yearned to offer reassurance, but he couldn't. Bella had to accept the reality of the situation. "With luck, the evidence will pile up for one of them soon." He reached over to touch her hand. "Humor me. I'm not working currently, but my lawman brain says to get the proof against me down to compare my status against the others."

She turned her hand to grasp his. "All right. It's a sensible idea."

When he noted a shiver rippling through her, Jax reluctantly pulled away. "Let me add some wood to the fire first."

As she watched Jax, Bella was reminded of her father stirring up the logs in the fireplace in their family suite at Ballantyne. He had always insisted her mother relax and rest while he got a roaring blaze going. Then, he'd sit across from her while Bella and Matt played on the floor as little ones. Later, they had done their homework at the gateleg table in the corner.

A similar table sat in front of the wide window looking out on the Hastings' side yard. Heavy drapes hung there. Jax had not closed them but, with his neighbor away for the holidays, as she always was, privacy was not a concern. Bella studied the room more carefully. In many ways, it reminded her of the family quarters at Ballantyne. Sturdy, well-worn furniture filled the space, and some of Mrs. Hastings' touches remained: the colorful knitted throw on the loveseat, lace doilies on the tables, brass candlesticks on the fireplace mantel, along with two photographs. One was the wedding portrait of Jax's parents. The other was the two of them with Jax as a toddler. Her family had chosen similar items for their living space, items that made Bella feel connected, even when they were all gone. The homey recollections warmed her as much as the glowing logs. Would she and Jax make similar memories in the future? Bella had felt confident about progress in nailing the killer as they went over details. The idea of delineating clues against Jax made her queasy. But he was right. A thorough investigation was essential, which meant reviewing every suspect—although Bella didn't consider him as one despite the murder charge—was part of the effort.

When Jax took a seat, he studied her face. "You look far away."

She smiled. "I was thinking about when I was growing up. In fall and winter, my dad always got a fire going at the end of the day."

"I remember. Back in the family quarters."

Her heart swelled. "Sometimes, you stayed overnight and did your homework with us."

"Whenever my dad was tied up with a case or had to go out of town, I did. Your folks always welcomed me any time, and I recall those winter nights, too." He glanced around the room. "My parents and I sometimes gathered here. Those are special memories of we three being together. I wonder how they'd feel now. When I was sitting in the cell, I thought about them a lot and wondered."

"They'd be angry you've been wrongly accused, and they'd both fight to clear your name." Certainty energized her response.

A half-smile tugged at one corner of his mouth. "I'm lucky to have you, Richard, and Jenny working on my behalf. I'm lucky the boys are in my corner, too. I've only spoken with Burton and with Nolen, who can't say much. But I felt the support."

"All the boys who were with you in France know you would harm no one. So do most townspeople. You have more support than you realize. Only a few people are like Lyle Fikeland."

Jax let his head fall back against the top of the chair. "I hope you're right."

His anxiety and fatigue were palpable. Both echoed inside Bella, but she couldn't let any doubt show even though a niggling finger of fear traced her spine. What if he went to trial and Fikeland's friends—or worse, Lyle himself—were on the jury? Could they sway others? Bella fought back doubt and focused on encouragement. "I am right, and we'll prove you're innocent. It's a matter of time and legwork." She cleared her throat. "Now, if you want to go over why you're a suspect, let's do it."

He sat straight up and squared his shoulders. "All right. First off, Celeste was blackmailing me. That's an issue in a couple of ways. Any man who married a woman, got her with child, and deserted them both wouldn't want to pay for their support. In addition, you and I were courting, which would give me reason to want her gone." His nostrils flared with a sharp intake of breath. "The one surefire way of not paying and getting rid of her is murder."

Bella noted Jax's effort to discuss his situation as an investigator, not as a suspect—a challenging task. She found it as difficult to maintain her perspective as a sleuth. And him mentioning their courtship in the past tense troubled her on a deep level. Not that they were stepping out now. But they would again soon. Wouldn't they? She shook off the dark worries. "Which goes to motive." She jotted a few notes before forcing herself to elaborate. "What you said to her could be construed as a threat. Richard is talking to Sam Push again, but Sam already told people what he heard. Then, prior to that, there was the confrontation immediately after the tree lighting." The memory danced on the edge of her mind. An ugly memory.

"And you heard much the same. If I go to trial, you may have to testify honestly."

Her heart hit her heels. For a moment, Bella could barely draw think. The observation was accurate but troubling. Terribly troubling. "We'll find the actual killer long before that can happen." They had to.

Although a slight smile played across Jax's lips, it didn't reach his eyes. "I know you'll try. As far as witnesses, there was a group at the park. Later, in the alley, I said she'd be sorry if she didn't get out of town, and I'd make her life miserable if she continued to make threats." He put the heel of one hand to his forehead. "Mostly idle warnings. I wouldn't have done anything to hurt her or the child, and I shouldn't have tried scaring her. I'm sorry for that." His lips flattened.

Regret resonated in his deep voice and shone in his green gaze. Neither echoed in Bella. The French-woman had not cared about Jax. "She tried to frighten you. She wanted a lot of money, and she was willing to hurt our relationship to get it. She even brought an accomplice with her. I'm sorry she was killed, but you shouldn't feel bad about warning her off. If she had left, she might still be alive." The vehemence in her voice filled the room. Jax shouldn't feel guilty about his words to Celeste. Not at all.

His faint smile returned. "You're a powerful defender, and I'm grateful."

Warmth rose in Bella's face. "Of course, I'm in your corner. I always will be." She clutched the pencil tighter. "Now, let's get back to reviewing the evidence against you, so we can remove you from the list."

His good humor again faded as he nodded. "We also know I had opportunity, since I was alone after Celeste left the alley. Very foolishly, I walked around trying to find her and the man. A couple of people saw me, which is a big reason I was arrested."

Bella rolled the pencil between her hands. "Being near the scene of the crime is circumstantial evidence."

"Maybe so, but bits of circumstantial evidence add up. I put the green mitten on my list of clues. I had a pair the same color. Nolen can testify to that fact. Probably a few of the other boys could, as well."

After he made that observation, Bella shrugged. "We already discussed how many soldiers received mittens. Thousands of pairs were sent overseas."

"But not so many were bright green. Besides, the point is every suspect, including me, could've dropped the mitten." Jax thrust his long legs out and crossed them at the ankles. "The issue is me having that color."

"Did you wear them much?"

"When we were standing around waiting to move out, and when we sat in the trenches. I wore them when I tried to sleep, too. You were close to the front, so you remember the chilly rain and frequent fog."

"I do, but I was never in a flooded, muddy trench." Jax never discussed the awful conditions, but Bella had heard complaints from other officers and soldiers.

"Thank heavens," he said with genuine feeling. "The wool mittens, scarves, and socks helped. Sometimes, I wore two pairs of mittens, especially at night. I couldn't fire my sidearm with them on, so I stuffed them in my pocket when we advanced."

"What about ambulance drivers? Did they get mittens from home?"

Jax rubbed his forehead. "Some did. I remember the driver who took me to the field hospital the first time had a pair. Red ones."

"So, Dewey could have some."

"He could, but it'll be hard to prove ownership of the mitten. I know for sure it wasn't mine, since I lost them the last time I was wounded."

"I'm sure Nolen and Newton have asked more about it. Finding the other one in the pair would be useful."

"Yep. As far as factors in my case, opportunity is definitely a problem. Motive, too. And means isn't on my side, either, since anyone could have grabbed a rock and hit her." A shudder racked him. "Such an awful way to die."

"It is," Bella agreed, but she fought off the image.

Jax seemed to shake off the dismay. "Which means all three major points are against me."

"Motive, opportunity, and method." Bella studied the notes. Each area had too many entries under Jax's name for her comfort. "I can make a comparison chart and fill in as we learn more about the others. We have quite a lot of information already." But nothing revelatory. Nothing to remove suspicion from Jax and put it solely on someone else.

He bowed his head. "I don't enjoy being sidelined, but I understand I can't investigate when I'm the top suspect." Once again, vexation was in his voice.

"Not to me, you aren't. Or to Jenny, Richard, and most of the town." Did Jax not believe her? Or was he worried about not gleaning sufficient support to convict the actual killer?

"I'm sorry. You shouldn't have to keep reminding me. Being in that cell for almost twenty-four hours affected my optimism. Knowing how much evidence is against me doesn't help. I keep wondering if the accomplice egged Celeste on. I wonder why no one else saw him. Only me."

His frustration echoed inside Bella. "The killer knew he murdered her, so getting away from the scene of the crime was foremost in his mind. As far as who came up with the plan, that's hard to say. We won't know for sure until we catch the killer."

"Yeah, you're right. I just wish someone else had seen a man in a greatcoat with Celeste. How did he stay out of sight to everyone except me? That's a big issue because, in court, it'll sound like I invented another person. If I was investigating, I'd be suspicious myself." Jax gazed steadily at Bella. "You would be, too."

The statement escalated her discomfort because it rang true. When she responded, Bella sidestepped agreement. "One of our major concerns is finding someone who had a greatcoat. Nolen checked the cottages and didn't find one with Patrick or Smithson, for that matter, but the killer probably would've ditched the garment.

You said they slipped down the alley. He might've taken the coat off right away." Bella turned her mind to what route the pair took. "You tried to find them that night. If only we knew where they went then. Patrick and Gaspard have vehicles. They could've driven to the park and suggested taking a walk to revamp their extortion plan. That would explain why no one saw a man walking with Celeste."

"True."

When Jax said no more, Bella went on. "Weren't most people inside when you met her?"

Jax laid his head against the chair back. "Yep. It was quiet in town."

"We've come a long way in a short time, and we only need one break. Richard said as much earlier, when he stopped at Ballantyne." Bella willed Jax to agree. "You've said the same in past cases."

"I have."

Bella studied his expression. Exhaustion lined his face. "You don't seem as certain now." And that worried her.

He shrugged. "My neck wasn't in the noose in those other investigations. Now, it is."

The graphic statement made Bella gasp. An image of the electric chair, which she had once seen in a newspaper photograph, flashed through her head. The picture had chilled her then. Now, ice formed around her, and she shivered with dread.

"I'm sorry, Bella. I shouldn't have said that."

"But you've been thinking it, haven't you?" Mostly, Jax had kept up a good front. But he need not do that for her.

"I have. Like I already told you, there's no guarantee justice will prevail. It doesn't always. We both know that, and we should prepare for the possibility. Despite most of the veterans and other townspeople supporting me, despite your work and the Jenkinses' involvement, hard evidence will tell in the end."

For a moment, Bella flipped to the front of the notepad and saw some scribblings for the first time. As she scanned his notes, grim certainty threatened to choke her. Jax had admitted to going over the suspects and feeling restless. But he had made additional comments about himself as the likely killer, comments written as if he was a lawman looking at evidence. Bold, forthright, chilling comments. He'd said they needed to do that, and they had—to a point. His writings went well beyond what they had discussed. When she looked back at him, Bella noted his wariness. "You actually believe you may be found guilty of a crime you didn't commit. It's what you went over and over after Jenny left." When he bowed his head, she knew she was right. "You shouldn't be alone at all. Too much time to think."

His chin jerked up, and his gaze met hers. "I don't need a babysitter. I'm not planning to do anything rash, like chase down the suspects and grill them for information."

"I didn't think you would. You're too self-disciplined to go off half-cocked. But you're trying to distance yourself by looking at the evidence like a constable would." She lifted the notepad and turned it toward him. "You'd already made a comparison chart before I got here, and it doesn't have what we learned today, which makes a long list of evidence under your name and scant clues under the others. Why, Jax? Why not wait until we have more details?"

He shifted to stare into the fireplace. "I appreciate you, Jenny, and Richard helping. I appreciate Nolen and the other boys believing in me…"

Bella cut him off. "So, you've said. But you wasted what—two or three hours—making a chart that no longer works because you didn't have all the information. Why did you do this?"

His troubled gaze met hers. "Because I don't want to harbor false hope, and I don't want you to harbor it, either."

The last assertion went to the core of the situation. "You think I should cut and run because you were arrested? Well, I won't. The charges against you will be dropped. Sooner would be better than later, but if it takes another week, or two, or longer, you won't be going to trial. Let alone back to jail." Bella took the notepad in both hands and tore out the pages with the long list of evidence against Jax, and short lists against the others, before tossing them into the fire.

Jax stared at the shards of paper as they became ashes. He glanced at Bella, who held up one hand.

"I'll make a new chart, and it will have all the pertinent information. Yours is absolutely worthless because you made a critical mistake, one an experienced lawman like yourself should never do."

"What's that?"

Since his query seemed sincere, Bella answered just as frankly. "A good investigator never lets personal feelings influence his or her work." She paused for a heartbeat. "And your summary of evidence is slanted because you're preparing for the worst." Her suggestion hung heavily in the air for several moments.

During that time, Jax glanced back at the fire before again facing Bella.

A heavy exhalation left him. "You're right. I've been on guard for the worst to happen ever since I saw Celeste after the tree lighting. Her accusations shocked me, and Lyle Fikeland didn't help. But you being there and hearing…the look on your face cut me to the quick. I felt like all my dreams and wishes were dying before my eyes." He braced his elbows on his knees and put his head in his hands. "Until then, I thought this was going to be the magical Christmas that I hoped for in 1916. I figured the worst was behind us."

His words matched her thoughts. Bella crossed to sit on the ottoman beside his chair and took his hands in hers. When he lifted his head, she saw anxiety and hope battling in his green eyes. Those same feelings filled her, but hope took precedence. Her life had been turned upside down and inside out since December 1916. His life had been, as well. Before Celeste's arrival and murder, Bella would have said clear sailing was ahead. Now, she and Jax were once again navigating choppy waters. "It still could be, and I believe it will be. I believe in Christmas miracles," she murmured, "but, most of all, I believe in you." Bella leaned forward to brush her lips over his. Almost immediately, he put one hand behind her head and deepened the kiss.

After long moments, Jax shifted back in the chair and took her hands again. "I've let myself harbor doubts about the future. We've had so many ups-and-downs in the past five years. More downs, really."

Bella squeezed his fingers. "We're almost past those."

A slight smile played across his lips. "I hope you're right. It's gotten a little too routine for me to brace for something bad instead of expect something good."

"All that will change soon."

"I hope so."

Bella pointed toward a stack of newspapers sitting off to one side. "The Moreley Monitor is a weekly. How long have you been saving the issues?"

"Those are old. You know my dad was a pack rat. Earlier, Jenny asked if I had Christmas decorations. We stored them in the attic, so I went up to look. After

Mom died, Dad and I had a tree, and I did later, too. At least until I left for France. I haven't since I came back. Anyhow, the ornaments were in those papers. Jenny will see to getting a tree next week, so I unwrapped a bunch and set them in a basket for her. We can use the old paper to start fires."

Something akin to Richard's gut feelings grabbed Bella, as did a faint memory. "Did you look through any of them?"

Jax shook his head. "They're from way back, probably 1916 since I didn't decorate after that. But no, I didn't look at them."

He need not repeat how that holiday had ended, but it echoed in Bella's heart. She had come home from school expecting to court, since Jax had made repeated trips to escort her to college events. With American involvement in the Great War on the horizon, he had virtually severed their relationship. In retrospect, Bella understood his attitude, although she did not agree with it. His voice broke into her reverie.

"Why did you ask?"

"My mom always kept the newspaper for me, so I could catch up with local news when I was home from college. I just remembered a big article about Dewey and the ambulance corps in one edition. There was a photograph of him just after he got to France. Let's see if that paper is in your bunch." Despite being unable to pull up a vivid image, Bella felt the pull of excitement. "You must recall the item. It was spread across the front page."

"All right. We can go through them." Jax handed a stack of papers to Bella, and kept the rest for himself.

Chapter Eleven

After twenty minutes, they had sorted through the entire supply without finding the newspaper with Dewey on the front page. Disappointment weighed Bella down. "The right edition must be gone."

"I suppose it got used for something else. Are you going to tell me why it was of special interest?"

She slumped back in the chair. "I only have a vague recollection of the picture. He was standing in front of an ambulance in a greatcoat. Since the photograph was black-and-white, I don't know the color, but it was the same shape and such as French army ones."

Jax's eyes widened. "I remember that issue now. I didn't read the article, and I spent very little time looking at Dewey's photograph, but I have a similar memory about his coat. I don't know why I didn't think about it before now."

"Because you were shocked and upset by Celeste's accusations. Then, you were charged, arrested, and jailed. Add that to our other strong suspects and your exhaustion, and it's easy to understand why you didn't remember. I wish I'd remembered it sooner."

"You've been upset, stunned, and exhausted yourself. All of that clouds the memory."

"True, but I wish we could find that edition. It could make a big difference." She chewed on her lower lip. "Mr. Yarken keeps at least one copy of every issue. He has them going back for years."

"You're right." Jax pulled out his pocket watch. "He may be in the office working late, since the next paper comes out the day after tomorrow."

Bella jumped to her feet. "Let's see."

For a moment, Jax hesitated. Finally, he rose from the chair. "Wait until I get my gun."

"Your gun? Why? We shouldn't have trouble with Mr. Yarken."

"No, we won't. However, I don't know who else we might run into. I didn't take the revolver the night I met Celeste, which could've been a deadly decision. Since you'll be with me now, I'm taking no more chances."

Jax fetched the gun and, within moments, he and Bella were at the newspaper office, where lights still burned. "He's here," she said. Hope bloomed as the pair approached the building. Jax wanted to stay out of sight from passersby, so Bella parked in the alley.

He tapped on the back door. Within a few moments, Yank Yarken, a small, spare man in his forties, appeared. "Good evening. What brings the two of you here?"

His benign expression eased Bella's mind. At least, the newspaper publisher wasn't acting suspicious of Jax. "We wondered if we could look at the archives," she replied. "We're looking for an issue from late 1916. It had a picture of Dewey Fikeland in it and an article about him being in France as an ambulance driver."

Yarken nodded. "I remember it well. His aunt was excited about it and asked for extra copies of the paper and two of the photograph. Last I knew, one is in their store, and the other is in their house." He stood back. "Come on in. I made an extra picture, just in case she wanted to send him one. Never did, so it's in my files."

Bella couldn't repress a smile when she looked at Jax, and neither could he. The pair followed Yarken to his office, which was near the front of the building, and waited for him to produce the photograph. When he did, Bella let Jax take it, and he held the image for her to see. "That's a French army greatcoat, and he's wearing mittens." Her voice trembled with excitement as she spoke.

"Right on both counts." Jax's tone was just as tremulous.

"I heard about a mitten being found in the park," Yarken said. "Never considered this photo as evidence since a bunch of you got those things from the knitting project, didn't you?"

"We did, but Dewey got these before we sailed for France," Jax replied. "The main thing is, I don't know of any other American who had a French army greatcoat." He briefly explained about the man he had seen with Celeste.

The publisher's eyes went wide. "Interesting. I understand why that wasn't revealed around town, but I wish

I'd known. I never figured you had anything to do with the girl, certainly not as her killer. I can find the issue pretty fast. The article might help you, too." He leveled his gaze on Jax. "I assume the two of you are doing another investigation."

"We are," Jax said without hesitation.

"Happy to help any way I can." Yarken got to his feet. "I won't ask questions, but I'd like to talk once the case is closed."

"Of course," Jax agreed. "We'll both help with a story." Bella agreed.

The older man nodded and smiled. "The archives are way back in a closet, but I shouldn't be too long."

When they were alone, Bella turned to Jax. "Dewey has to be the killer."

"Not much doubt about that. From here, we need to go to Nolen. He's most likely home now. We can call Richard and Newton from there." Jax gave a rueful smile. "Nolen can call them. He's the acting constable."

Bella started to reply but a thumping sound emanated from the back of the building. "I hope Mr. Yarken didn't fall down. Maybe we should check on him."

"Let me go first." Jax got up and headed to the door ahead of Bella. Before stepping into the backroom, he called out. "Mr. Yarken, are you all right?"

Silence echoed through the air until Jax spoke again. "Stay here and let me go alone."

"Of course." Bella wanted to follow Jax but being a distraction wouldn't help. In the faint light from the press room, she could make out his figure slowly moving away from her. Her pulse picked up when he reached into his pocket, the pocket holding his service revolver. Before his hand emerged, a figure approached Jax from behind. "Jax, watch out." He turned toward her, but it was too late. Bella's heart hit her heels when the other man brought the butt of a gun down on the back of Jax's head. Without forethought, she hurried forward and dropped to her knees beside him.

"Get up." Bella looked to see Dewey Fikeland, pistol pointed at Jax, hovering over her. "Do it now."

On shaking legs, she stood. "Where is Mr. Yarken?"

A humorless snort left Dewey. "In the back room. I followed the two of you here and waited to sneak in. When he came out of his office and went into the archives, I bashed him, too. But not too hard, since he's breathing."

A sliver of relief went through Bella. At least the newspaper publisher was still alive. "What do you want? If it's the old paper and photograph, your aunt has both. One is in the store. Taking the copy here won't make a difference."

"My uncle moved it to the storeroom, so it's not apt to be seen now. As for what I want, you need to come with me and find out." He yanked a set of handcuffs out of his coat pocket and thrust them at her. "Get Hastings' hands behind him and put these on. He's coming, too. Don't try anything. If you do, I'll shoot him where he lays."

While she wanted to object, Bella knew Dewey would make good on his threat. A gunshot might draw attention, but the newspaper was surrounded by shops that had closed hours ago, so she couldn't take a chance. "All right." Moving Jax's prone body wasn't easy, and he groaned as she did.

"You awake, Hastings?" Dewey asked.

In response, another moan left Jax.

217

"If you are, you better get on your feet fast or I'll have Bella pull you out of here. Meanwhile, I won't hesitate to shoot her or knock her out, either. I'd like both of you with me, but I definitely want her," Dewey snarled.

Somehow, Jax stood up, but he swayed on his feet. Bella reached out to steady him. "Are you all right?"

"Don't worry about me," he murmured.

"Bring your vehicle closer. Be quick and quiet about it. If you aren't, Hastings gets shot here and now. Then, you can be my sole hostage."

As Bella hurried outside and got the Ford in place, she scanned the area but saw no one.

Dewey pushed Jax into the backseat. "Head north out of town and don't pull anything funny."

Chapter Twelve

W ith trembling hands on the steering wheel, Bella headed out of the alley and to the town limits, which were near the newspaper offices. Summoning help got less and less likely as she drove north. In only a couple of minutes, they left Moreley behind. "Why follow us back to the paper? You were there earlier."

A humorless chortle left him. "When I heard talk about Celeste's accomplice wearing a French great-coat, I knew I had to get that edition out of the archives. I hadn't thought about it for a while. Not until I saw it at home."

Dismay filled Bella. "I suppose your uncle heard about the coat."

"Maybe, but Korbert Lannigan told me Hastings was looking for someone wearing a French army coat the night Celeste died. We talked earlier today."

"He and your uncle are friendly, so I suppose you got acquainted with him, too."

"Korbert befriended Uncle Lyle when he got to town, at my suggestion." Dewey sounded smug.

The statement heightened Bella's apprehension. "You knew Lannigan before he came here?"

"I suggested he come to Moreley, and I alerted him to your activities this evening. As soon as the Coopers go to their suite for the night, he'll join us."

A chill rippled through Bella. "I didn't see your uncle's truck near Jax's house. How did you know I was there and when we left?"

"Hastings' nosey neighbor, old Mrs. Adams, is at her sister's place, so I picked her flimsy lock and settled in the dining room, which has a splendid view of the Hastings parlor. You two were nice enough to have lamps on and the drapes open, and I saw you sorting through the papers. I'd parked in the back of her house, out of sight. When the two of you left, I followed and parked a ways from the newspaper. Once you went inside, I got in place. You know the rest."

Unfortunately, Bella did. Her mind wrestled with escape strategies. With Jax bound and semi-conscious, there were few viable ones. Still, she kept thinking.

About twenty minutes after they left the newspaper office, Dewey told Bella to stop at an abandoned house on the road to Boxwood. "Get out and open the door on Hastings' side. You get out then, too. Understand, Jackson?"

Bella turned in time to see Jax nod. When a groan rumbled out of him, she knew his head must be pounding. Fresh terror gripped her. He needed a doctor, but suggesting that wouldn't move Dewey.

"Go ahead of us. Try anything, and Hastings is a dead man."

Not for one moment did she doubt his threat, so Bella walked to the ramshackle front porch. Behind her, it sounded like Jax stumbled over the uneven ground.

After Bella mounted the broken steps, Dewey spoke again. "Open the door."

It took some effort, but she managed. Once they were inside, Dewey shoved Jax down on the floor. Unable to break his fall, Jax hit hard and moaned before going still and silent.

Dewey flipped on his flashlight. "Sit down, Bella."

In the thin beam, the dirt and disarray were obvious, but Bella settled on a battered, faded chair near Jax whose breath was fast and shallow. How hard had he been hit? A blow had killed Celeste. Would the same happen to Jax? Tears pricked her eyes. "What are you going to do with us?"

"Use you as a hostage. Korbert should be here within the hour."

"How did you get to know him?"

"We met in Cleveland. Both of us had crummy jobs and needed money. I suggested he move to Moreley. What with business here better, I figured he'd find something. And he did."

Shock made Bella gasp. "Why? Did you make plans with Celeste in advance, too?"

"Nah. I first figured on getting the hardware store from my aunt and uncle. Or working there and stashing as much money as I could. The two of them worked me like a servant all of my childhood, so I figured they owe me. Turns out the business isn't doing well. Not well at all, so I needed another plan."

"And you found Celeste? Or you stayed in touch with her all along?"

221

Again, he guffawed. "The latter."

"You've known her since 1916."

"I have. We met shortly after I landed in France. I was making runs from the front to field hospitals. Met her then, and I ended up at the one where she volunteered when I'd gotten wounded myself. She was beautiful and kind and attentive."

The man didn't have to say he had fallen in love with the French nurse because it was obvious in his tone and expression. Bella wanted to ask if Celeste had returned the sentiment but being circumspect seemed wiser. "How long were you in the hospital?"

"A week. We got well-acquainted, and I saw her a lot afterward, since I drove patients there pretty often. As often as I could." His jaw tightened. "The French army took a lot of casualties in 1916. The British did, too. Our local boys stayed safe here at home for far too long."

His repeated criticism came as no surprise, but it again missed a critical point. "President Wilson didn't declare war until 1917. The Ohio National Guard was called up soon afterward, which is when the soldiers from Moreley and the surrounding area reported." She had said as much before, but Dewey seemed to fixate on the theme.

A harrumph left Dewey. "Any of them could've volunteered like I did."

Arguing with him was futile, so Bella moved the conversation back to the original topic. "You stayed in touch with Celeste during and after the war?"

His gaze narrowed. "After the Americans came, I got moved to another area. I didn't know about her brother dying for a time. When I found out, I went to see her as soon as I could get off. By then, she was involved with Brewster." Anger burned in his eyes. "She was all starry-eyed about him and coming to the U.S. after the war. Never told me about him being betrothed to someone else. I found out from another ambulance driver later on. By then, Brewster was dead, but Celeste was carrying his child. She sent a message asking for my help. Took some nerve, but she knew I'd been sweet on her for a long time. Even when she was laying with another man. Fool that I am, I didn't get over her."

For a long moment, Bella debated what to say next. Dewey was clearly agitated. Although she couldn't blame him for being hurt about Celeste's involvement with Alan, his demeanor gave Bella pause. His hurt had evolved into anger, enough anger to seek revenge. But why involve Jax? Instead of asking those questions, Bella focused on why and how Dewey had stayed in touch with the French nurse. "What sort of help did she want?"

"With no family left in France, she wanted to get to her aunt and uncle in Cleveland."

"That's understandable."

He shook his head. "Because she figured she could get me to do her bidding after spurning me for a cad like Brewster? But I guess you always saw me as a buffoon, too."

"Of course not," Bella quickly replied.

A chortle escaped him. "You had Hastings tell me to stay away from you when we were kids."

Although Jax had done that on his own, Bella wasn't sure she should say so. Dewey was already prepared to kill him and kidnap her. At least she figured he'd leave Jax behind. And dead. Her gaze went to his prone form. He was so still. With Jax unconscious, it was up to her to find a way out of the dilemma. Could she? Bella wasn't at all sure, but she had to try. "I didn't think you were serious back then. We were both very young."

"I was fourteen when I first asked you to step out. You were only two years older."

"But my parents didn't allow me to step out with young men until later." Although the assertion wasn't precisely true, Dewey had no way of knowing. "I don't know what Jax said to you, but he was aware of my family's rules. You remember how he and Matt were best friends?"

Several seconds of silence passed while Dewey looked from Jax's limp form to Bella. "I remember. Why didn't your brother warn me away, if you weren't allowed to step out?"

An excellent question, and Bella couldn't give an accurate answer because doing so would give away too much. "I'm not sure, and we'll never know since Matt is gone." She cleared her throat. "So, you must've helped Celeste get to Cleveland." He still hadn't provided crucial information. Not that any of it would help now. Not unless the others realized Jax and Bella were in trouble.

"She couldn't just come. Besides, her condition was going to be obvious before long. The only solution was for us to get married."

Surprise momentarily held Bella mute. "The two of you have been together in Cleveland since the war ended?"

"We stayed in France until Xavier was born. The ambulance service allowed that, and our marriage gave me some status in the country. As did my work as a driver. People there appreciated our efforts. Here, soldiers get more credit even though they were there a lot less time."

His resentment continued to underscore his beliefs. But Bella still wanted answers. "When did you and Celeste come home?"

"Last February."

The reply surprised her. "You stayed in France until then?"

He nodded. "Xavier was sickly. Then, she got with child again—a girl."

"There's a son and a daughter." Two children were without a mother. One had no father, while the other's sire was a murderer. Her heart went out to both little ones.

"No. Xavier died before the girl was stillborn."

The statement was made with a complete lack of emotion, which only increased Bella's anxiety. Did the man have no feeling for his own offspring? "I'm sorry."

"Brewster's boy dying seemed like fate took a hand. As for the girl, it's too bad but she would've kept us in France longer. Celeste refused to travel with a small child. If she'd gotten in the family way again, we'd have been stuck there."

His callousness was appalling. "I thought you liked France."

"The entire country was a mess after the war. So much death and destruction. At least here, you can find food and housing easily enough. If you have a job."

"I thought you were working in New York."

"No, I only told my aunt and uncle I was there. I had a job in Cleveland, but the company went out of business. With so many out of work, I couldn't find anything decent. Celeste's aunt and uncle hired me as a delivery driver. Had to get up long before dawn and toil all day for a pittance."

As he spoke, Bella was hit with realization. "Which is why you tried blackmail after discovering the hardware store wasn't profitable. But why Jax? He barely knew Celeste."

"Maybe, maybe not. She talked about him often. All the doughboys were wonderful in her eyes. I'm sure she would've preferred to marry one of them."

"Did she suggest the two of you wed?"

"No, she just wanted my support. She planned to say she'd married a soldier who died. People would've believed her. Plenty of military cemeteries in France. After we had a liaison, it wasn't hard to convince her to wed me. She didn't want one scandal, let alone two."

The admission made Bella cringe. "You would have told people who Xavier's father was?"

"If she'd spurned me again, of course."

The French nurse hadn't actually spurned him at all, but Bella wisely withheld that opinion. "So, you chose Jax as a target because Celeste liked him?"

A half-shrug lifted one of Dewey's shoulders. "She'd spoken of him often enough, and he was right here where I had a good excuse to come on my own. And a helper in Korbert. No one in Moreley associated me with Celeste, and my aunt has wanted me to visit."

"How did you convince Celeste to go along with your plan?"

"That wasn't hard." A sneer curved his mouth. "The bakery isn't doing as well as it once did. Lots of people out of work and not so many interested in French concoctions nowadays, so her uncle started transporting booze to speakeasies. The delivery truck was a suitable cover."

Suddenly, an idea hit Bella. "You threatened to turn Celeste's uncle in." She made it a statement, not a question.

"I did, so my wife was willing to do my bidding. Besides, we needed money. Her uncle paying me poorly led to us owing our landlord and a few others."

"Coming on the same train seems risky."

"But it worked. That dolt Smithson Collier befriended Celeste. I didn't know about Orlington being at Ballantyne or the Frenchman in Boxwood. Just good luck until you started snooping."

"How do you know about all of them?"

"My uncle is a councilman and Cawlings keeps them all up-to-date."

"And your uncle told you."

"Me and my aunt." His gaze narrowed on her. "Once I arrived in town, I heard about you being an amateur detective. I figured you'd back off when Hastings got arrested, but I suppose you were sweet on him for years."

Bella wasn't prepared to deny the truth, so she tried to circumvent Dewey's assumptions. "Richard and Jenny Jenkins did a lot of the digging."

"That was also unfortunate." Dewey grimaced. "As was Celeste refusing to go along with all my plans."

Although she probably knew the answer, Bella asked a question. "What was the rest of your plan, and why wouldn't she agree with all of it?"

"Hastings refused to pay, as you must know. I didn't come here to listen to my uncle rant about how I should work for him and why I should never have left town. He was as bad as Celeste's uncle, who thought I ought to be grateful for a crummy delivery job." His nostrils flared with a sharp intake of breath. "We needed money, and I finally realized the only way Hastings would pay was if your safety was on the line. Word is he inherited money from his folks. Checked with an old schoolmate at the bank and found that out. Anyhow, I never planned to hurt you. I wouldn't have gone so far."

"But you will now. And you'll kill Jax in order to get away. Just like you killed Celeste."

A stricken expression fell over his face. "I didn't plan for her to die. I didn't want that. We argued after she met with Hastings behind the café. She refused to go along with kidnapping you, said she was going back to Cleveland and divorcing me. Can you believe that? After all I did for her." His voice rose as he spoke.

Placating him seemed like the only viable option, so Bella did her best. "You said it was an accident. How did it happen?"

Dewey stared at a point beyond Bella. "We went down to the water to talk. When she turned away, I grabbed a hold of her. She screamed. Even though it was late, I was afraid someone would hear her, so I put my hand over her mouth. She tried to bite me, and we ended up tussling on the ground. She was like a wildcat. I only wanted her to be still and quiet, but she kept fighting me. Finally, I got on top of her. I grabbed the rock, I guess. She stopped struggling after a bit, but I don't recall exactly what happened. I tried to wake her up. It was too late, so I pushed her into the water and ran home. I climbed up to my old room and went to bed."

His account of Celeste's murder horrified Bella. If he had really been distraught, why run? Why not say it was an accident? But then, how would he explain knowing her well enough to argue and tussle? "And hoped Jax got blamed."

"That occurred to me later. Him getting arrested took pressure off me. At least it did until the bunch of you started poking around."

Suddenly, he wasn't focusing solely on her participation. Not that Bella believed much of what he said. "You wanted to get the newspaper photograph with you in a greatcoat. How did you get the coat?"

"I'd made a special trip to get a wounded French captain to a field hospital. It saved his life. When he found out, he made sure I got a French officer's coat. Turns out his father was high in their government."

"And the mittens you had on in the photo?" Bella asked.

"Not the same ones I wore Monday night. Those in the photo got lost long ago. The green ones were knitted by Celeste."

Simple explanations. If only they had emerged sooner. "What's your plan now? You've grabbed both Jax and me. Killing him will only put more scrutiny on you. Richard, Nolen, and Newton are already trying to prove your guilt in Celeste's death."

A feral smile distorted his features. "Hastings is distraught about losing his temper and attacking Celeste. Even worse, he fears going back to jail and to the electric chair, especially when you confront him with your belief in his guilt."

"But I know he isn't guilty," Bella protested, "and many people are aware of how I feel."

"After collecting evidence, you changed your mind. At least that's what folks will believe when they read your note to him."

"I haven't written a note, and I won't write one." Abruptly, Bella recognized Dewey's new strategy. "Why would I? You're clearly planning to kill both of us. There's nothing to be gained by me penning an accusatory note."

Dewey's expression grew darker. "Nonetheless, people will believe he's guilty when he kills you and then, himself. Besides, Lannigan will vouch for me being with him all this time." He waved the revolver in the air. "This is Hastings' gun. He was foolish enough to have it on him just now. Of course, I had my own in my hand. His was in the holster. Getting it while we were in the backseat wasn't a challenge."

Jax wasn't foolish. He just hadn't grasped the depth of Dewey's depravity. Neither had Bella. A low moan broke into her troubled thoughts, and she turned to see Jax struggling to sit up. His bindings made that impossible. A look of confusion blanketed his face until his gaze met hers. Almost immediately, comprehension dawned in his expression. Before Jax could speak, Dewey did.

"Hastings, good to see you awake." Once again, Dewey sneered.

Jax turned to the other man. "You won't get away with this, Dewey. Nolen and Newton are looking into your association with Celeste. They'll find all the evidence needed to send you to the electric chair. Let us go, and you might get off with life in prison."

"Ha! You and I both know you'll press to have me executed if I let you go."

"I won't, especially if you set Bella free. You can keep me as a hostage, even take me along with you."

"Jax, no," Bella put in as fear gripped her. "He'll kill you as soon as you're away from here."

"And you'll go straight to the coppers if I let you go." Dewey focused on Bella as he spoke.

"She won't. In fact, you could tie her up here. Someone will be along later and find Bella." Jax kept his attention on the other man. "I heard you say Celeste's death was an accident. That also weighs in your favor, and I'm sure you don't want to hurt Bella, either."

Bella felt no similar sense of certainty on either count, but she could see Dewey wavering. She didn't want him absconding with Jax, so she intervened. "Just leave both of us bound. You'll be long gone before anyone locates us."

As Bella listened, she wondered how much Jax had heard and how long he'd been conscious. If he'd been awake for more than a few moments, he might have a solid plan. Being trussed would impede implementation unless she could figure out his strategy and help. They had been in other tight situations, but only once together. That had ended with Jax getting shot, something she wanted to avoid. Dewey was close enough to take dead aim, which made a shiver run through her. Bella studied Jax more carefully. Although his hands were bound, his feet were not. Could she distract Dewey long enough for Jax to get up and go after their captor? If Jax succeeded, Bella might grab the gun. What if it went off? Uncertainty plagued her, but doing nothing meant sure death for both of them. When she glanced back at Jax, Bella saw him wink. In reply, she gave a slight nod before focusing on Dewey.

"I know you don't really want to kill me. You're too good a person. Hurting Celeste was a mistake. It's easy to lose control during an argument." Although Bella was lying through her teeth, she kept her voice soothing. Convincing Dewey to try binding her was their only option. While he was distracted, Jax could jump him—if he acted quickly enough. He would try. She knew that. Try and succeed, or Dewey would shoot Jax before turning the gun on Bella.

Unidentifiable emotions played across Dewey's face. "You really think I'm a good person?"

Since he didn't sound cynical, Bella nodded. "You always were." That much was true. Dewey had been a nice boy. A pesky youngster, but never mean or cruel. She could see he wanted to believe her, so Bella pressed her point. "I'm sorry you felt like you couldn't talk to me after Jax warned you away. I always liked you but, as I said, I wasn't allowed to step out with any young men until I went to college. My parents didn't approve." Not at all true, since the Stewarts hadn't been especially strict. Out of the corner of her eye, Bella saw Jax's eyes widen slightly before he schooled his features. Some of her tension ebbed, since he must realize she was trying to placate Dewey.

"Yeah. Bella was angry with me when I butted in," Jax agreed. "She figured I could've explained why she couldn't step out with you."

Jax looked and sounded completely candid. If Bella hadn't known better, she would have believed him.

Dewey glanced from Jax to Bella. "I wish I'd known. I wouldn't have been so eager to leave town. I wish we'd crossed paths in France. Then, I never would've married Celeste. You and I might've gotten together."

Bella fought to keep her disgust from showing. Strict control helped her speak another fabrication. "Perhaps so. In any case, I know you don't want to hurt me. Why not tie me up and leave both of us? You'll be long gone by the time anyone finds us here. In a big city, you can get away and disappear. You could even escape to Canada. From there, you could go anyplace. You and Lannigan." Providing ideas for his getaway seemed wise. If she was persuasive enough, Bella might convince Dewey of a successful flight. No need to say the law would be on his heels no matter where he went. For long moments, Dewey was silent. Bella's heart raced while she waited for him to speak. Or for Jax to make a move, since their captor's attention remained on her alone. She maintained eye contact with Dewey but, when Jax struggled to his feet and launched himself at the other man, Bella jumped up, as well.

Having his feet free aided Jax a little, but Bella knew he needed help. She glanced around for some sort of weapon, something to stop Dewey from firing the gun. He had laid his flashlight aside after turning the oil lamp on, so she grabbed it. Since Dewey's back was now toward her, Bella used all her might to bring the torch down on the back of his head. Two sounds followed one another. First, a low grunt. Then, a gunshot. Dewey slumped to the floor with Jax underneath him. For what seemed like an eternity, but could have only been a minute, Bella stared in horror at the two prone bodies. Finally, Jax rolled into a sitting position. A grin curved his lips when he looked up at her.

"Good job." He sounded breathless but triumphant.

Bella smiled in return. "Let's get the handcuffs off you and get them on Dewey. With luck, the key is in his coat." She tried several pockets before meeting with success. Within moments, she had released Jax.

"Let's go. I want him in jail as soon as possible."

She could only agree.

As she headed back toward town, with a bound Dewey in the backseat, Bella glanced at Jax. "Are you all right?"

"I'm fine. The gun went off but the bullet didn't hit either of us. I'm just disgusted with myself for letting Dewey get the jump on me."

"I don't know how much you heard, but..." His voice cut her off.

"I came around when he was talking about following you and spying on us. It took a bit for me to get my bearings and figure out if I could put him out of action."

"Which you did. He plotted thoroughly, except he didn't know the hardware store wasn't making a lot of money."

"He might've sold it after his aunt and uncle were out of the way."

Fresh alarm filled Bella. "Do you think he was going to kill them?"

"I don't know, but that's my guess. He sounded out-of-control back at the shack. Hard to say what he might have planned. He was desperate. At least he isn't going anyplace."

"Except to jail, which is where he belongs."

"I couldn't agree more." His jaw tightened. "The sooner we alert Nolen and Newton, the better. Lannigan needs to be arrested, too. If he gets to the abandoned house, he could still escape. I definitely don't want you going home now. Stay with me until they're both in custody."

Bella laid a hand on his arm. "Dewey was more interested in you. I'm not sure he would've harmed me."

A harrumph left Jax. "You give him too much credit for decency, but you were smart to pin the blame on your parents, as far as not accepting his invitations. That mollified him a little."

"I said that when I first ran into him. Of course, it wasn't true. Mom and Dad would've thought I was foolish to step out with Dewey." She withdrew her hand and sat back in her seat.

A moment passed before Jax replied. "Why? I recall you going to a dance or two with boys in your class." The words were out before he considered them.

"You've never mentioned that before."

The surprise in her voice made Jax regret the admission. "It never came up. Those boys were in your class, so I suppose you mean your folks would've thought Dewey was too young for you."

"Not necessarily. I'm sure they both realized I had a crush on you, maybe before I knew it."

Her admission made Jax consider what the Stewarts had probably recognized—in Bella and in him. "I suppose they knew I was sweet on you, too. That may be what led your brother to encourage me."

"Maybe so. In any case, I wasn't interested in Dewey."

The comment reminded Jax that they should discuss the case before getting to town. "Let's stop at the constable's office. With luck, Nolen or Newton will be in. If not, let's go to the Rogers place, and the sooner we get in touch with Richard, the better."

"If he's already at the café, we'll see his Winton when we drive into town."

"Probably so. I'll be happy when Dewey and Lannigan are behind bars."

"I will, too."

Within a few minutes, Bella pulled to a stop in front of the constable's office, where the lights were on. "Someone is here, and I see Richard's vehicle. Let's get help to haul Dewey to a cell." After hurrying around to assist Bella, he took her by the elbow and led her inside.

Jillian and Nolen were behind the counter, while Richard stood in front of it. "Thank goodness, you're here." As the senior constable made the observation, he smiled. "Yank Yarken's son went to the newspaper office and found his dad on the floor. He saw me driving by and flagged me down. Got Yank to Doc Smedlay's office. He's got a lump on his head, but he should be fine. And he was able to tell us about the two of you being in his office."

"Jax probably should see Doc, too." Bella's statement elicited a host of questions, which she and Jax answered.

Newton walked in the door as they were wrapping up. "Dewey Fikeland is making a lot of noise in the back of the Ballantyne vehicle. I assume he's the guilty party."

"You assume correctly. Let's get him in a cell. "I'm going to deputize both of you." Nolen looked from Jax to Richard. "I know that seems backwards, but we don't have time for anything else."

"It's a fine solution," Richard said.

"We'll go after Lannigan as soon as Dewey is secured," Nolen suggested.

"I agree," Jax put in.

As soon as Dewey was behind bars, the other men got ready to leave.

"Lannigan probably hasn't left the hotel yet, since Dewey didn't expect him right away.

He'll wait until the Coopers go to their suite." Jax turned to Nolen. "What's your plan?"

"Two of us can go to the front desk and the others to the back door," Nolen suggested. "We shouldn't have any trouble nabbing him."

"I hope not," Jax murmured.

The thought echoed inside Bella.

An hour later, both suspects were in cells. Jax slumped with relief once the door clanged shut behind Lannigan. Bella, who had waited with Jillian, slid her hand into his. "You can really relax now."

A weary grin lit his face. "Yes, I can. Thanks to you." He looked around the group. "All of you."

Richard grabbed Jax's shoulder in a half-hug. "Happy to help, son."

"All of us are glad to find the real killer," Nolen added.

"We sure are," Newton said.

"I better call the mayor because word will spread quickly," Nolen said. "Sam's café is staying open late from now until the first of the year, and several folks were leaving when we just pulled up outside. In the meantime, why don't the rest of you go into the office?"

"I made fresh coffee," Jillian said, "and Mrs. Jenkins dropped off cookies on her way out of town this afternoon."

"Sounds great," Richard replied. "Jenny will be sorry to have missed the big arrests but happy to provide much-needed refreshments."

Everyone except Nolen retired to the other room. When he entered a few minutes later, Jax asked, "What did Cawlings have to say?"

"He's glad the killer is under arrest." Nolen shrugged.

"He believes Dewey murdered Celeste?" Bella made the inquiry. "Not that he shouldn't, but he was quick to pin the blame on Jax."

Nolen leaned back in his chair. "You know how the mayor is. He always takes the simple path. Now that there's ample evidence—which I explained in part—against Dewey, he's fine with the arrests."

"It's about time." Bella still found the mayor's earlier attitude toward Jax to be disgusting.

"He was ambivalent from the start. When a lot of townspeople spoke up for Jax, the mayor was even more uncertain about the arrest," Newton put in. "I'm sure he regrets it."

Bella glanced at Jax, who looked weary. Being accused and jailed had weighed on him. The hit on the head didn't help. "How are you feeling? Do you have a headache?"

A soft smile touched his mouth. "Not really. I was only out a couple of minutes."

"Enough time that you ought to see Doc Smedlay," Richard suggested.

"I will," Jax promised.

Before anyone could respond, a commotion ensued in the outer office. Nolen got up, but Lyle Fikeland appeared in the doorway simultaneously. The man glanced around the table with a scowl. "The bunch of you are plotting together, I see." His gaze riveted on Jax. "I want him arrested right now, and I want my nephew released."

"Mr. Fikeland, please calm down," Nolen said. "I can't release Dewey when there's ample evidence to charge him."

When Jax said nothing, Bella spoke. "Dewey waylaid Jax and me. Your nephew hit him over the head, knocked him out, and threatened both of us."

A harrumph left Fikeland. "Of course, you'd make excuses for Hastings."

Bella lifted her chin. "Are you accusing me of lying? Because I'm not. Jax has a lump on his head from where Dewey bashed him, and marks on his wrists from the manacles." Her attention went to where his hands rested on the table. Jax's efforts to get loose had left abrasions. "You can't argue with clear-cut evidence."

The intruder scowled. "I want to see Dewey."

"I'm sorry, Mr. Fikeland, that's not possible right now." Nolen spoke with the authority of his temporary office. "You can come back in the morning."

"Young man, you'll regret this. I planned to support you in becoming our permanent constable. Taking sides with him," Fikeland gestured toward Jax, "is a terrible mistake. A council meeting is scheduled for tomorrow night, and I'm making it my mission to see neither of you sets foot in this office again unless you're under arrest. As for you, Hastings, you shouldn't be in this office discussing the case. The charges against you haven't been dropped, have they?"

"No, sir," Jax replied.

"But they will be," Richard put in.

Nolen nodded. "They will, and yet tonight."

Fikeland's face flushed beet-red. "Sticking together won't help when you're all in the wrong. You'll get your comeuppances. Wait and see." Then, he stomped out of the room.

"I'll do the paperwork for the dropped charges tonight." Nolen sat down again.

"It can wait until tomorrow," Jax told him.

"I agree with Nolen. Doing it tonight is best," Richard said. "Lyle is in the minority, but he'll stir up as many people as he can before the meeting. Having the charges against you dismissed is a good idea, just in case..." His voice trailed off.

A knot formed in Bella's stomach. Just in case Nolen and Newton got fired, which could happen if Fikeland drummed up all his supporters. Council meetings weren't well attended, especially during the holidays when folks were busy with other activities. A minority could hold sway, if others didn't come. The expression on Jax's face revealed his thoughts were much the same as hers.

Nolen ran a hand over his face. "I need to get the details from both of you about what happened tonight." He looked from Bella to Jax. "That'll help in keeping Dewey and Korbert in jail."

"Of course," she murmured while Jax nodded.

They took the next few minutes to review what had happened. Nolen jotted down notes and asked some questions. "Is there anything else either of you want to add?"

Jax shook his head. "That's all."

His flat tone bothered Bella, but she answered with the same response. Before the group broke up, Nolen made a request. "Could we all meet here in the morning? We'll question the pair more tonight, and I'd like to go over everything we know together."

The others agreed. When Bella and Jax left, Richard stayed to talk with Nolen and Newton.

"I'd like to follow you back to Ballantyne," he said. "Dewey and Lannigan are locked up, but I'd feel better. If you drive me home, I'll get the Chummy."

While she appreciated his concern, Bella had her own worries. "You should see Doc. I could tend the wrist abrasions, but you were unconscious for a while. I'll go with you. Then, you can follow me home."

A weak smile pulled up one corner of his mouth. "I wasn't out too long."

Bella searched his face. "It can't hurt to be checked out. Please."

A resigned sigh escaped him. "All right. We'll go there first."

An hour later, they arrived at the resort. Jax parked behind Bella and hurried to help her out of the Ford. She murmured her thanks before continuing. "Come in and I'll fix something to eat. I don't know about you, but I'm hungry."

"As long as you don't go to any trouble. I never ate any of the food Jenny left, just the cake from you."

"I'll fix sandwiches and tea."

"Sounds good."

While Bella fixed their snack, Jax got plates out. In short order, they were at the table. "You got an excellent report from Doc, but you need to rest. The last week has been hard, I know."

After taking a bite of the sandwich, he nodded. "For you, too. I don't know how I would've managed without your help and support."

"I'm glad the charges against you were dropped. It's such a relief." She bit her lip to keep from saying how hard seeing him in jail had been. "Now, it's behind us, and we can get back to normal." Her Christmas wish had changed over the last few days. Courting during the holiday season, with the possibility of an engagement to cap it off, had been on her mind. Once he had been jailed, she only wanted Jax to be free.

Jax laid his food aside. "That remains to be seen."

Confusion overcame Bella. "What do you mean?"

"You heard Lyle Fikeland. He plans to stir up trouble ahead of tomorrow night's meeting. If he gets enough people to come who agree with him, I may not have a job in the future. At least not in Moreley."

His observation reignited Bella's apprehension because the warning had validity. Even so, she offered reassurance. "Most townsfolk support you."

"Maybe. Maybe not, but some of the support comes from women, and they aren't welcome at council meetings."

"Which is ridiculous. Women got the vote last year."

"True, and I agree with you," Jax said, "our female neighbors should have the right to attend. Unfortunately, that won't be the case tomorrow night."

Bella couldn't refute the observation, so she tried another tack. "Most of the men are in your corner, too. More will be when they hear the complete story, which should spread quickly."

He shrugged. "With holiday festivities getting back to normal, people are busy with last-minute preparations. I'm not at all sure there will be a big turnout, and that may bode ill for my future employment."

Since she had already worried about that prospect, Bella couldn't argue. For long moments, she considered whether to ask the question hovering in her head. Finally, she did. "What will you do if you don't get your job as constable again?"

Jax put one hand to his head. "Amos would welcome me back to the Prohibition Bureau."

The answer didn't surprise Bella, but it sent her spirits plummeting. "You said your arm is healing well. Maybe you should reconsider going back to being a golf pro."

His gaze moved to his plate. "It's too soon to tell, and I've played little since before I left for France. My attempts since I got home were hardly reassuring."

"But you might play in the future."

"No one will hire me as a golf pro based on might."

"We would." The words were out before Bella considered them.

He reached across the table and took her hand. "I appreciate it, but you have a pro. Two with both Griff and Mac. If I could pull my weight, I'd consider the offer. I don't know if I can, and I won't for weeks. Then, I might discover I'll never be able to play well again. I don't want to be deadwood or take charity." Bella opened her mouth to object, but he raised a hand to stop her. "Let's wait until after the meeting to talk seriously. Maybe it'll go better than I think."

With all her heart and soul, Bella hoped so, but she let him move the conversation to less emotional ground.

Chapter Thirteen

The next morning, Bella drove into Moreley. Jax, Richard, Nolen, and Newton had already reconvened at the big table in the inner office, so she j o i n e d them.

"We haven't started our discussion yet," Nolen told her.

She sat next to Jax and fished the notepad and pencil out of her pocketbook. "I'll take notes, just in case you need them."

Nolen nodded. "Thanks, Bella."

She took a sidelong glance at Jax, who looked like he hadn't slept. His green eyes were red-rimmed and heavily shadowed. Was he so worried about the up-coming council meeting? Surely, the town would hire him back. With effort, she focused on the discussion.

"We checked out the other suspects, just to ensure we have the details when the case goes to court,"

Nolen began. "We found out Patrick Orlington was telling the truth about visiting his grandmother, and Smithson Collier went back to the hotel after the tree lighting."

"Do you know if he saw Lannigan when he did?" Jax asked.

"Lannigan finally admitted he did," Newton replied.

"You were right to check their alibis, since that may come up in court." Richard gave the younger men his vote of confidence, which made them smile.

"What about Victor Gaspard? Do we know where he went? Or if he's back?" Bella asked.

Nolen nodded. "He called his landlady to say he'll be home next week, probably to close his business. Another former French soldier moved to Quebec, and Victor drove up there to see him. As things stand now, he's planning to move there."

"Understandable. Most people in Quebec speak French, so he may feel more at home there." Bella glanced at Jax. "It doesn't explain why he acted so strangely toward you in the Boxwood diner."

"From what Burton and Mrs. Cotton said, Victor is very reserved. Having a failing business probably didn't help. Besides, I never knew him well," Jax replied.

"I suppose so," she murmured.

"Do Smithson Collier and Patrick Orlington know we caught the killer?" Richard asked.

"I drove out to Ballantyne and talked to them again," Nolen said. "I explained why they came under suspicion. Smith was gracious. Patrick was annoyed."

A chuckle left Jax. "No surprise."

"I suppose I should talk with them, too," Bella observed. "They're resort guests, and I want to make sure they're comfortable. Especially Smithson."

"Do you care if the Orlingtons come back?" Jax asked.

She frowned at him. "As a co-owner, I want to be hospitable to all our visitors."

He shrugged. "I'm glad I don't have to be." If his arm and shoulder kept improving, he might return to his old career as a golf professional. Then, Jax would need to be gracious with guests, too. And he would. For Bella. Not that he didn't normally try to be pleasant, but Orlington was a troublemaker, even though he wasn't a killer. "What about Lannigan? How did he and Dewey meet?"

"My friend in Cleveland helped with that," Richard replied. "Lannigan worked at the bakery run by Miss Bouchard's aunt and uncle. He made deliveries, even after they were mostly to speakeasies. When he started drinking some of the booze in his truck, the uncle fired him, but he and Dewey stayed in contact."

"So, Dewey initially planned to take over the hardware store," Bella suggested.

"That part seems to be true," Nolen agreed. "At least Lannigan is sticking with the same story. He says Dewey figured on either taking over the business or siphoning money out of it."

"But there wasn't much money to get," Jax put in.

"Right. I can't say I'm surprised about the business going downhill," Newton said. "Lyle antagonized plenty of folks. Since there's a hardware store in Boxwood, more people go over there."

"Others say Lyle's stock is down, and they can't find what they need." Nolen drummed his fingers on the table. "Lannigan said Dewey was pretty upset over the business failing."

Jax leaned back in his chair. "Lannigan has been talkative."

"He has," Nolen agreed. "He's hoping to get a lower sentence."

"And he might," Richard said.

"What about Dewey? He claimed he didn't lure Celeste to the park, intending to murder her." Bella looked around the table. "I'm not sure if I believe him. Does anyone else?"

"It could be the truth," Richard replied.

"It could," Jax agreed. "That's for a jury to decide."

Nolen and Newton concurred.

"And the marriage license?" Bella asked.

Nolen picked up his notebook before looking at her. "I spoke to Celeste's uncle again late last night. Mostly about arrangements for her. I also asked if he used a print shop for flyers and such. He gave me the name of the business, and I passed it along to Richard."

"I called my friend right afterward," the older man said. "He went to the shop early this morning. Turns out they also use their truck to make deliveries to speakeasies. Although my buddy is no longer on the police force, he has connections to it. Not sure exactly what he told the printer, but the man admitted creating the fake certificate."

Bella turned her attention to Jax. "At least we know how they got it, and we have proof that it's not genuine."

"What a tangled web," Jax said.

Richard nodded. "But we've untangled it, so there's a strong case against both Dewey and Lannigan."

The group wrapped up their discussion in short order. Following the meeting, Bella walked outside with Jax, who didn't look as relieved as she felt. "Did you get any sleep at all?"

One corner of his mouth lifted in a weak attempt at a smile. "Not a lot."

"Did your head hurt?"

"No." He shoved his hands into his coat pockets. "I'm concerned about tonight's meeting."

His answer wasn't surprising. "Lyle Fikeland is one of a handful of folks who believed you were the guilty party." Bella could not make herself use murderer and his name in the same sentence.

"Maybe so, but I'll be glad when it's over. Until it is…" His voice trailed off.

"Until it is, you don't want to make plans." The certainty overwhelmed her.

"I don't."

As long moments passed, memories surfaced. "You didn't want to make plans for Christmas of 1916, either."

Jax bowed his head. "I didn't with good reason. The reason now isn't the same, but it's just as valid. If I'm not rehired, I'll have to consider other possibilities. We've already talked about all this. Now, let's wait until after the meeting. I'll come out to Ballantyne right away."

Uneasiness rippled through Bella, but what choice was there? Until the council decided, they were stuck.

At the evening meal, Bella found herself unable to do more than play with her food. After she and Ida cleaned up, her friend suggested a game of checkers. Since Griff and Mac had gone to the meeting, the ladies were alone in the family quarters. Bella lost every game and, when the men came home, she jumped up.

"What happened?" She looked from Mac to Griff and back.

The men exchanged a glance. "Jax is coming, and he'd like to tell you himself," Griff replied. "We agreed to let him."

"Aye, lass," Mac said, his gray gaze soft with empathy.

Bella studied their faces but gleaned nothing. Forcing the news out of them would be impossible, since they wouldn't go against Jax's wishes. "All right." Although she offered to make cocoa for everyone, Bella had no takers. Instead, Griff headed to his space above the golf shop while Ida and Mac, both telling her to wait patiently, went to their respective rooms.

Patience proved elusive. After a while, Bella headed to the inn's wide foyer and curled up in one of the leather chairs. The dying embers in the fireplace mimicked the ebbing hope in her heart. Where was Jax? Why wasn't he here? What would keep him in town?

Finally, as the grandfather clock struck ten times, a tap sounded at the inn's main door. "It's unlocked," Bella called out from her seat. Either a guest or Jax was there. She hoped for the latter, since Griff and Mac had arrived home more than an hour ago. Anxiety had built to a crescendo since the two men got back. It still was escalating. All her attention riveted on the entrance. When Jax came in, she stood up. "I've been waiting for you."

"I'm sorry. I expected to get here sooner. Otherwise, I would've let Griff and Mac tell you at least part of what happened."

He crossed the distance between them in long strides and opened his arms. She went into them immediately. Her hands rested on his shoulders while her head nestled against his chest. Even with his thick coat and her heavy sweater between them, Bella felt his heart pound. Fresh apprehension flickered along her nerve ends. Did he have bad news? Was that why he was late? If so, what did it mean for their future? Would they have a future together if the town council voted not to rehire him as constable? For long moments, she clung to Jax. Dewey Fikeland was guilty of murdering Celeste, and Korbert Lannigan was his accomplice. Bella didn't need the results of a trial to convince her, and neither did most people, but Lyle Fikeland had threatened to get like-minded men to the meeting. Last night, Jax had worried about suspicion lingering on him. Was it? Did the councilmen want someone else as the head of their law enforcement agency? How could she stay in the area if that happened? Her love of Moreley would disintegrate.

He loosened his grip and stepped back. "Let's sit down and talk. Maybe in a more private place, just in case a guest comes."

A shuddering sigh left her. "We can use the family quarters." On trembling legs, Bella led the way. As they entered the suite, one oil lamp eased the darkness. When she went to turn on an electric one, Jax stopped her.

"This is fine."

His features weren't clear, but she agreed and took a seat on the sofa facing the hearth. Jax spent some time stirring up the banked fire and tossed another log on it. Before sitting down, he took off his coat and laid it aside.

Bella cleared her throat. "You're later than I figured. Griff and Mac were home an hour ago. They said you wanted to tell me what happened." She tried to sound composed.

"I do, and I didn't think I'd be stuck so long after the meeting ended," he replied. "A lot of townspeople showed up, and some wanted to talk afterward. Quite a few, really."

Her pulse raced. Had some of Lyle's buddies cornered Jax after Mac and Griff left? Surely, they wouldn't have deserted him if he'd been under duress from undue criticism. She wouldn't have. "I should have been there, too. Women should be allowed to attend those meetings. After all, we have the vote now." More than that, Bella wanted to be with Jax in every situation—good or bad.

Jax gently cupped her cheeks. "I agree with you, and you'll be happy to know ladies can attend from now on." A grin curved his lips.

"We can?" The answer surprised and pleased her.

"Yep. Not sure when they'll be able to serve on the council, but it was discussed. Before I get to all that, let me sum up what happened regarding me."

"Of course." As far as Bella was concerned, that was of the utmost importance. He sat back but put his arm around her shoulders. Bella again let her head rest on his chest. "Don't keep me in suspense." A chuckle reverberated under her ear. "It feels like far longer than an hour since Griff and Mac got back, and I've been on edge the entire time."

"I'm sorry. I should've called, but I wanted to tell you myself, and in person. Lyle maintained Dewey's innocence and claimed his nephew was framed to keep me out of the electric chair. People immediately protested, which disrupted the meeting for a short time. The mayor told Lyle to be quiet more than once."

"Really?"

"Really," he repeated with a chuckle. "Cawlings never thought I was guilty, and neither did the three other councilmen at the meeting. Many townsfolk, almost all who came, gave me their vote of confidence."

Bella lifted her head and looked into his eyes. "I'm so glad. You deserve their trust and respect." Jax ranked with her male relatives and Mac as one of the best men she had ever known.

"I was awed by some of what was said." His voice was ragged with emotion. "Doc stood up and revealed how Dewey ambushed us. He offered the lump on the back of my head and the marks on my wrists as proof."

With her fingertips, Bella traced the bruises. "What did Lyle say to that?"

"He got even more furious, but others shouted him down. I was amazed by the outpouring of support. I wasn't at all sure what would happen, but the entire council voted to rehire me as constable and everyone yelled out their agreement."

Shock struck Bella. "Even Lyle?"

Jax shook his head. "No. By the time the vote was taken, he'd left. The mayor asked him to resign from the council, and Lyle did. But he stormed out along with his buddies. All four of them."

"Good." Bella turned into Jax's arms. "The mayor hid his feelings well. I've been angry and upset with him ever since you were arrested."

His lips quirked. "I wasn't happy, either, but he explained about wanting to appear unbiased. He didn't want any doubt when I was proven innocent. He hoped I understood, so we'll let bygones be bygones."

"You're very forgiving. I'm not sure I feel as charitable toward him."

"I'm sure you'll get over that, eventually. Besides, Cawlings was the one who immediately insisted I get my old job back."

"That's in his favor," she said a bit grudgingly. "In any case, I'm happy for you."

"It's an enormous relief. I really wondered what would happen, especially since Dewey and Korbert haven't gone to trial yet."

Bella was relieved, too. More than words could say. "The evidence against Dewey is overwhelming. He's guilty, and he'll be convicted of murder and of kidnapping me along with assaulting you. I'm not sure what Korbert is charged with, but he'll be found guilty, too." She felt certain about her assertions.

"I agree, and so do most other people."

His lighthearted tone lifted her spirit. "When do you return to work?"

"January first, so I have some free time." His voice softened. "We can still make the dance and the play. And I can help around here, if you don't mind."

"Mind? I'd love to have you at Ballantyne more." Was he joshing? She wanted to spend as much time as possible with him. When he resumed his job, he'd be busy and, come spring, the resort would absorb a lot of her time. "As for events, I don't care about those. We can spend quiet evenings together." She shifted to look at him. "After all, you're still recuperating from surgery. All the stress and strain of the investigation didn't help, I'm sure. Neither did Dewey bashing you in the head and trussing you up."

Jax shrugged. "The bump will disappear in a few days. As for the case, you did most of the running around. Without you, Jenny, and Richard, I might still be in jail."

"I assume he was at the meeting, so he got the good news right away."

"He did. He went home to share it with Jenny."

Bella smiled. "She'll be thrilled, too."

"I'm lucky to have so many people who believe in me." His expression grew solemn. "As far as spending time together, we only started stepping out in October. Then, I had surgery at Thanksgiving, which put me out of circulation. I haven't courted you properly yet." He sat up and levered slightly away from her. "At the end of September, we talked about social engagements over the holidays. We haven't had as many as I hoped, mostly due to Celeste's arrival and murder."

"We discussed you filling my calendar, and you've done that." Bella aimed for a light tone.

His mouth flattened. "Not in the way I planned."

Over the past few weeks, Bella had grown more and more certain she and Jax were meant to be together, forever and always. Because she didn't like the idea of more delays in their relationship—they'd had too many already—Bella posed a question. "How long is a proper courtship in your mind? Is there a set number of social engagements? Or a certain time period?"

His brow furrowed. "I don't know. I can't put a number on it. Don't you want to be courted and wooed?"

A chuckle left her. "Wooed? How are you planning to woo me? With flowers? Except when you were stuck in town, you've brought some every week since your surgery. Maybe candy? You've brought me plenty of that, too. And you've taken me to moving pictures, out to dinners, on picnics when the weather was pleasant. What else do you have in mind?" Bella couldn't keep the amusement out of her voice. "Books of poetry? Or maybe you'll write poems for me yourself."

He rolled his eyes. "Very funny. We haven't been to the town Christmas dance together, ever. Surely, you want to go. It's tomorrow night. Griff is taking Ida. Before the whole business with Celeste, we planned to go with them." His tone and expression held a note of perplexity. "Is that off?"

"We still can go. I just wondered if you'll have time to court after you go back to work, when who knows what else might happen?" She released a long breath. "It's been one thing after another since you and Matt got called up in 1917. That's almost five years ago. Even before you left, you didn't want to step out because we all knew war was coming." Bella hadn't seen that as a hindrance, but Jax had worried about being badly wounded and becoming a burden to her. Not that he could ever be a burden.

His expression grew solemn. "You're right." He searched her face. "Christmas of 1916, Matt urged me to court you. He knew I wanted to, and having his approval meant the world to me. I just couldn't do it with war on the horizon."

Warmth spread through Bella. "He always approved of you and me being together." In September, Jax admitted her brother had championed the idea of marriage for them going back a number of years. Matt had been more subtle with his sister. Much more subtle. Perhaps, he hadn't wanted to pressure her to wed his best friend. Bella didn't know and never would now. The thought weighed on her heart. How she wished Matt was still here. Matt and her parents.

A soft smile touched Jax's lips. "He did."

"But you were against the idea then."

He gnawed on his lower lip. "I feared something terrible might take place. What I didn't count on was us growing apart."

Bella hadn't considered that, either. "Neither of us could have predicted all that happened. But we've been in a good place since last April. Unfortunately, various circumstances have kept us apart since then, too, and that's what bothers me now. What else might happen? Looking back, we could've navigated everything better if we'd been a couple." When he didn't speak, she continued. "Do you disagree?" Uncertainty impinged on her confidence.

"Not at all." Jax reached into his pocket as he slid off the sofa and went to one knee.

Bella stared at him. "What are you doing?" Could he be doing what she thought? Her heart raced at the idea.

He beamed up at her. "Until this evening, I figured I'd wait until tomorrow night after the dance. I figured on taking you outside near the town Christmas tree, but I'm not sure if we'd have privacy. Not after the council meeting. We may be subjected to plenty of well wishes and attention going forward, so I brought this tonight." He placed the small box in the palm of his hand and snapped it open. Before continuing, he inhaled sharply. "Bella Stewart, will you do me the honor of becoming my wife?"

For several seconds, she stared at the diamond glittering in the firelight. Then, Bella looked into Jax's beloved face. "Yes. Absolutely, yes." When he plucked the ring from its resting place, she extended her hand and Jax slipped the band on. "It's beautiful."

"Do you really like it?" he asked. "It was my mother's, so if you want to choose your own…"

Bella put one forefinger to his lips. "That makes it even more special."

A grin lit his handsome face. "I love you, Bella. Always have. Always will."

"I love you, too, Jax," she murmured, her heart near to bursting. "Always have. Always will." Echoing his assertion came without forethought. Her next statement didn't. It was one she'd considered for a long while. "I hope you aren't planning on a lengthy betrothal."

"It can be whatever length you like." Jax got up and sat next to her again, but he continued to hold her hand.

"We haven't courted very long, but we've known one another for most of our lives."

"We have," Bella agreed. A recent discussion with her best friend came to mind. "You already know Ida and Griff plan to announce their wedding date on Christmas Eve."

"I do," he replied. "She won't be upset that we're betrothed, will she? I wasn't trying to upstage Ida and Griff. It's just that we've waited so long already. I couldn't hold off until after their marriage."

"Ida agrees we've waited too long, and she'll be thrilled for us. Griff will, as well." Bella clasped his hand tighter. "She and I were talking, and Ida said it'd be wonderful to have a double wedding. At the time, I didn't see how it would be possible, since they plan to marry in March. Now..." Her voice trailed off. "Maybe you want to wait longer."

He beamed at her. "Not one day too soon for me."

Joy spread through Bella. "I'll tell her tomorrow, and we'll start planning. After Christmas, we won't be busy here, and Ida is resigning from her teaching position next month at the end of the semester. Things will be calmer for all of us."

"I hope so. You've had a busy year, what with resort business being good and working three cases with me. Four, counting this last one, but you did a lot of the investigation on your own this time. I wasn't much help."

"Richard and Jenny were great, and you pitched in when you could. The main thing is that the actual killer is behind bars where he belongs, and you've got your job back." Bella didn't think she would ever get over seeing Jax sitting in a jail cell. He'd looked despondent, desperate, and alone. And she'd felt fear like she had never known, wondering if he would end up being executed for a murder he didn't commit.

"I can take a few days off after the wedding, but I may be busy before then. I'm not sure how much help I'll be, preparing for the big day."

His statement sent a spear of anxiety hurtling through Bella. Since her return from France two years ago, she and Jax had been involved in six major investigations. A number of months had passed between the second and third, but the others had been close together. Would something else happen before March? Surely, fate wouldn't be so unkind.

Jax's voice broke into her thoughts. "Is something wrong?"

"No, of course not." Bella made the reply with a smile. When they were together, everything was possible. She laced her fingers with his. They were together now as an engaged couple. In less than four months, they'd be husband and wife. Again, she looked down at the sparkling gem on her left hand. Soon, a gold band would join it. And nothing would impede that.

About the Author

D.S. Lang started making up stories to entertain herself as an only child, and she is still making them up. Now, she puts them in writing. Her books are historical mysteries with intrepid amateur sleuths bent on cracking cases and upholding justice.

After earning Bachelor's and Master's degrees in education, D.S. worked as a golf shop manager, teacher (junior high, high school, and college), program manager, tutor, and mentor. She has a lifelong love of history and often gets sidetracked on research when she should be writing.

When she is away from the computer, D.S. enjoys reading, swimming, spending time with family and friends, and walking her dog Izzy.

Visit my author's web page at https://www.dslangbooks.com
Readers find news books and authors through reviews. I greatly appreciate all ratings and reviews! Thank you

Books in the Arabella Stewart Historical Mystery Series

For more information on the series, please visit https://www.dslangbooks.com